"Please don't say

Slade's heart stalled.
her. About anything. Ever. He'd happily be her
yes man.

But that wouldn't be the best way to avoid
Raquel. Or Hunter. Coaching Hunter would
weave him more tightly into their lives. And
then the time would come to give them up. And
he wasn't sure he'd be able to. Better to keep his
distance.

"It's only for three months." She made it sound so
easy.

"I only leased the house for three months."

"That's perfect." Raquel's eyes lit up, making him
want to do whatever it took to make her happy.
"Your lease goes through May and the season goes
through May."

His heart clunked back in place in his chest. If he
coached Hunter, he'd automatically spend more
time with Raquel. They'd grow closer. But he
couldn't let the attraction grow.

Shannon Taylor Vannatter is a stay-at-home mom/pastor's wife/award-winning author. She lives in a rural central Arkansas community with a population of around 100, if you count a few cows. Contact her at shannonvannatter.com.

SHANNON TAYLOR VANNATTER

Rodeo Reunion

HEARTSONG
PRESENTS

LOVE INSPIRED BOOKS

ISBN-13: 978-0-373-48785-1

Rodeo Reunion

Copyright © 2015 by Shannon Taylor Vannatter

Trust in the Lord with all thine heart; and
lean not unto thine own understanding. In all thy
ways acknowledge him, and he shall direct thy paths.
—*Proverbs* 3:5–6

To my parents for their unconditional love and support.

Acknowledgments

I appreciate DeeDee Barker-Wix, director of sales at the Cowtown Coliseum; former Aubrey City Hall secretary Nancy Trammel-Downes; Aubrey Main Street Committee member Deborah Goin; Aubrey librarian Kathy Ramsey; and Allison Leslie and Steve and Krys Murray, owners of Moms on Main for all their help and support. Thanks to Stephanie Pedigo, Aubrey Youth Sports communications director; school nurses Sandra Cissell-Bryant and Jennifer Davenport Olivarez; and RN Ginger Smith Harris for helping me get the details right. Any mistakes are mine.

Chapter 1

"Isn't there anyone who makes your heart rev?"

Raquel swallowed hard. Her friend was only trying to help.

Three years since Dylan's death and no one had made her pulse speed up since he'd been gone. She searched the familiar restaurant for something, anything, to change the subject to. But Caitlyn wouldn't give up that easily. She might as well be honest.

"It's been years since my heart revved over anyone other than a certain seven-year-old."

"Uh-uh. This is your mom's day out. No talking about Hunter." Caitlyn wagged a finger at her and Raquel tried not to squirm on the booth seat. "And no changing the subject. You know Dylan wouldn't want you to be alone."

"He did make me promise to find someone else if anything ever happened to him." Raquel shrugged.

"You've even got permission from the love of your life to move on. So what's stopping you?"

"Right now—" Raquel traced the condensation on her tea glass with her fingers "—my focus is Hunter and baseball. I want him to have fun and be happy living in Aubrey. Even though I'll admit I'm lonely and I know my son needs a father, if God has someone out there for me, I'll trust Him to make it happen in His time."

"You know I'm no good at waiting on God's timing. I ask Him to forgive me daily for trying to rush things without Him." Caitlyn's stomach growled and she pressed a hand to her huge baby bump.

"Sounds like Juniorette is hungry." Raquel glanced toward the door as it opened, letting in mid-February evening air. "Mitch should be here anytime and he wouldn't want you to keep his baby girl waiting. We should order."

"It might take a crane to unwedge me from this booth." Caitlyn groaned.

Raquel winced. "Why did you pick a booth?"

"I wanted to prove I could still squeeze in here. May not get out. But I'm in."

"Don't get out. I'll order." Hopefully, by the time she returned, Caitlyn would have forgotten her line of questioning.

"Good idea, but only if you let me pay." Caitlyn held out a twenty.

"You can buy next time."

Raquel placed their orders, then moved to the register, dug her money from her wallet and waited for her change.

The man behind her in line ordered and she turned to see if he was anyone she knew. He looked familiar. Inky waves, sage-green eyes, chin cleft. Where did she know him from? Parent from school? Church?

He smiled.

And her brain kicked in. Slade Walker.

Her mouth went dry. Her wallet slipped from her fingers. Coins danced and rolled; bills fanned around her feet;

credit cards bounced, spun and slid across the hardwood floor.

In most places, people would dive in and steal as much as they could. But this was Aubrey, Texas.

Slade knelt at her feet along with the lady behind him in line and helped her pick everything up. A man she didn't even know handed her one of her credit cards.

"Thank you."

In minutes the contents of her overstuffed wallet were back in place as Slade gathered stray change.

"Don't worry about the change."

"Is that everything?" He stood.

"You're Slade Walker."

"Yeah. Got all your cards and money?"

She tugged her gaze away from his long enough to flip through the bills and cards, then nodded. "Yes, thanks."

A slow smile tugged at his lips. "I'm sorry, but have we met? I usually remember beautiful women, but I'm drawing a blank."

Her face heated. "You were my husband's favorite base-ball player."

"Wow." He blew out a soft whistle and rubbed his right shoulder. "That was a long time ago and my career was short-lived. I can't say I've been recognized for baseball in a long time."

"Well, you should be. You were great. If my son was here, he'd be beside himself. Could I get your autograph for him?"

His face turned red.

"I mean, I don't want to bother you."

"No, it's fine. It's just been a long time since anybody asked. Got any paper?"

She scurried to the booth where Caitlyn waited and grabbed her purse. "Caitlyn, this is Slade Walker. *The* Slade Walker." She must have sounded like an idiot.

With a confused frown, Caitlyn offered her hand. "Nice to meet you."

"Not a baseball fan, I take it? No worries. It's been a few years." Slade accepted the grocery receipt Raquel handed him as several people brought her quarters, nickels, even pennies. Small-town proof there were still good, honest people in the world.

"What's your son's name?"

"Hunter Marris. I mean, you can just make it Hunter."

"Marris? I went to elementary school with a Dylan Marris."

Raquel nodded like a bobblehead. "My husband."

"No wonder you know who I am. We were best friends until fifth grade when I moved. How is Dylan?"

Her heart squeezed. He didn't know.

"Raquel!" Caitlyn's face contorted with pain. "I hate to interrupt, but I think I might be in labor."

"Oh, my goodness. Let's get you to the hospital."

"Should we wait on Mitch?" Panic dwelled in Caitlyn's eyes. Everyone was looking at them.

Calm down, Raquel. She was a nurse. But this was her friend and treating anyone she loved in medical distress rattled her. Ever since Dylan.

"I'll call Mitch." Deep breaths. She could do this. "He can meet us there. Everything will be fine. Remember, I'm a nurse."

"Let me help you up." Slade offered his arm to Caitlyn.

She managed to unwedge herself from the booth, but as she stood, she quickly doubled over as another contraction rocked her.

More deep breaths.

"Maybe I should drive you." Slade's voice was calm. "That way you can sit in the back with her and keep an eye on things."

"Good idea. Don't worry, Caitlyn. I'll be right there with

you to monitor the baby's progress." *Oh, Lord, please let everything be all right.*

"No." Caitlyn clenched her teeth against obvious pain. "I appreciate your help, Mr. Walker, but I don't even know you."

"I've never had a speeding ticket or been in an accident." Slade pressed his free hand to his heart. "I promise."

"And he's a Christian. He led Dylan to Christ. I know who he is." At the moment Raquel didn't care if he was an ax murderer. She was much too shaky to drive.

"Okay." Caitlyn moaned.

Slade helped Caitlyn with her jacket, then supported her as she hobbled to the exit. "Where's the hospital?"

"In Denton." Raquel held the door open.

"Do you need me to carry you, ma'am?"

"No." Caitlyn wailed. "I'd break your back for sure. Ooooh!"

Another contraction already? Denton was only fifteen minutes away, but this was happening too fast. Would they make it?

"Caitlyn?" Raquel used her most soothing nurse voice. "Have you been having contractions for a while?"

"I thought it was false labor like last week."

Please, Lord, let me keep it together and help Caitlyn through this.

The hospital was chilly. Slade zipped his jacket. Why was it always so cold in hospitals?

Doctors and nurses scurried past the waiting room. Families and friends dotted the chairs surrounding him. Probably some of them were here for Caitlyn. He kept expecting to see Dylan, but no sign of him yet. Caitlyn's husband had met them en route and given them a police escort. It obviously came in handy to have a Texas Rangers husband.

Slade was out of place. Probably should leave. But since he'd been a part of this drama, he couldn't bring himself to go.

Besides, maybe his sister would show up. What would he do if she did? He pulled the two clippings from his pocket.

First their father's obituary. He ran his fingers over the grainy publicity image from years gone by. Back from his father's heyday before the boozing had sabotaged his career, before the numerous comebacks, concert tours and rehab stints.

Raised by his grandparents, Slade had never known who his father was. His mother had been an inconsistent menace in his life until she finally gave his grandparents guardianship when he was seven. After that she'd just been inconsistent. Over the years, he'd often asked about his father. His grandparents had claimed not to know who he was. When his mother came around, and he asked, she never answered.

Then a lawyer called his grandparents claiming Slade's father had died and left him a sizable inheritance. He'd thought it was a scam, but the lawyer wouldn't leave him alone until he finally agreed to a meeting. That day he learned his father was famous, a jerk who'd paid Slade's mother to keep silent about his paternity. But he'd left Slade a fortune. A man of contradictions.

He folded the first clipping and slipped it back in his wallet. Through the obituary, he'd learned he had a sister. Though his grandparents were awesome, he'd always yearned for a real family. His throat constricted. A sibling. A younger sister. But an older sister might do in a pinch.

Months had passed before he'd gotten the nerve to search for her on Google, which had led him to her wedding announcement—and the second clipping.

Fair coloring, nothing like him. She looked happy. The

dark-haired man at her side smiled at her as if she made his world go round. Slade hoped so. Hoped she was still as happy as when that picture was taken. What was she like? Would she be glad to learn she had a brother? Or angry that her father had cheated on her mother?

There was no way to know. Other than to track her down. Which he'd done. Which had brought him to Aubrey.

"Mother and daughter are both fine." Raquel stood in the doorway, looking tired but smiling. "The baby's in the nursery, if anyone wants to come see."

Cheers and amens went up and the waiting room cleared out. Clearly Caitlyn had lots of friends and family. Slade folded the clipping and put his wallet away.

"You're still here?" Raquel sank into the seat beside him.

"I wanted to make sure your friend was okay."

"Thanks for driving us." She shivered. "I'm really not sure I could have."

"Why is it always so cold in hospitals?" He shrugged out of his jacket and offered it to her, even though the cool threatened to raise goose bumps over his flesh.

"So the doctors and nurses are comfortable. You can't imagine how hot it gets in the OR rooms with all the lights. Keep your jacket—I'm fine. Just wound up."

"I thought nurses had nerves of steel."

"Not since…" She swallowed hard. "Let's just say my days as an ER nurse are over."

"You're not a nurse anymore?"

"A school nurse now." She shrugged. "It suits me better and I have the same hours as Hunter, including summers off."

"I thought I'd see Dylan here."

"How's Caitlyn?" A dark-haired woman hurried into the room.

"Fine. The ultrasound was right. The baby's a girl. They're both fine." Raquel stood. "I can take you back to see the baby."

"Is that where the crowd rushed off to down the hall?" At Raquel's nod, the woman settled into a chair. "Since everything's fine, I'll wait till things clear out a bit."

"Thanks again for driving us, Slade. I really appreciate it, and Caitlyn did, too. She was just a bit panicked. I'm going to check on her."

Dismissed. He should have left already. "Maybe I'll see ya around."

But she was already gone. Should have gotten her and Dylan's number. He'd love to catch up with Dylan. At least he knew where they were now.

And his sister, too.

"Star Marshall." The dark-haired woman handed him a business card. "You a friend of Raquel's?"

"Not really." He glanced at the card. Real estate agent. "I just ran into her in Aubrey and her friend went into labor, so I offered to drive."

"New to the area?"

"Just visiting. But Aubrey's a nice town."

"Well, if you ever think of relocating, just give me a call."

"I'll keep that in mind." He stood. "Nice meeting you."

His old friend Dylan Marris lived in Aubrey. His sister lived in Aubrey. And a real estate agent had landed right in front of him. Was God trying to tell him something?

Maybe none of the cowboys could tell how distracted Slade was during his sermon this morning. Except Frank— his mentor.

With his Bible tucked under his arm, Slade stood at the outdoor arena exit shaking hands, smiling, making small talk as the well-wishers and preacher-duckers emptied from the arena. The sun was working overtime at warming the morning air, but they'd still had a good crowd.

A few volunteers lingered to make sure there were no coffee cups left behind, freeing his mind to stray to his visit to Aubrey earlier in the week.

After the fifth grade, he'd seen Dylan only a handful of times. But they'd always taken up right where they'd left off as if no time had passed. The last time they'd seen each other was after high school graduation.

"Good sermon." Frank clapped him on the back.

"Not my best, but I'm glad you came. I hope my lack of focus didn't show."

"Not at all. Surely I don't make you nervous." The older man's knowing gaze appraised him. "What's got you so distracted?"

A couple left the arena—the cowboy's arm around his wife's shoulder, nestling her against his side. Their laughter blended as they shared a private joke.

A painful knot lodged in Slade's throat. He wanted that. Someone to share life and laughter with. Someone to settle down and start a family with. For months now, the road had been wearing on him.

"The road getting long and lonely?"

"How did you know that?"

"God knew it wasn't good for man to be alone, so He created woman to keep us out of trouble. Somehow Eve didn't get the memo."

Slade smiled.

"Traveling the circuit is a surefire way not to have a family or a place to call home, since most of the women hanging around are attached to the cowboys." Frank propped his booted foot on the fence rail. "Unless you go for the buckle bunnies."

"Trust me." Slade chuckled. "They're not interested in the chaplain or anything I have to say."

"You need an Irene. She was as happy as I was traveling the circuit with me while I was a rodeo chaplain. The kids were grown and gone and we found a fulfilling way to spend our twilight years."

Over two years had passed since Irene lost her fight with cancer, and Frank had recently remarried, but the pain of losing his first wife was stamped in every wrinkle lining his face, every silver streak in his hair.

"How's Meredith?"

"Keeping me happy. Don't change the subject. Tell me what's really bothering you."

"Let's not keep Meredith waiting. We're still on for lunch, right?"

"One of the many things I love about Meredith is her patience."

There was no sense trying to hide anything from Frank. He'd even told Frank about his inheritance and discovering who his father was. Slade's shoulders slumped. "I found out I have a sister."

Frank blew out a big breath. "Kind of knocked you for a loop?"

"I can't stop thinking about her, and I don't know what to do." Slade leaned his elbows over the fence's top rail. "It's driving me nuts. Yesterday I went to Aubrey, where she lives."

"Did you talk to her?"

"I didn't even see her. I guess I just kind of wanted to feel it out. See if I just happened to run into her, but I didn't."

"Maybe you should call her."

"And say what? I'm your younger brother from an affair your father had on your mother."

"Hmm." Frank stroked his silver beard. "That complicates things."

"I did run into a friend's wife there. Dylan and I were

best friends until the fifth grade, when I moved to my grandparents' house, and we kept in touch for a long while. He called weekly after my baseball injury and was a big encouragement until I went on the circuit and eventually lost touch with him. Seeing his wife got me thinking about him again."

"So Dylan grew up with you in Garland. Where's your sister from?"

"From what I've found on the internet, Ponder originally, and Fort Worth for a while."

"Kind of odd that your sister and your friend ended up in the same tiny town."

"I even met a local real estate agent." A lump formed in Slade's throat. "It's like God's trying to lead me there or something."

"Ever thought of giving up the circuit?" Frank shielded his eyes from the sun with one hand. "You could preach at a church."

"I've thought about it." Slade shrugged. "But I don't want to let these guys down. I mean, let's face it—some of these guys will never darken the door of a church, but they'll come hear a sermon at a rodeo arena."

"Find somebody to replace you, like I did."

"But you didn't quit. You retired and you probably wouldn't have if Irene hadn't been sick." He couldn't turn his back on his rodeo ministry. Or on the cowboys.

"The circuit's a worthy ministry." Frank scratched his chin. "But if your heart's not in it anymore, are you fulfilling God's call?"

"Good question." Yet just this morning, three cowboys had come forward to accept Christ. "But my work here is still bearing fruit."

"True. But someone else with a fresh fire for it might bear more fruit. Maybe you need a sabbatical."

Sabbatical? That might help. Visit Aubrey. Slow down.

Think. Regroup. Refuel. Decide whether to contact his sister. Or not. Maybe settling down would wear thin after a while and he'd come back with a fresh fire in his belly for his ministry.

The breeze stirred the manure scent. He wouldn't miss that.

"You might be onto something." But who could take over the ministry? "Know any preachers dying to take on the circuit?"

"Boy howdy, sometimes seeing God work makes my head spin." Frank clapped him on the back. "Meredith and I aren't here by accident. We're testing out the motor home we bought recently. Planning to do some traveling and even talked about taking up chaplaining again."

God had known he needed a break—even before Slade had. His chest tightened. Was it just a break or could God be nudging him to make a change?

"Why the third degree if you want back in?"

"I wanted to see where you stood on the subject. Under no circumstances would I want you feeling like I moved you out. It's your decision." Frank put an arm around Slade's shoulders and they walked toward Meredith. "Take three months off, then see how you feel. If you want to come back, Meredith and I can work another area. Texas is a big state with plenty of rodeos and cowboy souls for the both of us."

Just like that—Slade was free.

He could rent a house in Aubrey. Catch up with Dylan. Decide what to do about his sister. See what it felt like to settle somewhere. See what came next.

In the first weeks after Dylan's death, the photo album had become a daily ritual for Raquel. As Hunter had gotten older, they'd pored over the family pictures at least once a week. Slowly, it had become a monthly thing. And slowly, she was losing Dylan.

Hunter leaned against her on the couch, fresh from his bath, the scent of lime shampoo clinging to him. Warm and cuddly in his pajamas with logs crackling in the fireplace.

"I can't really remember him anymore." Hunter peered at a picture of Dylan holding him when he was an infant.

"I know, sweetie. You were so young when we lost him—only four." Her eyes misted.

She'd thought following their dream of living in Aubrey would make her feel closer to Dylan. But Dylan had never lived in this house with them. He had sat on this couch with them and his woodsy cologne had once been captured in the cushions. But not anymore.

"Tell me about the picture."

It had always been Hunter's favorite picture and he had a copy in his room. Though she'd told him the story countless times before, it was their way of holding on to Dylan. "You were only a few weeks old. We still lived in Garland then and I woke up to a quiet house."

"And that was weird, cuz I usually woke you up crying." Hunter snuggled closer.

"I found y'all on the back deck of our apartment. Daddy was sitting crisscross-style with you cradled in his arms." His brown eyes focused solely on their son.

"And he was so focused on me he didn't even see you."

"I hurried to get my camera—" she kissed the top of his head "—snapped the picture through the glass patio door and watched y'all for several minutes before Daddy realized I was there."

"He finally looked up, you opened the door, and he said he wanted you to get some extra sleep cuz you deserved it for giving him such a perfect son."

"That's right." Her eyes singed. She glanced at the clock.

Getting late. Hating to interrupt such precious memories, she gave him a good squeeze. "It's bedtime."

"Aw, Mom. I like sitting here with you and we're not done with the album."

"I like sitting here with you, too. But you have school tomorrow. Tell you what—tomorrow night we'll do it again."

"Promise?"

"Promise." She kissed his cheek, thankful he was still young enough he didn't shrug off her affection just yet.

What would she do when he got older and didn't want to cuddle? When he grew up? When he got married and left her alone?

The whirring furnace knocked the chill off in the rental house. Second day of March and Slade had three months to figure out what came next.

"You're sure the landlord is okay with a dog as large as Blizzard in the house?" Slade gestured to the huge white fluff-ball inspecting every nook and cranny.

"He okayed pets." Star, Aubrey's Realtor, grinned. "And didn't mention size restrictions."

"Blizzard will be either outside or in the laundry room when I'm gone."

"So does that mean you like it?"

He scanned the house. Sheetrock walls painted taupe with hardwood floors and simple furnishings. No bells or whistles. Perfect for him.

"When can I move in?"

"Today."

"I'll take it."

"Great." Star went over the deposit, how much he needed to pay up front, when the rent was due and the exit policy.

"I plan to stay through May. Can I just pay it all in advance?"

"Sure, if that's how you want to handle it." She tapped numbers on her tablet and gave him the grand total. "So my husband recognized your name. He said you were a major-league pitcher for the Rangers and you were really good."

"I wasn't bad." He rubbed his shoulder. "Until I tore my rotator cuff in the first season. My first surgery was a success, but against my doctor's orders, I rushed my recovery and tore it again during off-season practice."

He'd sacrificed everything to follow his grandfather's footsteps into baseball. His laser focus had gotten him a baseball scholarship to college and then a ticket to the major leagues. But he'd been so focused he'd never even had a girlfriend in high school.

So ten years later, here he was with just Blizzard to keep him company. No wife, no family except his grandparents and a sister who didn't even know about him.

He signed the check and handed it to Star in exchange for the keys. "I hope my neighbors won't have any problem with Blizzard."

"I don't think you'll have any problem with the neighbors." Her phone rang. "I need to get this. Let me know if you need anything." She waved and backed out the front door.

Hmm. Did the neighbors have a bigger, noisier dog than Blizzard? Or maybe fifteen dogs?

"Woof." Blizzard's bark echoed through the sparsely furnished house.

"Want outside, boy?"

The dog's ears perked up and his bushy tail thumped.

"How about a walk?"

"Woof." The huge dog quivered with anticipation.

And people thought dogs didn't understand. He clipped the leash onto Blizzard's collar and headed for the front door.

* * *

"Mom." Hunter got two syllables out of the word. "Throw it right."

"I'm trying, sweetie." Raquel concentrated on the spot where the seven-year-old's bat would swing and threw the baseball with all her strength. Her shoulder protested. She'd probably thrown it out of socket.

The pitch looked good. Right height, but it sailed two feet out of Hunter's reach.

"Mom." Two syllables again.

"I'm doing the best I can." She massaged her shoulder. "I never pitched. Maybe Uncle Brant can help."

"He's on tour, and besides, he never pitched either." Hunter poked at the piece of two-by-four—their make-shift home plate—with his bat. His shoulders slumped. "It doesn't matter. I can't do it anyway."

"Don't say that." His defeat squeezed her heart. "You can do anything you set your mind to." With Hunter's first baseball practice next week, she'd wanted to encourage him. Instead she'd discouraged him with her lousy pitching skills.

Why, why, why did Dylan have to die? Hunter needed his father. If Dylan had been here, Hunter would already have been hitting home runs. But Dylan wasn't here. And Raquel had to do this alone.

"I wish my dad was here."

Her vision blurred. "Me too, sweetie." But all Raquel had left of Dylan was his seven-year-old spitting image waiting for a decent pitch. And Hunter would never really know his father, no matter how hard she tried.

"Surely there's somebody in this town who can pitch a baseball. We'll find somebody."

Like Slade Walker. He'd pitched for a short time in the major leagues. What were the odds of running into him a few weeks ago? But he'd probably been only passing through.

"Who's that man?" Hunter looked past her.

Raquel turned.

A man and a large white dog stepped through the line of dormant crepe myrtle trees lining her property.

She stiffened, ready to protect her cub, but recognized the familiar smile.

"Did I hear something about needing a pitcher?"

"Mr. Walker?" As if she'd wished him into existence.

Chapter 2

"The one and only." Slade grinned.

And his grin revved her heart. She clasped a hand to her chest. Maybe it was the surprise.

"What are you doing here?"

"I was taking Blizzard for a walk." He stopped beside her and patted the dog's head. The dog settled in at his feet. "And I heard some baseball going on."

"Can I pet your dog?" Hunter cut around her to get to the dog.

"Sure, he's a big softy."

"Hi, Blizzard. My name's Hunter. What kind of dog are you?"

"Great Pyrenees. They're bred to protect sheep." Slade knelt beside the pair and scratched the big white head. "I knew from the size of his feet when he was a pup he'd end up being too big to be called Snowball."

"You have sheep?" Hunter giggled as the dog licked his cheek.

"No. But I used to work with a lot of horses, and Blizzard's breed is good with livestock, too."

"You live here?"

"Just rented the place next door." Slade glanced at their ranch-style house. "You live here?"

"We moved here last May." Hunter grinned as Blizzard crouched in his "wanna play" stance.

Next door? Raquel had seen vehicles and a camper earlier but hadn't had time to be neighborly. She'd never dreamed Slade would move in.

Slade seemed to remember Raquel was there and stood.

"Mr. Walker just happens to be a pitcher, Hunter. A major-league pitcher. Remember that autograph I gave you?"

"Really?" Hunter's eyes grew wide.

"That was a long time ago." Slade rubbed his shoulder.

"Can you pitch for me?"

"I'm sure Mr. Walker doesn't have time right now."

"It's not a problem. It's what I came over for. Unless you think Dylan might have a problem with me helping Hunter."

Her gaze flew to Hunter, but he'd forgotten about baseball for the moment and was rolling and giggling in the grass with Blizzard.

"Dylan died three years ago," she whispered.

"Oh." Slade swallowed hard. His eyes reddened. "I'm sorry. I had no clue."

"I tried to contact all of his friends." Something went soft inside her and tears burned the backs of her eyes. After three years sometimes it still hit her as if she'd just lost him. Especially when she had to tell someone new. And especially when that someone had known and loved Dylan, too.

She blinked hard. "Hunter, baseball. I'm sure Mr. Walker doesn't have all night."

Hunter jumped up, ran toward home plate and picked

up his bat. Blizzard lay content in the grass where Hunter had left him.

"Come here, Blizzard." Raquel clicked her tongue. The large dog followed obediently and she settled on the porch steps. Blizzard rested at her feet and she scratched around his furry ears.

Why hadn't she thought to get Hunter a dog? While they'd lived in Garland, their apartment wouldn't allow pets. But she'd fulfilled her and Dylan's dream by moving to the country. Ten months after the move and she hadn't even thought of getting a dog.

"Choke up on the bat. Set your feet apart a little wider and line 'em up with the plate."

Hunter squeezed the bat, adjusted his stance and looked even more awkward.

"Here, let me help you." Slade jogged over to Hunter. "*Choke up* means move your hands higher on the bat." He adjusted Hunter's grip, then moved to the other side of the plate and showed Hunter the proper stance. Hunter mirrored Slade's posture, and all his awkward angles were gone.

"That's so much better." Raquel clapped her hands. "You look like a pro."

"Thanks, Mr. Walker." Hunter's wide grin put a smile in her heart.

"Just call me Slade." Slade returned to the pitcher's mound—another piece of wood. "Ready?"

Hunter nodded and Slade fired the ball—the perfect pitch. Hunter swung but didn't connect. His shoulders slumped again.

"Swing your bat level. You swung under and then up. Practice before I pitch again."

The bat made an undercut and then veered up again.

Slade jogged over to him. Standing behind her son, he

clasped the bat and swung in a straight line. "Like that. Now do it without me."

Hunter swung the bat in a straight line.

"That's it—keep it level just like that." Slade jogged back to the mound and lobbed a pitch.

Raquel's fists curled and her nails dug into her palms.

Hunter swung. Thwack. The ball sailed into the air.

"Woo-hoo!" Raquel jumped to her feet, clapping.

Red splotches stained Hunter's cheeks, but his grin was a mile wide.

"That's it. You've got it."

"Can you pitch me some more?"

Raquel checked her watch. "Homework time. Besides, Slade probably needs to get going."

"Aw, Mom."

"Don't argue with your mom." Slade patted the boy's shoulder. "And appreciate her for trying to pitch for you. At least she tried."

"Yes, sir." Hunter shot her a sheepish grin as he climbed the porch steps. "Thanks, Mom."

The screen door slapped closed and Slade sat down beside her. "He's a great kid."

"Thanks. We do pretty good most of the time." Until he'd signed up for baseball. "I never played softball, so I'm not much help. But Hunter loved baseball in Garland, so I thought signing up here would get him out of his shell and help him make some friends."

"Why did y'all move here?" Slade scratched Blizzard's ears.

She dug her fingers into the soft white fur along the dog's side. "A child changes things. After an incident at school, Dylan and I decided we wanted to raise Hunter in the country. But then Dylan died." And her parents tried to convince her to move home. But she'd wanted Hunter to feel secure and know they could make it on their own. "I decided I should fulfill Dylan's dream."

"Why Aubrey?"

"Dylan and I brought Hunter to a dude ranch here when he was three. He doesn't remember it, but Dylan and I both fell in love with the town. Last year my brother ended up moving here because his best friend lives here and helped him get a job." She shrugged. "There was an opening for a school nurse here and everything fell into place as if it were meant to be."

"Hunter seems well adjusted."

"He tends to be shy around other kids and so far he's only made one friend since we moved here. It's been worse since my brother's job took him on the road. He was reluctant to go because of Hunter, but I convinced him we'd be fine until he gets back."

"What happened to Dylan?" His voice came out tight. "I mean, if you don't mind telling me."

"It's fine." She cleared her throat. "He made it as a Texas Ranger like he always planned, but he died in an off-duty car wreck."

"I'm sorry."

"Yeah, me too." Her gaze scanned the horizon. "What brings you to Aubrey?"

"I'm taking a sabbatical from my rodeo chaplaincy. My mentor thought I needed a break and after I ran into you, I decided to move here and catch up…"

"With Dylan. I wish you could." She sighed. "I remember Dylan talking to you on the phone about being a rodeo chaplain. I imagine it can be frustrating, like any ministry." She still couldn't picture him at the rodeo.

After watching old games with Dylan, she'd have never imagined Slade wearing any kind of hat other than a baseball cap. But his cowboy hat somehow fit.

"It's not exactly what I set out to do with my life." He

shrugged. "But it's been more fulfilling than anything I've ever done."

"So, how long will you be here?" The house next door was a rental house.

"Three months. Maybe I'm getting old, but the road's rough and it's not really a good place to find someone to settle down with. Most of the ladies are attached to the cowboys traveling the circuit."

Settling down? Slade Walker wanted to settle down. And he couldn't find anybody single and willing? The breeze blew through his dark waves, a sharp contrast to those sage-green eyes.

"So God gave me the opportunity to take a break. Relax in quiet little Aubrey, Texas, and hopefully get my fire back for the road." He turned to face her. "I thought I'd catch up with an old friend and never dreamed…"

"Yeah, me neither. If you'd have told me back when I met Dylan that I'd be a widow by the age of twenty-four, I'd have laughed."

"Even with him being in law enforcement?"

"I never worried about his job." She shrugged. "A lot of the wives and girlfriends do, but I just didn't. And in the end…the job didn't cause his death."

"How's your friend Caitlyn?"

"She and Michaela Natasha Warren are both fine."

"That's a pretty name, but it's a mouthful."

"After her father, Mitch, and her aunt Natalie." A brown butterfly with yellow-lined wings flitted about the bluebonnets. The first she'd seen this spring. Butterflies always gave her a sense of tranquility. "I hope she's a good speller." Raquel laughed.

"Did you know Caitlyn before you moved here?"

"Mitch was Dylan's partner."

"Ah. I thought y'all seemed close."

"Mitch was great when Dylan died. He spends as much

time as he can with Hunter. And once he married Caitlyn, we became friends."

"I'm glad you haven't remarried."

What?

"I mean…" Slade stuttered. "I've known people who marry the first person to come along and end up making mistakes."

Oh. Not because he was interested in her. But sweet that he cared.

"I love the sounds of the country. Listen." Slade closed his eyes.

Grateful for the change of subject, she relaxed. The frogs struck up a chorus as the sky darkened. Dylan would've loved it, too.

From the time she and Dylan had started dating, he'd worried about dying because of his occupation. He'd worried about leaving her alone and always made her promise to find someone new to love if anything happened to him. Especially after Hunter was born. He'd made her promise to find a new love who'd be a good father to their son.

After Dylan died, she'd made a promise to herself. She would eventually find a good father for Hunter with a nice safe occupation. She wouldn't even think of bringing another man into Hunter's life if his odds of dying young were high.

Why was she thinking about that promise now?

"It was nice seeing you." She stood. "But I'd better go check on Hunter. Thanks for helping him."

"No problem. He can come over and play with Blizzard anytime." He patted the dog's head. "And I'd be happy to work on his baseball skills whenever he wants to."

"Thanks, but I'm sure you're busy."

"Actually, I'm not."

"Oh, right. I'll tell him. I'm sure he'd like that."

"Good night, Raquel." He clicked his tongue. "Come on, Blizzard. Let's go home."

Home? Right next door. Slade Walker was right next door. He disappeared through the line of bushes.

The few times she'd dated since Dylan's death, it had felt forced. As if she was just looking to fulfill her promise to Dylan. But she'd known of Slade since she'd met Dylan. Had even answered the phone a few times when he'd called in the early years of her marriage.

Now, after meeting him in person, she was at ease with him. She stepped inside and locked the door behind her. And she'd always thought he was handsome. Yes, Slade had always been a nice guy, a Christian and a hunk. And a girl couldn't get any more safe than a rodeo chaplain.

But he might not stay in Aubrey. She couldn't allow Hunter to get attached to a man who would leave in three months. And she couldn't afford to have such silly thoughts. If only he'd keep going and stride right back into her past.

Dylan was dead. He wasn't here anymore. It didn't compute.

But his widow lived next door.

Slade's heart hurt for her, but her strength appealed to him. The strength that kept her going after her husband's death. The strength that had given her the courage to move somewhere new for her son's sake without running home to her parents. Her determination to give him a small-town childhood, even if she had to do it alone.

It was her strength that made him want to help her—so she could relax for once and not have to be so strong.

Slade climbed the porch steps and unlocked the door. Blizzard bolted inside and headed for his food bowl. Chunks clattered against the stainless steel bowl as Slade filled it.

When she'd told him Dylan was gone, it had knocked the wind out of him. Sitting on the steps together remembering a man they'd both loved seemed to bond them.

Everything had lined up perfectly as if God was directing it all. The little town of Aubrey had drawn them both here, her son needed help with baseball, and Slade had nothing but time on his hands. He could be there for Dylan's widow. Be there for Dylan's son.

Thwack. The bat made contact, the ball sailed past second base, and Raquel and her friend Lacie jumped to their feet cheering. As his team rooted for Hunter, her heart swelled and he made it safely to first base. After his almost nightly batting practices with Slade, Hunter hadn't struck out like last year. His grin was brighter than the afternoon sun.

"That was awesome." Lacie sat back down on the aluminum bleacher. "Did you teach him that?"

"No way." Raquel laughed. "I played basketball."

"Duh." Lacie rolled her eyes.

The tiny blonde's petite build made Raquel feel like an Amazon woman at five-eight. Caitlyn had introduced her to Lacie back when Raquel had first moved here. Since Lacie had been widowed before she married Quinn, and her son, Max, was in Hunter's class, she and Raquel had bonded and Hunter had made his first true friend in Max.

"Good job, Hunter." The coach applauded. "Everybody's been up to bat, so let's wrap it up for the day. Boys, pair up and play catch while I talk to the parents."

The coach and his two assistants exited the field and the parents circled them.

"Could any of you parents volunteer to coach?" The coach kept his voice low.

"Isn't that you?" Lacie asked.

"I just got news that I'll be deployed in a week."

Raquel's heart sank. For the soldier and his family but also for Hunter. He'd be so disappointed.

All of the parents shook their heads.

"I'd like to break the news to the team after I find a replacement so they won't worry. Anybody know anyone who might volunteer?"

The parents shook their heads again.

"I hate to say this—" the coach propped his foot on the bottom bleacher "—but if we don't find someone, we won't be able to have a team."

"What about your assistants?" Raquel gestured toward the two men flanking the coach.

"I've never coached before." Lacie's husband, Quinn, kicked at the dirt. "I played hockey in school and only signed up to help out since Max is playing. I'm totally not qualified to coach. In fact, I'm still learning the rules."

"I might be willing." The man with the potbelly scanned the parents. "But I don't have any experience."

"I appreciate that, Sam." The coach studied the parents as if hoping for a better solution. "I'm really sorry about this. If I'd known I would be deployed, I'd have never signed up to coach."

"It can't be helped." Raquel tried not to let the disappointment show in her tone. "We appreciate your willingness and your service to our country."

"Ask around and see if you can come up with anyone. I'll do the same. Sam, you think about it and we'll see what happens."

The move had been harder on Hunter than she'd expected. Especially since her brother, Brant, was gone so much. Hunter had looked forward to the move because of his uncle. But Brant's frequent touring was wearing thin. If his baseball team lost all season, Hunter would miss his old friends and teammates even more.

She cleared her throat. "I might know someone."

All eyes turned to her as if she'd saved the day.

And she had. If she could convince Slade.

Lunch at Moms on Main had gotten Slade out of the house. Made him stop watching the clock. Made him stop waiting for Raquel to come home. And the meal had been much better than anything he could have come up with in his rental-house kitchen.

Saturday was usually the busiest day of his week, as he prepared for the rodeo and his sermon. Now the weekend stretched before him.

"Slade Walker?" A man met him on the sidewalk pushing a baby stroller with a petite redhead on his arm.

Slade's eyes widened. His chest constricted. The fair-complexioned woman from the clipping in his pocket. His sister. And her husband.

How does he know me? Had the lawyer let it slip?

"Have we met?" Slade cleared his throat.

"No. I followed your career with the Rangers. I'm Brant McConnell."

"Oh." Slade's relief poured out in a trickle of sweat down his back. Despite the early-March chill.

"You just passing through?"

"Actually—" his gaze strayed to Tori...his sister "—I'm here for a few months."

"I'm Tori." She stuck her hand toward him.

He clasped her delicate hand. "Nice to meet you, ma'am." Who'd have ever thought he'd have a redheaded sister?

"My wife." Brant stated his dibs out loud.

And Slade realized he was still holding her hand.

Chapter 3

Slade dropped Tori's hand as if burned by fire.

Great. It looked as if he was hitting on this guy's wife. Hitting on his sister. Ugh. *Come on, brain—kick into gear.*

"Congratulations." His gaze settled on the baby dressed in pink. Probably six months old or so. His niece.

But his brain did the math. He knew from the clipping in his wallet that Tori and Brant had gotten married on Thanksgiving Day. Which meant she'd been hugely pregnant or had already had the baby by the time their wedding came around.

"Thanks." Tori's smile trembled. He'd made her uncomfortable hanging on to her hand because she had no idea who he was. Great.

"It was nice to meet you." He tipped his hat at Tori and kept walking. Before he did something stupid. Like punching her husband for taking advantage of her. Before telling her right then and there who he was.

* * *

She'd been gone most of the day and set Slade's imagination on edge. Where had Raquel been? On a date? Had she dropped Hunter at a sitter's and gone to dinner with someone?

He needed something to do other than sit around and think about Raquel's social life. What she did with her Saturday was none of his business. He clicked the TV on, then off again and let Blizzard out.

A knock sounded at the front door. He hadn't heard a vehicle. Maybe it was Hunter wanting to play with Blizzard or practice batting. Hunter had been over almost every day, but he'd only seen Raquel supervising from her yard.

He hurried to the front of the house and swung the door open. Raquel stood on his porch, kicking his pulse into overdrive.

"Hey."

"Hey." He managed to speak around his heart lodged in his throat.

A flowery scent entered his space. Tantalizing and soft—like Raquel. Did her long blond hair feel as silky as it looked? His fingers itched to learn, so he shoved his hands in his pockets.

"Come on in."

"Thanks, but I can't. I've got dinner on. My brother and his family have been out of town for the last three months and just got back. They're coming over for a celebration dinner in a bit. I thought you might like to join us."

"It's real nice of you to ask, but I don't want to impose on your family dinner."

"You wouldn't be imposing. I cooked a roast with carrots, potatoes and green beans. There's plenty."

His taste buds fired up. "I don't know."

"Come on—it'll be fun. And I'm a great cook."

"I remember Dylan saying that."

"Hunter would love it if you came."

"I don't have a thing to contribute to the meal."

"You don't need to bring anything but yourself. Supper is ready and they should arrive anytime."

"I'll be over in a few minutes, then."

"Sounds good." She turned away.

Slade raked his hand through his hair. For the first time, he'd noticed her long blond hair. Hair that begged a man to run his fingers through it. Her willowy lithe figure—even after giving birth—that begged a man's arms to hold her. Her blue eyes that twinkled when she laughed. And her laugh that sounded like music.

Admittedly, Slade was drawn to her. And attracted to her.

What kind of jerk would allow himself to be attracted to his friend's widow?

Raquel booked it across his yard to hers while her legs would still work. Her heart was about to beat out of her chest and her mouth had gone dry when he'd opened the door. How could a man make jeans and an undershirt look so good? How could a man have that many muscles?

Why did he have to be so stinking good-looking and nice on top of that? Maybe this wasn't such a good idea after all.

But she had to think of Hunter.

And she had to refrain from staring when Slade brought his fine self to dinner. Surely he'd put a real shirt on.

Oh. My. Goodness.

He'd made her heart rev. Again.

No. No. No. He was here for only three months. Her heart could not rev over him. She'd just been nervous about asking him to coach Hunter's team. Yeah, that's what it was.

Calm down. Butter him up with supper. Resist looking at him unless she had to. And everything would be fine.

As she entered through the back door, cartoons blasted from the living room. "Hunter, turn down the TV and go wash up."

"Yes, ma'am."

The television faded into background noise and she checked the roast, then transferred the fork-tender beef and vegetables to a serving platter. The onions and celery added a savory aroma to the gravy and made her mouth water as she covered the dish with foil to keep it warm.

"They're here!" Hunter called.

Raquel squealed as she hurried to the front of the house and followed Hunter out the door to meet Brant.

Hunter beat her to him and hugged Brant until he knelt to scoop up his nephew.

"I'm so glad you're home." Raquel hugged him around Hunter. "But you're gonna hurt your back."

"Not with this squirt."

"I'm not a squirt. I'm one of the tallest in my class." Hunter giggled as Brant tickled his ribs, then set him down.

Raquel hurried to hug Tori and coo over her baby niece. "Oh, Lorraine, you get prettier and prettier, just like your mama."

"Nope. She's prettier than I ever thought about being." Tori grinned.

"Obviously, you haven't looked in the mirror lately, 'cause you're one smoking-hot mama." Brant winked at his wife.

"Little ears," Tori whispered.

Brant covered his mouth in mock dismay and focused on Hunter again. "So, were you surprised?"

"About what?"

"That I'm here. That I'm home from my tour."

Hunter shook his head. "Mama told me you were coming to dinner tonight."

"Rock." Brant shot her a stern scowl. "Will you never learn to keep a secret?"

"I tried." She winced. "It slipped out in something like 'We'll save this roast for Saturday when Uncle Brant comes home.'"

"No secrets around my little sis." Brant shook his head and scooped a pie out of his truck. "I'm starving."

"You were born starving." Raquel linked arms with her brother. "Tori, you weren't supposed to bring anything. You just got home."

"We stopped for lunch at Aunt Loretta's." Tori rolled her eyes. "She did her best to sabotage my postpregnancy diet and insisted we bring you her blueberry pie."

"Pfft, you don't need a diet." Raquel got a whiff of the pie. "Yum. Tell her thank you. How was the tour?"

"It was the most awesome thing I've ever been part of." Brant's eyes shone.

"I'm so glad." She squeezed his arm. Brant had achieved his lifelong dream and she couldn't be happier for him, but goodness, she missed him when he was gone. "I'm so glad you're home for three months, though."

"Me too."

"I got a new baseball bat to show you." Hunter grabbed Tori's hand and tugged her toward the house.

"Careful, Hunter. Don't pull Aunt Tori. You might make her drop Lorraine."

Hunter eased up and followed his aunt inside.

"So, after we eat, could you and Tori entertain Hunter for a bit while I talk with our new neighbor? You'll never guess who lives next door."

"Who?"

"Slade Walker."

"Slade Walker?" Brant scowled.

Scowled? In disbelief? Brant had watched Slade play baseball right along with her and Dylan.

"As in former Texas Rangers pitcher. How cool is that? Just when Hunter needs a new coach. That's what I want to talk to him about."

"Wait a minute. I thought Hunter had a coach."

"He's getting deployed, so I'm hoping Slade will agree to coach his team."

"That's not a good idea." Brant's tone held bridled anger.

"Why?" Raquel frowned as she perched on the porch swing. It creaked when Brant settled beside her. "How awesome would it be to have a former Texas Rangers pitcher coaching Hunter's team? He helped Hunter with his batting and Hunter hit the ball in his first practice the other night. You should have seen his face."

"You can't just go asking some guy you barely know to get involved with your son."

"So I barely know him." Raquel shrugged. Brant had been a fan during Slade's Rangers days. What was his deal? "But Dylan knew him well. They were best friends in Garland until the fifth grade, when Slade moved away. After that they saw each other a few times over the years and Slade led Dylan to the Lord. They talked on the phone often. He's a nice guy."

"A lot can change in a guy between the fifth grade and late twenties, little sister."

"You act like you know something I don't." She elbowed him.

"I do. Tori and I ran into him in Aubrey a little earlier. Lorraine was getting fussy in her car seat, so we stopped for a walk and—"

"Hey. I hope I'm not late." Slade strolled toward them from the path Hunter had already worn between the bushes separating their houses.

"Perfect timing." Raquel stood.

"You invited *him* to dinner?" Brant's whisper verged on a growl.

"Be nice." She elbowed him in the ribs. "We'll talk about this later."

"Just proceed with caution, Rock. Do not ask him to coach Hunter until we get a chance to talk."

Slade stopped a few feet from the porch. Recognition dawned in his eyes and he looked as if he might turn and go back home. But then he closed the gap and climbed the steps.

What on earth had happened between Slade and Brant?

"It's Brant, right?" Slade offered his hand. "You're Raquel's brother?"

Brant clenched his jaw and tension roiled through the air. Raquel jabbed him with her elbow again and he clasped Slade's hand.

"We ran into each other earlier in town." Slade's gaze bounced from her to Brant. "I didn't realize there was a connection between y'all."

"Yeah, me neither." Brant's tone held a warning.

"Dinner's ready." Raquel stood. And not a moment too soon.

The day just kept getting better. Slade had managed to tick off Brant—his sister's husband. And now Brant turned out to be Raquel's brother. Great.

Despite the tension, Raquel's house was warm and inviting, not bare like his. Her decor had cowgirl flair, just like her. Somehow the touches of burlap and lace didn't look too girly.

While Brant fed Lorraine, Slade snatched glimpses of his sister and his niece. That and the roast and vegetables drowning in succulent gravy made the tension worth it. It would take more than Brant's glare to scare Slade's appetite away.

Tori seemed nice, gentle, kind. And she was a great mom—attentive to Lorraine's every sound and move. Not the kind of person to be upset at learning she had a brother. Under different circumstances, Brant would probably be all right, too. He seemed to be a hands-on dad and a caring brother and uncle.

He'd still gotten Tori pregnant before he married her. But once Brant learned who Slade was and that he wasn't making moves on Tori, maybe they could build a relationship.

"This roast is awesome." Slade stuffed another bite in his mouth.

"Thanks." Raquel glanced from Brant to Slade, clearly wondering what was up.

"I need to stop. I'm stuffed to the gills, but this stuff is just too good to leave on my plate."

"Raquel loves to cook and she's great at it." Tori shrugged. "Maybe between her and my aunt, they can teach me a thing or two now that we're home."

"Where were y'all for the last three months?"

Brant glowered at him.

"Brant is touring with Garrett Steele." Raquel cleared her throat.

"*The* Garrett Steele?"

"Uh-huh." Hunter giggled. "They've been friends for years."

"Do you have an album out?" Slade risked directing the question to Brant.

"Recording one," Brant growled.

"Brant has wanted to be a Christian country singer for as long as I can remember." Raquel filled empty tea glasses. "And he's finally living his dream since Garrett Steele blazed the trail with the new genre."

"How often do you tour?"

"Three months on, three months off." Raquel filled the silence, the perfect hostess.

"All that travel can't be easy with a baby."

Tori seemed as uncomfortable with him as Brant did when he asked specifically about their family.

"Lorraine's the best baby I've ever seen. I've never even heard her whimper." Raquel scooped up her niece and held her up in the air. "Isn't that right, sweetie? I've been wanting to get my hands on you all night. I thought your poky daddy would never finish feeding you."

Lorraine gurgled and Raquel pressed her nose against the baby's smaller one, then tucked the squirming bundle into her shoulder and rhythmically patted the tiny back.

And she was good with babies. Perfect wife material. Why did the only woman he'd met who drew him like a moth to a flame have to be his friend's widow? On top of that, her brother hated him, and his calling was up in the air.

Definitely not a good time to pursue Raquel. Why couldn't she just stop being so friendly, so strong, so appealing, so perfect, so beautiful?

"First my wife, now my sister. What are you, some kind of stalker?" Brant's glare could have pierced steel.

Tori smacked him in the shoulder. "Hush."

Busted. Slade hadn't even realized he'd been staring at Raquel.

"Not at all." He pushed his chair back. He should have left as soon as he saw Brant on Raquel's porch. "But I think it's time for me to go."

Hunter looked wide eyed from one man to the other.

"Hunter, if you're finished with your pie, go study for your spelling test."

"Aw, Mom."

"Go."

"Yes, ma'am." The boy reluctantly scurried from the room.

"Slade, you haven't even had your pie yet." Raquel turned a sharp look on her brother. "Stop being a jerk and be nice to *my* guest. Maybe you and Tori could go help Hunter with his studying."

"I'm not leaving you alone with this guy."

Raquel held Lorraine up between them like a shield and the baby squealed and kicked her feet. "Lorraine will chaperone. Now go, before I kick you out of my house for bad manners."

Though Tori tugged on Brant's arm, he clearly wasn't ready to back down. The phone rang.

Saved by the bell.

"I'll get it," Hunter called from the front of the house.

"I really need to go." Slade headed toward the back door.

"Oh, all right, but at least let me send you a piece of pie home. And I need to talk to you about something soon."

"Sure. Anytime." He could feel Brant's glare burning a hole through him.

Raquel sliced the pie, set it on a disposable plate and wrapped it in foil.

"Mom!" Hunter blasted into the room. "Max said Grady said Fletcher said Coach James is quitting us. And when Max asked Coach Quinn, he said it's true."

Great. Just what she needed. A steaming brother and an upset child. "It is true, sweetie. But he has a good reason. Coach James is a soldier and he has to go back to work."

"But what about the team?"

"Don't worry—we'll find another coach."

"Hey, what about Slade? Will you be our coach?"

"Hunter! Calm down and don't put Slade on the spot like that. Please go back in the living room and study. The team will be just fine."

The little boy's shoulders slumped. "Okay."

"Come on, sweetie." Tori patted his arm. "I'm sure your team will find another coach."

Hunter and Tori trailed toward the living room, but

Brant stayed long enough to shoot Slade one more evil eye. "I'll be watching you."

"Brant!" Raquel snapped. "Out."

"I don't trust him, Rock. When we ran into him earlier, he made a move on my wife and he's gone back and forth staring at her, then you all night. Just watch him." With reluctance obvious in every step, Brant left them alone.

"I'm so sorry." Raquel covered her face with her hands. "This evening has been a disaster from the moment you arrived. You'll have to overlook Brant—a man tried to hurt Tori last year and Brant has been in overprotective overdrive ever since."

"Hurt her?" Slade's heart pounded.

"It's over now."

"I'm glad." Slade forced a grin to get things back on a light note before she got suspicious of him, too. "Rock fits you."

And got a laugh out of her. "He's called me that since we were kids. He says I'm strong and stubborn."

"I can see that." He rolled his shoulders. The tension of the evening had taken its toll. "Listen, Brant and I got off to a bad start. He recognized me on the street in Aubrey and Tori introduced herself. We shook hands and she…" He winced. "Let's just say she reminds me of someone. I may have held her hand a little too long, but I didn't mean anything by it. I don't go after married women."

"So that's what happened." Raquel shrugged. "He's always been overprotective and territorial—he's just worse now. I'll explain things to him and he should be fine. In the meantime, I apologize for his extreme rudeness. He has a bit of a temper."

"It's fine. So, is the coaching thing what you wanted to talk to me about?"

"Yes. But I wanted to do it privately so you wouldn't feel coerced by a pitiful, sad child." She sat on a stool at the breakfast bar. "I can't believe Fletcher's parents broke the news. Why upset the team when we could have just quietly found a replacement? Why do some parents seem to thrive on drama and angst?"

"Not a clue." Slade stood across from her. A safe distance with a bar between them. "Look, I'd love to help out, but I don't think I can."

"Please don't say no."

Slade's heart stalled. He didn't want to say no to her. About anything. Ever. He'd happily be her yes-man.

But that wouldn't be the best way to avoid Raquel. Or Hunter. Coaching Hunter would weave Slade more tightly into their lives. And then the time would come to give them up. And he wasn't sure he'd be able to. Better to keep his distance.

"If we can't find a new coach, all they'll have is an assistant who's never coached before."

"I'd love to help you, but—"

"It's only for three months. We practice on Tuesdays and Fridays during March. Then the games are on Mondays and Thursdays beginning in April and last through May. But if other days would be better for you for practice, that would be fine, too. And we could practice less once the season starts if you want."

"I only leased the house for three months."

"That's perfect." Raquel's eyes lit up, making him want to do whatever it took to keep her happy. "Your lease goes through May and the season goes through May."

His heart clunked back in place in his chest. If he coached Hunter, he'd automatically spend more time with Raquel. They'd grow closer. But he couldn't let the attraction grow.

She was still tender from losing her husband. And she had a son to think about. With his calling up in the air, nothing could happen between him and Raquel. Not if he wasn't staying put.

Besides, there was his sister to consider. He still didn't know what to do about Tori.

On top of all that, coaching Little League baseball wasn't part of his doctor's prescribed treatment. He shouldn't even have pitched for Hunter at all; forget taking on a coaching position.

"I can't."

"You can't?" The light dimmed in her eyes.

"I'm sorry."

"Oh. Um… Okay." She stood, stepped over to the stove and ladled roast into a plastic bowl. "Take some leftovers with you. I guess I need to get back to my other company anyway."

"I'm sorry."

She waved a hand through the air as if it didn't matter. But her eyes said it did. "It's no problem. I shouldn't have asked."

"I'd help if I could." He sighed. "I can still get together with him for batting practice."

"It may not be necessary if he ends up without a team."

"I'm sure the assistant will be fine."

"Probably. I just want Hunter to have a good year." She sealed the bowl and pushed it to him across the granite counter. "The move was tough on him. He had to leave all his friends and his baseball team. And in Garland, he happened to end up on a really good team and they won their league championship. I'm worried if his new team doesn't do well, he'll miss Garland even more."

"I'm sorry." No matter how many times he said it, he could never show her how sorry he was.

"It's okay. I understand." She hurried to the back door and placed her hand on the knob. Ready to open it for him. Ready to be rid of him.

And the disappointment in her eyes would haunt him. For days. Maybe even for months.

Could he go against every instinct he had and sign up to coach Hunter's team? He'd help Hunter and make Raquel happy, but he'd surely lose his heart in the process. And what if at the end of May, God still wanted him back on the road?

Maybe he could keep his feelings in check, keep Raquel at a safe physical distance and take on the coaching position. Just to help Hunter. That way he'd have to worry only about his shoulder. A much easier task. Besides, they probably used a pitching machine.

"I'll do it." He made no move for the door.

"You will?" Her eyes lit up. "Hunter will be so excited. We can change the schedule up however you need to. Whatever is convenient for you."

"I think the current one will work."

"You have no idea what this will mean to Hunter. He'll be big guy on the field. The kid who got a former Ranger to coach. This will do wonders for his friend-making issues." She spoke faster and faster and did a little bounce, then launched herself into his arms. "Thank you."

Slade's heart rocketed in his chest.

Yes, her hair was that silky. Yes, she fit perfectly in his arms. Yes, he really wanted to kiss her.

Chapter 4

Slade's arms around Raquel warmed her from head to toe. What had she been thinking—throwing herself at him? She hadn't thought past how excited Hunter would be about his new coach.

Why was she still in his arms?

"Sorry." She pushed away from him, but her brain was mush from the feel of him. Resting her hands against his rock-solid chest, she risked looking up at him. "I get a little excited sometimes."

"Not a problem." His gaze latched on her lips.

"Ahem." Brant cleared his throat.

Raquel sprang away from Slade.

Her brother leaned against the kitchen door frame, glowering.

"Slade agreed to coach Hunter's team. I was just thanking him." She patted his shoulder.

Wow, he was solid. Shouldn't have touched him again. No touching. Definitely no touching Slade.

More space between them was in order. She took another step back. Lots of space between them.

"It was only a friendly hug." Slade held his hands up in surrender. "But in case you haven't noticed, Raquel's a grown woman. I think she can hug whoever she wants."

The space she'd made between them cleared her brain. "You go on, Slade. I'll handle this."

"I'm not sure I should leave until your brother calms down."

"His bark is worse than his bite." She waved her hand as if to wave away his concerns. "And I'm pretty sure he got his rabies shot this year. We'll be fine. I've been defusing Brant since we were kids."

Slade grinned. "I guess I'll see you at the ball field Tuesday night?"

Brant's scowl grew deeper.

"Yes. And thank you so much. You have no idea what this will mean to the kids. I'll call Hunter's coach and he'll probably bring a form for you to fill out. You can meet us at the ball field."

"Where is it?"

"I'm terrible with directions. Why don't you just ride with us? We'll leave about a quarter till six."

"It's a date." Slade's mouth tightened. "I mean…see ya then."

"I really appreciate this. The kids will, too." She handed him the bowl of roast and the pie.

"It'll be fun."

Fun. Keeping her heart from revving for three months in Slade Walker's presence. Not Raquel's idea of fun.

"Can I trust you to play nice if I leave?" Slade turned to Brant.

"My *nice* will come out when you leave."

Slade blew out a sigh and left them alone.

"Didn't I warn you about him?" Brant barked. "I turn my back for two minutes and he's all over you."

"It was a hug. An innocent hug. And I instigated it. You know how I am when I get excited about something. I'm a hugger."

"And I love that about you. Just be careful who you hug. But that wasn't a hug I saw. It was 'I wanna kiss you' written all over his face. I tell you, that guy's a womanizer or a stalker."

Her face flushed. She'd read the look, too. "He told me what happened with Tori. She reminded him of someone and I guess it kind of threw him. He didn't hold her hand to make moves on her." She rolled her eyes. "He's a rodeo chaplain. Not a womanizer. Or a stalker."

"He wouldn't be the first preacher to sample the congregation."

"Brant!"

"Well, it's true. You hear about it all the time in the news."

"And you don't hear about the millions who don't." She took her frustrations out on the counter, scrubbing it hard with a dishcloth, trying to forget the way Slade had looked at her. "Dylan became a Christian because of Slade. He's spent years on the rodeo circuit preaching sermons. He's a good man."

"And you know this because?"

"Dylan only had good things to say about him. And I can just tell."

"The people who live next door to the serial killer always say, 'He was such a nice guy.'"

"Brant, please."

He sighed. "You're my baby sister and I don't want you to get hurt. Didn't you caution me when I was falling for Tori?"

"True. But I was wrong. Look how great that turned out."

"Really great." Brant's mouth curved into a goofy grin but then flatlined. "But think of Hunter. He's been through a lot. More than any kid his age deserves."

"Yes." Raquel leaned her hip against the counter and folded her arms across her chest. "But what does Slade coaching Hunter in baseball have to do with either of us getting hurt?"

"Say he's not a womanizer or a stalker and he is a nice guy. There's something stirring between you and Slade. If you two end up dating and getting involved, and then he leaves… You can't raise Hunter traveling the rodeo circuit. And you don't deserve a long-distance relationship."

Brant was right. Even if Raquel could handle it, Hunter couldn't. She didn't need him getting attached if Slade was leaving.

"Hunter just needs a coach and Slade's the best baseball player around. That's all there is to it."

"I still want you to be careful. I wish you'd taken that self-defense class I sent Tori to. Just keep it about baseball with Slade. That's all I'm saying."

Could she keep her heart out of things? With the only guy who'd made her heart race since Dylan?

"Truce?"

"Truce." Brant gave her a hug.

"Awww." Tori chuckled as she entered the kitchen. "Isn't that the sweetest thing, Lorraine? Maybe someday you'll have a brother."

The sweet moment misted Raquel's eyes.

"I like the sound of someday." Brant pecked Tori on the cheek and scooped Lorraine from her arms. "Ready to go home, my beautiful wife?"

"Yes." Tori yawned. "I'd like to sleep for three days."

"I can keep Lorraine one night next weekend if you want." Raquel tickled Lorraine's chin and the baby gurgled.

"We might just take you up on that." Brant shouldered the diaper bag.

It all reminded her of Dylan when Hunter was little. How attentive he was and how he always carried the diaper bag or car seat for her.

Having her brother home with his happy family warmed her heart. And made it ache with loneliness.

She and Dylan had planned to have another baby. But Dylan was gone. And Hunter was an only child.

And the only man she'd felt anything for since then lived right next door—temporarily. Totally out of reach.

Slade had tried to make small talk during the short drive to the ball field. But his brain didn't seem to fire right with Raquel next to him in her car. He couldn't stop thinking about the hug. About wanting to kiss her and her not seeming to disagree with the notion.

He'd been tired of traveling the circuit for a while now, but not tired of preaching. Could he fulfill his calling and stay in Aubrey?

Could he preach in a regular church? He was used to being surrounded by the smell of manure, with horses stamping and whinnying in the background and his congregation wearing cowboy hats under the Texas sky.

Churches were definitely more comfortable. Yet he couldn't imagine the cowboys he ministered to being comfortable with carpet and padded pews.

But he could definitely be comfortable riding to Raquel's rescue. At a slow but steady pace.

Focus on baseball.

"Got any power hitters on the team?"

"Power hitters?" Raquel laughed. "We're talking second grade here."

"Okay. Anyone who can hit the ball?"

"Three or four kids," Hunter piped up from the back-seat.

Raquel turned into a parking lot and cut the engine. The field teemed with Little Leaguers and supportive parents.

"I can work with that." Slade opened his door and they all piled out.

"And thanks to you, Hunter's one of our hitters now." Raquel pulled the cooler she'd packed with Gatorade out of the backseat.

"Let me get that." He wrestled the cooler from her.

"Watch for cars." Raquel called as Hunter ran across the parking lot. The boy obediently slowed down.

Once on the field, Hunter spoke to a boy and they both turned to look at Slade. Hunter's teammate passed the word and soon the team huddled in the middle of the ball field staring at Slade.

"This is priceless," Raquel whispered. "He just went from zero to hero in five seconds flat. Thank you."

"I just hope I live up to whatever hype he gave me." Slade grinned.

They neared the bleachers and a man met them at the edge of the field.

"What's this I hear about a former Texas Ranger agreeing to coach the team?" A tiny blonde ran to meet Raquel.

"This is Slade Walker." Raquel stopped and Slade did, too. "He and Dylan were friends and he played for the Rangers."

"I know." The man offered his hand and Slade clasped it. "I mean, I know who he is. James Johnson, former coach. Commentators used to crack jokes about the pitcher named Walker who never walked anybody."

"I wouldn't say never." Slade winced. "And the Rangers was a long time ago."

"Not that long ago." Raquel's elbow brushed his as she

twisted off the cap of her bottled water. "He helped Hunter with batting."

"You can put the cooler in the dugout." The blonde pointed him in the right direction.

Grateful to put some distance between himself and Raquel, Slade fell in stride beside the coach. This was turning out to be harder than he'd thought.

"He's cute," Lacie whispered, and waggled her eyebrows at Raquel.

Raquel's cheeks heated and she was glad Slade was busy setting up the cooler in the dugout.

"Hunter, introduce Mr. Walker to everyone," the coach called.

"This is my friend Slade Walker." Hunter stood tall and proud. "He used to play for the Texas Rangers and he's gonna be our new coach."

Gasps and whoops echoed through the gathering.

"Let's get started with batting practice so Coach Walker can see what we got." Coach Johnson smiled at Hunter. "You're up first since you saved the team."

Hunter's pride warmed her heart as he stepped to the plate and took his pro stance.

"Where's the pitching machine?" Slade scanned the mound.

"Eight and Under is coach pitch. But we can get a machine for practice, if you want."

"It's fine." Slade rotated his shoulder. "Guess I'll pitch, then."

Slade warmed up and wound up on his pitch. It was perfect. Thwack. The ball sailed into outfield and Hunter made it all the way to second base.

She and Lacie cheered, then settled alone on the guest bleachers.

"So what's the story on Slade?" Lacie bumped Raquel with her elbow.

"No story. He happened to move in next door for the spring, happened by when I was trying to pitch for Hunter and helped him with his batting. So when the coach thing came up—" she shrugged "—I asked him."

"That's a lot of happening. Is he an old flame?"

"No." Raquel shook her head decisively. "I never met him before. He and Dylan were friends until the fifth grade, when Slade moved. After graduation he got a scholarship and went to college and then the major league. But an injury in his first season ended his career. They were great phone friends for a few years and always planned to get together but never managed it."

"Quinn and I knew each other before he came to Aubrey." The sound of the ball hitting a glove punctuated Lacie's statement. "I was already head over heels for Mel when Quinn came to our school, but he was crushing on me back then and I had no idea."

"That's sweet."

"It's funny you never met Slade until he ends up in Aubrey. Tiny little Aubrey." Lacie pointed heavenward. "I think there's something divine going on here."

"Like coincidence. Caitlyn and I ran into him at Moms on Main a few weeks back. Caitlyn went into labor and he drove us to the hospital." She shifted her position on the aluminum bleacher.

"So, he knew you lived here before he moved here?"

"Yes, but he didn't know Dylan was gone until after he happened to move in next door."

"Oh." Lacie scanned the ball field. "Okay, maybe you weren't in Slade's plan, but maybe it's God's plan."

"I don't think so. Slade's a rodeo chaplain. He travels the circuit and he's only here for a three-month sabbatical."

"If he needs a sabbatical, maybe he's looking for a

change. Like something permanent. With someone permanent." Lacie bumped her elbow again. "I know it's hard. Trust me."

Raquel released a sigh. "How did you put everything you had with Mel aside and allow Quinn room in your heart?"

"I don't know." Lacie shook her head. "Time, I guess. And Quinn was persistent. At first I felt guilty, like I was betraying Mel's memory. But Quinn was patient and it just happened. We had some major issues to work through before we married, but I can't imagine my life without him."

"Dylan made me promise—" Raquel's gaze dropped to the sunflower hull–littered ground in front of the stands "—from the beginning of our relationship and especially after we had Hunter that if anything happened to him, I'd find love again and remarry."

"It's awesome that he gave you permission to be happy without him." Lacie patted her hand.

"Yes. But I can't risk opening up to someone new who's not sticking around." She focused on Slade encouraging the kids, coaching them on batting and catching. He was a natural at this. He was a nice guy. A great-looking guy who made her pulse race. But he still wasn't Dylan. And he was just passing through.

"Maybe you could give him reason to stick around."

"You want me to drag him away from God's calling to be a rodeo-circuit chaplain?"

Lacie winced. "Well, when you put it that way… I just want you to be open to something new. God didn't call him into the priesthood. And there aren't many godly unmarried men out there."

"With safe professions."

"A safe profession? That's a requirement?"

Raquel drifted back to the emergency room the night

they'd brought Dylan in—the night she couldn't save him. She shivered. "Yes."

"But you said Dylan died in an off-duty car wreck."

"Yes. But why complicate things with a dangerous job? If I'm going to start over with someone new, someone to be a stepfather to Hunter, I don't need him dying on us."

"You know, I never really worried about Mel bronc riding." A wistful lilt entered Lacie's tone. "I thought it was so much safer than bull riding. But Mel died riding a bronc."

Raquel squeezed Lacie's hand.

"And Dylan was a Texas Ranger and he died in a car wreck that had nothing to do with his job. Don't you think God's in control of life and death and when it happens?"

"Definitely." Raquel's voice cracked. "But why increase the odds?"

"Well, that makes Slade the perfect candidate. Even when he was a Texas Ranger, he was the safe kind and you can't get much safer than a chaplain."

Slade was looking more and more perfect all the time. If only he could stay, put down roots in Aubrey.

A shadow fell over them and she looked up to see her brother. "Hey, I didn't know you were coming."

"I'm home now, so I get to see Hunter play ball." Brant sat down beside her. "Hey, Lacie. Nice seeing you."

"You too. Tori and the baby okay?"

"She wanted to come, but she thought it was a bit cool this evening for Lorraine."

"Tell me about it." Lacie pulled her sweater tighter. "I left Cheyenne with my sister."

"I see Walker's here?" Brant scowled.

"You heard him agree to coach." Raquel rolled her eyes.

"I was hoping he'd change his mind."

"He seems nice and he's really good with the kids." Lacie frowned. "Quinn was really relieved he signed up."

"I don't trust him. And besides, Rock and Hunter don't need a rambling man."

Raquel squelched her laughter. "That sounds like a country song."

But Brant glowered at her, obviously missing the humor.

"We might get a pitching machine for the next practice unless someone else can pitch." Slade's voice echoed from the pitcher's mound. "I'm not supposed to do much pitching. My doc says he might not be able to fix my shoulder a third time."

Raquel's heart stilled. Slade had agreed to help Hunter when it could cost him his arm. What if he'd hurt himself all those times he'd pitched for Hunter at the house?

"See, he shouldn't be coaching the team. For y'all's sake and his," Brant whispered. "This is the perfect opportunity to let him off the hook."

Hunter would be disappointed. But surely there was someone else who could coach.

Slade could walk back out of her life and she was beginning to think Brant was right—maybe that would be best. For everyone.

Why was Raquel so quiet? Had Slade done something to upset her?

Silence echoed as she drove them home. But Hunter filled it.

"We're gonna have the best team ever." Hunter tossed his ball back and forth into his glove.

"I hope so." Slade grinned. "I see definite promise. You've got a great arm. I see pitching in your future."

"Really? Maybe you can teach me."

Slade would love to. But it would be another two years before Hunter would graduate to a team with a kid pitcher instead of the coach. By then Slade would be long gone. Back on the circuit. His throat closed up.

"Can you teach me?"

"I think Slade has to be really careful with his shoulder." Raquel's voice startled him as she turned into her drive, pulled into the garage and killed the engine.

"Can you run around the side and open Blizzard's gate for me, Hunter?" Slade undid his seat belt.

"Sure." Hunter jumped out of the car. "He doesn't need his leash?"

"No. He's getting used to the place and doesn't run off."

Hunter scurried out the side door of the garage.

"I heard you tell Quinn you weren't supposed to pitch because of your shoulder." Raquel got out of the car. "You should have told me that. All the times you've pitched for Hunter, what if you'd hurt yourself?"

"You must not have heard all of what I said." Slade got out and faced her over the top of the car. "We can use the pitching machine for practices, just not games. Since I don't pitch with my full steam for kids, it shouldn't hurt me."

"But it could. Maybe it's not a good idea to coach Hunter's team. If you want out, I understand."

"I don't want out. And I plan to train Quinn and Sam to pitch."

"Look, I appreciate your help, but if you reinjure your arm, I'll never forgive myself."

"Then I'll just have to be extra careful. I'm not letting these kids down."

A flicker of a smile played across her mouth. "I better get supper on. Send Hunter home." She turned toward the house.

"Can he stay and play with Blizzard for a little while?"

"I guess. It'll take me thirty minutes or so to get supper ready." She disappeared into her house.

Slade longed to follow her. To set the table while she cooked. To share a meal with her and Hunter. To tuck

Hunter in and spend the evening watching some sappy chick flick with Raquel.

Man, he was going soft.

Raquel turned the burner off under the rotini noodles and stirred sautéed mushrooms and zucchini into the bubbling spaghetti sauce.

It was rude not to invite Slade over for supper.

After all, he was doing her a favor. Doing Hunter a favor. And all against the advice of his doctor.

Raquel stomped her foot. If only Hunter would come home without her calling. No way around it—she had to invite Slade. She dug her phone from her pocket and found his number in her address book.

"I'm kicking him out the door right now." Slade's grin resonated in his tone.

"Want to come with him and have supper with us?"

Silence. One, two, three seconds…

Chapter 5

Raquel held her breath. *Please say no.*

"You sure it's not too much trouble?" Slade asked.

"Not at all." Raquel crossed her fingers. "I would have asked earlier, but I wasn't sure what I was making." That part was true. "Turns out it's rotini with spaghetti sauce. Hope you don't have a problem with mushrooms or zucchini in the sauce. The only way I can get vegetables down Hunter is to drown them in tomato sauce or cheese."

"Sounds great. We'll be right there."

Raquel closed her eyes. Why couldn't he have just turned her down? She set another place at the table, drained the water off the pasta, and poured the tender noodles into her favorite red bowl and the sauce in a separate matching bowl. She set the meal in the middle of the table just as Hunter barreled inside with Slade a few paces behind.

With practice on Tuesdays and Fridays and games on Mondays and Thursdays, this could get to be almost a nightly thing—having Slade over for dinner.

"Perfect timing."

"What can I do to help?" Slade strode to the kitchen.

And her kitchen suddenly wasn't big enough with him in it.

"Ice." She pointed to three glasses sitting on the counter. "I'll take the tea pitcher to the table. I hope you like sweet tea. It's all we drink."

"I don't see the need for anything else. Sweet tea goes good with everything." Slade held the glasses under the dispenser and the racket of ice against glass killed any chance of conversation.

What would they talk about over dinner?

"Wait until we pray." Raquel hurried to the dining area, slapped Hunter's hand away from the garlic bread and took her seat beside him. "Did you even wash your hands?"

"Slade made me before we left."

"Good. It's your turn to pray."

"Where should I sit?" Slade carried all three glasses of ice to the table with ease.

"That was Dad's spot at our table." Hunter pointed to the empty chair on his other side.

An awkward silence shrouded them.

But Slade didn't bat an eye and sat down across from Hunter. "This spot must be for guests, then."

Hunter bowed his head. "Dear Lord, thank You for this food. Thank You for baseball. And thank You for my new coach. Amen."

Passing the food around the table occupied them for a few minutes.

"Mmm, this is great." Slade rolled his eyes in ecstasy.

"It's just spaghetti with fancy noodles." Raquel's face warmed. "I started making it this way when Hunter was little. Spaghetti noodles were way too messy."

"I like fancy noodles."

"Hey, Mom said I could get a dog. We're going to

Adopt-a-Pet this Saturday. Can you come with us? Can he, Mom?"

"Sure. If he has time." Having a truck would be nice. If only her pulse would settle.

"I'll make time. Where is Adopt-a-Pet?"

"Here in Aubrey. A friend of Caitlyn's is a vet. She takes in strays and finds them homes."

"Max wants you to show him how to bat, like you did me." Hunter talked around his food.

"No talking with your mouth full."

"I'm planning to make the next practice just batting. I'll work with each team member on stance and swing."

"Awesome."

At least Hunter had swallowed before speaking that time.

Baseball stayed the hot topic and Raquel didn't have to worry about contributing much to the conversation.

It felt like a family, the way it would if Dylan were here. But Dylan wasn't here. They weren't a family and Slade probably wouldn't stay. He was here for only three months. Then he'd be gone again. And she and Hunter would be alone again.

The phone rang and she checked the screen. Mitch's mom?

"Um, normally I'd let it ring, but it's a friend I haven't heard from in a while."

"Go ahead. Just don't expect any food to be left when you get back." Slade's smile sent her heart off-kilter.

She stepped into the living room. "Hey, Audra, what's up?"

"Cody's coming home for the weekend."

"Oh, that's wonderful. I know he doesn't make it this way often."

"I'm planning a big gathering with lots of food, of course, and I want you and Hunter to come."

"Sure. When is it?"

"Saturday around noon. Cody will arrive Friday evening late."

"Sounds good. We'll be there. What should I bring?"

"I'd say nothing, but I know you love to cook, so why don't you whip up some yummy dessert?"

"Will do."

"We'll look forward to seeing you."

"See you then." She ended the call.

Raquel had often wished she and Mitch's younger brother had ended up more than friends. She loved his family. She loved Cody. They got along so great and laughed themselves silly when they got together. But there was just nothing there—other than a really great friendship.

Besides, Cody was never home and he was idiotic enough to ride bulls for a living, which broke both of her rules. And he was just a big overgrown kid. She already had a son to raise and didn't need another.

She returned to the kitchen. Hunter wore a guilty smile. So did Slade. Both had gotten another heaping helping of the rotini and sauce.

Great. Another big overgrown kid. Just what she didn't need in her life. Best if Slade passed through their lives. And kept going.

Dogs yipped a cacophony as Slade pulled his truck next to a long barn.

A brunette wearing a long braid shielded her eyes from the mid-March sun as she stepped out to meet them. "Hi, I'm Ally."

"Nice to meet you, Ally. I'm Slade. This is Raquel and Hunter."

"I called a few days ago about adopting a dog for Hunter." Raquel set her hands on Hunter's shoulders.

"Of course. We went over all the caring-and-preparing-for-a-pet stuff on the phone, so it just comes down to which one you want. I'm glad the whole family could come. Picking a dog should be a family decision."

"Um, we're not—" Raquel stammered. "Slade is a friend, our neighbor, Hunter's baseball coach."

But he wanted to be more. Did that count?

"Oh, my bad. So what did you have in mind, Raquel?"

"I want a Great Pyrenees," Hunter piped up.

"I'm afraid I don't have any of those. But I've got a lot of other nice dogs who need good homes."

"My concern is this." Raquel winced. "If Hunter and I see all the dogs, we'll want to take them all home. And we can't."

"I understand completely." Ally grinned. "That's exactly why I'm in the shape I'm in. Tell you what—give me an idea of what you have in mind and I'll see what I have that might fit your needs."

"I'm not crazy about the puppy stage." Raquel laughed. "So if we could skip all the chewing and jumping, that would be great. I'm thinking larger breed, but not necessarily purebred. And I want a gentle dog, a good playmate for Hunter that I won't have to worry about getting too rough."

"I think I have just the dog. A yellow Lab. Two years old, past the puppy stuff. They're great with kids and she's a light yellow, so she's almost white like a Great Pyrenees. She's female and spayed. Is that okay?"

"I figure she'll spend time with Blizzard," Slade whispered to Raquel. "Spayed females get along well with neutered males. Another male might want to fight."

"Yes, but you and Blizzard won't be here forever."

Ouch.

"Can we see her, Mom?"

"Sure."

"I'll be right back." Ally disappeared into the barn.

Barks intensified into a frenzy followed by Ally's soothing words too low to understand.

"She's got a big heart." Slade scanned the long barn. "I wonder how she funds this place."

"I don't know." Raquel kicked at gravel as Hunter chased a yellow kitten. "Don't scare him, Hunter. Coax him to you."

A big white dog rounded the side of the barn with a leash and Ally in pursuit. "She needs to work on her leash skills, but other than that, she's a great dog."

A lonesome howl began in the barn and Ally cringed as Hunter petted the big white head. "I call her Snow, but you can give her a new name if you decide to take her home."

Snow licked Hunter's chin and he giggled.

"What do you say, Hunter? Want to take Snow home?"

"Can we?"

"Sure."

Hunter hugged his arms around Snow's neck. "Can we get the yellow kitten, too?"

"Um, I'm not sure he's up for adoption."

"He is." Ally smiled. "But your mom may not be up for that."

"How is Snow with cats?"

"She doesn't bother them."

"How is Blizzard with cats?" Raquel turned to Slade.

"Fine." He lowered his voice. "But Blizzard and I won't be here forever."

Her mouth tightened. "Well, I have a big unused barn perfect for a kitten. I'll take Snow and the kitten. Does he have a name? Is he neutered?" Raquel whispered.

"His name is Tigger and he is neutered. All of the animals I have up for adoption are spayed or neutered."

"Could I ask how you fund this place?" Slade picked the kitten up.

"This was my family farm, so I own the property. My vet practice and pet gift shop pay the bills. I also charge adoption fees, which Raquel and I discussed on the phone. And I have a few local investors."

"Do you—" Slade lowered his voice "—put any animals down?"

"Not unless they're too sick or injured to save."

"I'd like to make a donation." Slade handed Tigger to Raquel and slipped his checkbook out of his back pocket.

"That's wonderful." Ally grinned. "I appreciate it—you can make the check out to Ally's Adopt-a-Pet."

"Does Snow by chance have a sibling?" he whispered.

"Yes." Ally flinched. "That's Flurry howling. I basically flipped a coin on which sister to show Hunter. They've never been separated. Poor thing. Several of the kids from the church youth group come by to walk and play with the animals each evening. I'll make sure she gets some extra attention tonight."

"This should cover a donation." Slade handed her the check. "Plus adopting Flurry?"

Ally scanned the check and her eyes widened. "It certainly will. Thank you, so much. Are you sure you don't want to see Flurry first?"

"Nope, Flurry's coming home with me. Blizzard needs company. And Snow can visit her."

"I'll go get her. And I'll make y'all receipts." Ally left them alone again.

Hunter paid them no attention as he cuddled and played with Snow.

"That was very sweet of you." Raquel had the kitten purring.

"Too bad I won't be around forever." He cleared his throat. "I mean—for Snow and Flurry's sakes. But maybe the next few months will transition them until I have to leave."

In the meantime, he had to resist Hunter's innocent invitations. And Raquel's charms.

Slade scanned the hallway and saw the sign—Office. How had he gotten roped into this? Career Day for the eighth-grade class—talking pro baseball, when he'd barely gotten his feet wet in it. One of the kids on Hunter's team had an older brother, and here he was.

Hopefully, the kid wouldn't be disappointed when he showed up to encourage the kids not to depend on sports for their future but to have a backup plan. Just in case. Just in case they ended up like him.

He ducked into the office and a gray-haired lady looked up at him. "I'm Slade Walker. Career Day. Eighth grade."

"Yes. Of course. You're in Ms. Newman's class today. That's four doors down."

"Thanks." He stepped back into the hallway just as a door marked Nurse opened.

Raquel stepped into the hall and her eyes widened. "Slade? What are you doing here?"

"I got wrangled into Career Day." Slade shrugged.

"Ahh, I heard Mikey plotting that." She shifted the files she held. "Have you checked in?"

"All checked in." He pointed down the hall. "Third door down?"

"Fourth. I'm headed that way."

Just admit it—he'd agreed to Career Day on the off chance of running into her. And it had worked. He slowed his pace to prolong their walk together.

He lived next door to the woman and saw her every Tuesday and Friday night. For the past two weeks, they'd fallen into a comfortable routine: Raquel cooked on Tuesdays and he took her and Hunter to Moms on Main on Fridays.

But on Mondays, Wednesdays, Thursdays and week-ends, he missed her. March couldn't be over with fast enough to suit him. At least in April he'd see her at games on Mondays and Thursdays, too.

Her heels clicked with each step and her perfume stamped its scent on his heart.

How had this happened? He'd tried to keep his distance. But Raquel was everything he'd always dreamed of. Smart, strong, beautiful, kind, a great mom and a great cook.

When March wrapped up, he'd be a month closer to going back on the circuit and leaving Raquel behind. He needed time to slow. Not speed up.

"Here we are—Ms. Newman's class." She gestured toward the door. "You might pop your head in to let her know you're here, but when the bell rings, step back or they'll flatten you. It's like they all charge the corral at the same time."

"Thanks for the heads-up."

"Good luck." She hurried down the hall, leaving him to stare—and dream. How had she wrangled her way into his dreams?

And sidetracked him from Tori? His sister was the reason he'd come to town, and after meeting her, he longed to tell her who he was. But deep down, he got the feeling he should keep his distance for a while and pray Brant would warm up to him.

So instead of thinking about Tori, he dreamed about Raquel. A woman he very probably could never have.

"Can me and Max sit at our own booth?" Hunter's question caught Raquel off guard.

Last week he'd sat with her and Slade at Moms on Main. But tonight Hunter had invited Max, while Lacie and Quinn had turned down her invitation—leaving her to sit with Slade. Alone.

"May Max and I?" She tousled Hunter's hair.

"You want to sit with Max?" Hunter frowned and Slade snickered.

"No." Raquel rolled her eyes. "Your grammar."

"Oh. So, can we?"

"May we? Yes, you may."

"Tell me what y'all want, sport." Slade turned to Raquel. "Then y'all can go ahead and find a booth, if it's okay with your mom."

The boys rattled off their orders and even though Hunter loved cheese, once Max said cheese was yucky and not to put it on his burger, Hunter agreed.

"I'll pay for ours." Raquel dug out her wallet.

"I'll get it. Tell me what you want and go have a seat."

It was easier not to argue, so she told him what she wanted and went to supervise the boys.

Minutes later Slade claimed the seat across from her a few tables away from Hunter and Max's booth. "He's a great kid."

"Thanks." She kept her gaze on the table.

"He seems well adjusted to me."

"He was so young when Dylan died. I worry he won't remember him."

"I mean adjusted to the move."

"Oh. Well, he became Mr. Popular when you agreed to coach his team."

"How did you and Dylan meet?"

Her gaze bounced up to meet his.

"I mean, that is, if you don't mind talking about him."

"I love talking about him." She closed her eyes. "We met in the emergency room. He cut his hand on a rusty fence pursuing a suspect. It got infected and he finally came in for treatment in the wee hours of the morning when I was on duty."

"Love at first sight?"

She couldn't stop the smile and nodded.

"Do you miss the emergency room?"

"No." She swallowed hard. "I was on duty the night Dylan had his wreck. His mother had cancer and he'd been at the hospital visiting her. I didn't realize how tired he was when he left to go home. Thirty minutes later they brought him in on a stretcher." Her voice cracked. "He'd fallen asleep at the wheel."

"I'm sorry." Slade covered her hand with his. "I didn't mean to bring up a painful subject."

"You didn't know." She swiped at her eyes. "There wasn't a thing I could do to save him and I decided I never wanted to feel that powerless again."

"Looks like I'm just in time." Brant's voice cut into Raquel's thoughts.

She jerked her hand away from Slade.

Striving for casual, Raquel turned her best smile on her brother. "In time for what?"

Brant's hardened gaze bore into the back of Slade's head. "Just in time to eat supper with my favorite sister."

"Sure. Come join us." Slade cleared his throat. "I thought about asking if you wanted to come at the ball field, but I figured you had a wife and baby to get home to."

"My lovely wife texted me a few minutes ago. Lorraine's already asleep and Tori's going to bed, too."

"Uncle Brant, come sit with Max and me."

At least Hunter was attempting to work on his grammar. Why did the English language have to be so complicated?

"Maybe in a minute. I need to talk to your mom." Brant slid in beside Raquel. "Hope I'm not interrupting anything."

"Of course not." Raquel's cheeks heated. She wasn't exactly sure what Brant had interrupted.

Chapter 6

Too clean, too comfortable, too churchy. Slade scanned the interior of the third church he'd visited during his sabbatical. Would he ever get used to a regular church again after spending so many years preaching in sale barns and arenas?

But the emptiness had begun churning inside him—proof his calling wasn't over. He needed to preach.

"Slade, you came." Star scurried to his side, dragging a blond man behind her.

"You found me a house, lickety-split. Figured I owed my favorite real estate lady a favor."

"Ahem." The man cleared his throat. "I'm your favorite real estate lady's husband."

"He didn't mean anything." Star whacked her husband on the shoulder.

"No, I didn't." Slade held his hands up in surrender. "Honest. If I'd been flirting, I'd have said something like 'the most beautiful real estate agent in Aubrey.'" Why did other men always think he was flirting when he was simply being complimentary?

"Wyatt Marshall." The man offered his hand. "Sorry 'bout that. But when you're married to the most beautiful real estate agent in the whole world, sometimes you have to stake your claim."

"Not if you keep sweet-talking me like that." Star laughed up at her husband.

Great. Another bliss-filled couple to remind Slade what he was missing. But Slade remembered Wyatt from the circuit. And the Wyatt he'd known would never have stepped the toe of his boot in church. "I'm Slade Walker."

"I know." Wyatt tore his gaze away from his wife and turned back to Slade. "You pitched for the Texas Rangers."

It always came back to that. "For a short time."

"So, you moving here?"

"Sort of a pit stop. I'm on a three-month sabbatical."

"I heard you preach a few times on the circuit." Wyatt shrugged. "Back before I wanted to hear you. It took some stuff in my personal life for God to finally get through to me. But you planted some seeds."

"I'm glad." Slade's eyes burned and he blinked. Hearing he'd touched a life for Christ in some small way always got to him. And drove home that he still had a calling.

"You rode broncs on the circuit, too."

"Not as well as you rode bulls. Didn't you end up winning the Championship Bull Riding title?"

"Twice." Star linked arms with Wyatt. "Come sit with us. Max is really excited you're coaching his team. Lacie's my sister and they're here somewhere."

That was why Lacie had seemed familiar to him the first time he met her on the ball field. A blonde version of Star.

"I hope we have a good year. The boys play hard."

"You looking to do any bronc riding while you're here?"

Wyatt clapped him on the back as they strode deeper into the sanctuary.

"Maybe."

"Come to the Stockyards. Broncs every Saturday night at Cowtown Coliseum. Rodeo starts at eight o'clock."

"Will you be there?"

"Planning on it."

"Maybe you could introduce me around."

"Sure. Get in with the cowboys by competing and then maybe you can help me do some witnessing. A lot of those guys still don't want to hear."

"Coach Slade." An excited voice came from behind him.

Slade chuckled. "Let me guess. Max?"

"How'd you know it was me?" Max circled around in front of him.

"Turns out your aunt Star invited me and she told me you were here. How ya doing, champ?"

"Awesome. I can't wait for our first game."

"Me neither."

And he couldn't wait until Saturday night. It wasn't a preaching gig. But once he got to know the cowboys, he could at least witness to them. And the best way to get to know the cowboys was to meet them where they were.

That, Slade could do. God had put him right where he needed to be when he'd followed up Star's invitation to her church.

The song service was great. The sermon was interesting and powerful. But the pews were just too cushy.

Slade parked his truck close to Moms on Main. *God, help me find a church I can feel comfortable in—or maybe uncomfortable.*

Even though he probably wouldn't be back next week, he'd accepted Star and Lacie's invitation to eat at his favorite café. He could almost taste the chicken-fried steak as he strode down the sidewalk.

"There you are." Wyatt ushered him in. "The ladies already ordered and are saving us a seat on the other side where the big tables are."

The two men got in the long line. Despite the length, it seemed to be moving pretty fast.

"So, what did you think of church?"

"It was nice."

"Nice? Doesn't sound like you'll be back."

"Maybe. But it isn't the church. It's me. I'm used to dust and manure while I preach. I'm like a man fresh out of prison who can't sleep on my own comfy mattress anymore."

"Hmm." Wyatt frowned.

"It's an analogy." Slade chuckled. "Don't worry—the only experience I have with prison is preaching a few prison rodeos and witnessing to some cons."

"Sounds like you need a cowboy church where they meet in a barn or a sale barn. Seems like I heard of one starting up somewhere close, but I can't remember who was telling me about it."

"That actually sounds interesting."

"I'll ask around and see what I can find out."

"Thanks."

They placed their orders and strode to the next room, with all the long tables where he'd heard the church groups sat on Sundays.

At a long table, Star had two seats saved for them among a dozen faces he'd seen in church this morning. And though she'd introduced him to several, he couldn't come up with any names. Not a one, other than the pastor and Max. He scanned the next table, hoping to remember somebody.

Raquel.

His heart sped.

With Hunter beside her. And Tori and Brant on her other side.

Hunter waved at him—giving him the perfect opportunity to go speak with Raquel. If only her glowering brother hadn't been around.

"We're over here." Wyatt gestured to him. "We don't mix with their kind."

"Don't listen to him." Star smacked Wyatt's shoulder. "We're all the same denomination—we just go to different church buildings."

"Wanna sit with us?" Hunter asked.

"I'd like to, but Ms. Star already saved me a seat."

"Can I sit with them, Mama? I wanna sit with Coach Slade and Max."

"I don't think there's room." Raquel didn't meet his gaze.

"We can steal your chair and slide you in somewhere. That is, if it's okay with your mom."

Her eyes finally met his and his heart sped even faster.

"I don't want to make everyone shuffle around."

More than anything, he wanted to swap chairs with Hunter and sit by Raquel. But that would be rude and his grandma had taught him never to be rude. Besides, Brant would glower even harder if he sat with Raquel and probably insist on sitting between them.

"Please, Mom."

"You better be good." Raquel pointed at Hunter.

"I will." Hunter's chair scuffed against the floor as he wiggled out of his spot at the table and scurried over to Max. And Slade's excuse to stand by Raquel disappeared.

"Guess I better get this over there." He picked up the chair and returned to his table.

"Coach Slade came to our church this morning," Max

announced as everyone scooted to make room for Hunter. "I got to sit with him and everything."

"Maybe you can come to church with us next week." Hunter plopped into his chair.

"I just remembered." Wyatt snapped his fingers. "It was Garrett Steele telling me about the cowboy church."

"Garrett Steele—the singer?"

"Exactly. He's a hometown boy. Born and raised right here in Aubrey. Somebody was wanting to use one of his barns to start a cowboy church." Wyatt scanned the next table. "He kind of sticks to himself. You know, the whole celebrity thing."

"He goes to my church." Hunter covered his mouth with his hand. "But I wasn't supposed to tell, so his fans won't tackle him there."

"I won't tell anybody." Slade winked at the boy.

"He's just a normal person—" Hunter whispered "—and his wife is friends with my aunt Tori."

"There you go." Wyatt gestured to Tori at the next table. "Maybe she could get in touch with him and find out who it was."

Or maybe he'd just attend Raquel and Tori's church next week.

Quite a productive Sunday. A rodeo opportunity. And another reason to spend time with Raquel. But before he could spend any more time with Raquel, he needed to clear the air.

"Does Tori work outside the home? I don't want to bother her during lunch, so I'm wondering when and how to contact her about it." Now, that was some smooth fishing.

"She's a clothing designer and owns Tori's Threads." Star dug in her purse and handed him a business card. "I think she's usually in her office two or three days a week when she and Brant are in town."

"Thanks." He tucked the card in his pocket and chanced a glance at his oblivious sister at the next table.

Tori needed to know the truth.

Brant's glare bore into him.

They all did.

"I'd like to see Tori McConnell." Slade swallowed the knot threatening to choke off his words.

"Could I get your name, please?" The secretary's tone was all business, her smile placid.

"Slade Walker."

"I'm not sure if Mrs. McConnell is in." The secretary wrote something on her notepad. "Have a seat and I'll check."

Translation: she's here, but I'll check to see if she wants to see you.

He settled in a cushy nail-head wingback in the waiting area and flipped through the magazines. Fashion, fashion, fashion. No sports or outdoors magazines. He gave up and twiddled his thumbs.

"Yes, Mr. Slade Walker is here to see Mrs. McConnell. Is she in?" The secretary tapped the end of her ink pen on her desk. "Yes, I see. Of course. I'll tell him."

Slade stood.

"Mrs. McConnell is very busy. You'll need to make an appointment."

"I only need a few minutes of her time. I'll just wait and maybe she can squeeze me in."

"Mr. Walker, it would be better if you made an appointment."

"I'll wait." He plopped in the wingback.

"Excuse me—I'll be right back."

I'm sure you will. "Go ahead. I'm fine."

The secretary opened a door to the right of her desk and disappeared. The phone started up and rang incessantly with only a few pauses. Just so his nerves wouldn't shoot straight out of his body, he grabbed one of the fashion magazines and flipped through it. A picture of Tori caught his attention.

Tori's Threads Takes the Fashion World by Texas Tornado. He skimmed the recent article. She'd started her company only last September. Shortly after their dad had died, so she'd probably funded her company with her inheritance. Smart and savvy. The article made it sound as if she was already a roaring success—Tori's Eaton Up Fashion.

"You know—"

Slade looked up.

Tori stood in the doorway with both hands on her hips. "I'm trying to work here. I don't have time for whatever game you're playing."

"No games. Trust me. It's not what you think at all. Just give me five minutes."

"Should I call security, Mrs. McConnell?" The secretary's hand hovered over the phone on her desk.

Indecisiveness deepened Tori's frown. She tapped the pointy toe of her high heel. One. Two. Three times.

"No. But check with me in two minutes, Carol." She quirked an eyebrow at him. "You coming?"

Slade stood and followed her through the door. She ushered him to a chair and sat down at a rustic desk with cowhide-lined panels. A Texas flag on the wall, a set of longhorns and a leather couch. Tori was all about Texas.

"Time's wasting." She checked her watch. "You now have ninety seconds."

"It's a long story." Slade took a deep breath. "But I promise I don't want anything from you. I just want to get to know you—to have a relationship with you."

"Hello? I'm married. Very happily married." She placed

her hand on the phone. "And your time is up. Now. Don't make me call security."

"Not that kind of relationship."

She picked up the phone.

"I'm your brother."

Her eyes widened and she set the phone down. "What?"

"I never knew who my father was until last September. My grandparents got a call from a lawyer who said my father had died and I was in his will." His words got faster and faster as the story rushed out of him. "I thought it was a joke and tried to ignore him, but he wouldn't leave me alone. I finally agreed to an appointment and he told me my father was Walter Eaton, better known as Slim Easton."

Tori didn't say anything, but he had her full attention.

"I promise you, it's true. The lawyer showed me the paternity test from after I was born. I can give you the lawyer's number."

"What's the lawyer's name?"

"Houston Lancaster."

"You know—" Tori clasped her trembling hands "—back when my aunt told me I needed to see Houston after my father's death, I thought, he's probably got a dozen kids we don't even know about."

"So you believe me?"

The phone rang and Tori jumped, then grabbed it. "I'm fine, Carol. Clear my schedule. I need to leave early. Yes. Thank you."

"I'm not here for money or anything else." He put a hand to his heart, striving to convey complete honesty. "I got way too much in his will and to be honest, I didn't want it. The lawyer had to talk me into it and it's sitting in my bank account as we speak—untouched except for a recent charitable donation. All I want is a sister."

She straightened the papers on her desk. "Let's get out of here. Somewhere quiet."

"My place."

"That sounds good. We'll get Raquel in on this and figure out how to break the news to my husband."

"He doesn't like me."

"He's overprotective."

"So you're just gonna trust me." Slade splayed his hands palms up. "Enough to go to my house with me? I could be some lunatic who read about your inheritance and came here to kidnap you or Lorraine or both."

"But you're not. Your story makes too much sense to be a lie." A tiny grin threatened. "Besides, I've already been kidnapped once and lived to tell about it. Brant made me take a self-defense class a few months ago and I'm licensed to carry. So maybe you're the one who should worry."

"Maybe." Slade swallowed hard for effect. The more he saw of her, the more he liked her. Smart, funny and tough. "I'll be on my best behavior."

"I need to wrap up a few things first. Give me twenty minutes or so."

"Sounds good."

While he waited, he'd dig out his paternity test results. Should have brought that to begin with. But he'd been so nervous he'd forgotten.

He turned toward the door.

"And, Slade, I'm really looking forward to talking to you."

"Me too." Now that she knew who he was, no one would keep him from getting to know his sister better.

Not even her husband.

The elevator doors closed and Raquel's stomach stayed on the ground floor while the rest of her ascended to Tori's office. Some building. She was so proud of her sister-in-law. A little over a year ago, Tori had been a party girl pregnant by an abusive boyfriend. Now she was a Christian, a great wife to Brant and an awesome mother, and she'd sent the fashion world into a tizzy for Tori's Threads.

Lorraine gurgled at her over Brant's shoulder as the elevator stopped, the doors slid open and Brant launched down the hall.

"Lorraine, tell your daddy to slow down so I can keep up."

"Sorry, but we miss Mama. Don't we, Lorraine? We had three months—just the three of us—spending every moment together except for concert time. I can't get used to her being gone all day."

"She loves this." Raquel scanned the upscale office complex. "And she's only here three days a week."

"I know. And I'm proud of everything she's accomplished. I'll get used to it."

Tori's no-nonsense secretary looked up from her desk with a pleasant smile. "Mr. McConnell, how nice to see you."

"Thanks, you too. Could you tell Tori we're here?"

"I'm sorry, but she left about half an hour ago."

"She did? Did she say where she was going?"

"No, but she asked me to clear her schedule and said she wouldn't be back in until Wednesday."

"Maybe she missed y'all, too." Raquel shrugged. "And decided to meet us at the restaurant."

"Maybe. I'll give her a call. Thanks, Carol."

They headed back toward the elevator, but Brant stopped before they got there. "She's not answering."

"Text her."

"Can you? Somebody's getting wiggly." Brant blew a zerbert on Lorraine's arm, sending the baby into a fit of giggles.

"Sure." Raquel pushed buttons on her phone. "'Still on for lunch? We're at your office.'" She read her message aloud.

Seconds passed.

"Nothing?" Brant frowned.

"Give her a minute."

"This isn't like her."

"It's her first day back. She's not in the swing of things yet. Maybe she forgot and took a client to lunch or something."

"Maybe." Brant vaulted back to Carol's desk. "Was Tori alone when she left?"

"Yes, sir."

"She didn't mention meeting anyone?"

"Just you for lunch, but that was early this morning."

"Did she meet with anyone who might have changed her plans?"

"There was that guy." Carol's gaze dropped to her desk.

"What guy?" Raquel frowned.

"Let me find his name. I wrote it down." Carol flipped through the pad on her desk. "He made me nervous."

"Why?" Worry sounded in Brant's voice.

"Because he was nervous. He didn't have an appointment, but he acted like he was going to stay until she saw him. Here it is——Slade Walker."

"Slade Walker was here?" Brant growled.

"I wanted to call security." Carol winced. "But Tori agreed to see him. She told me to call and check with her in two minutes. I did, but she said she was fine."

Why had Slade been nervous? Raquel's stomach tilted. Why had he insisted on seeing Tori? Could Raquel be wrong about him?

"She didn't leave with him." Carol shook her head. "He only stayed in her office about five minutes and then he left. She left about twenty minutes later."

"Did she seem okay?"

"She seemed——" Carol's eyes narrowed as she searched for the right word "——rattled."

Brant wheeled back toward the elevator and Raquel practically ran to keep up.

"Where are you going?"

"To find my wife. I knew I was right about him. If he touched her, I'll rattle his teeth."

Lorraine whimpered in his arms.

"If he touched her, I imagine she rattled his teeth. Now hush. You're upsetting Lorraine. Here, let me have her." Raquel stopped him long enough to take the baby from him. "It's okay, sweetie."

But even as she soothed her niece, her heart pounded. Had Slade made moves on Tori? Could Raquel really be that wrong about him?

Her phone buzzed as they stepped in the elevator with three men in suits. A message. She pushed the button to retrieve it. From Tori.

"She just texted me this. 'I'm so sorry. Forgot all about lunch. Tell Brant not to worry. I'll be home in a while.'"

Brant jabbed buttons on his phone, pressed it to his ear and waited. "Where are you?" he barked.

The men in suits looked up at Brant.

Calm down, Raquel mouthed.

"I was just worried." Brant lowered his voice. "Carol said Slade was in your office today."

Raquel's heart continued to pound.

"Okay." Brant's jaw tensed. "Yeah. I'll see you at home. Yeah, Lorraine's fine." He hung up and shoved the phone in his pocket.

The elevator stopped on the second floor and the suits got off.

"What?"

"She said not to worry about Slade. It wasn't what I think and that she'll tell me all about it when I get home."

"So where is she?"

"Said she's at the grocery store and she'll be home soon. But we just went grocery shopping yesterday."

"Maybe she forgot something."

"Does Slade have a big dog?"

"Yes. Why?"

The elevator stopped and Raquel put it in high gear to keep up with Brant.

"Because I heard a big dog bark."

"You don't think she's at Slade's?"

"That's exactly what I think." They exited the building.

"Why would you think that?" Raquel whispered. "Tori would never cheat on you. She loves you."

"I know that and I trust her, but I don't trust Slade. What if he lurked around until she left and took her against her will?"

"Okay, maybe I was wrong. Maybe Slade does have a thing for your wife. But he's no Russ Dawson. I think I'm an accurate enough judge of character to know that Slade wouldn't kidnap Tori."

"Then why did my wife just lie to me?"

They reached Brant's truck and got in.

"Just because you heard a dog bark and Slade has one doesn't mean she's there. Maybe she was in the parking lot at the grocery store."

"We'll see." Brant started the engine.

And Raquel's pulse continued to race.

Tori would never cheat on Brant, and Raquel couldn't imagine Slade forcing a woman to do anything against her will. Besides, Tori knew self-defense. But what was going on?

Please, Lord, let Slade be the gentle soul he seems to be. Let this whole thing be a misunderstanding, and most of all, let Tori be okay.

Chapter 7

A gentle March breeze wafted through the air, fluttering the paternity test results as Slade handed them to Tori.

Sitting on his porch steps with his sister while Blizzard and Flurry roamed the yard. The sister he hadn't known he had until six months ago. Surreal.

"So you don't know anything about our father?" Tori handed the paper back to him.

"A little. Once I saw the lawyer and learned who my father was, I searched his name on Google and read a few articles. Mostly about his career—the highs and lows, the rehab, several comebacks."

"And the fans rode the roller coaster right along with him." Tori rolled her eyes. "They never gave up on him."

"What about you? Did you give up on him?"

"Slim Easton may have been my father." Tori's tone turned bitter. "But he was never a father. He was rarely home and when he was, he beat my mother mercilessly."

Slade winced. "I didn't know. Did he hurt you?"

"Not physically. But words do hurt. He never had anything good to say about anyone—including me."

"I'm sorry."

"Yeah. Me too." She cleared her throat. "I'm sorry you finally found out who your father was and you ended up with Slim Easton. What about your mom?"

"She was a drug addict and an alcoholic." He tried to keep his tone matter-of-fact. Even after all these years, his mother's neglect still hurt. "My grandparents got custody of me when I was seven. She showed up every once in a while over the years, usually wanting money, until she overdosed five years ago."

"Both your parents overdosed. I'm so sorry."

"Yeah. Me too." Slade shrugged. "We keep saying that."

"Not much else to say when Slim Easton's your dad. I know as a Christian, I'm supposed to forgive him, but I'm still praying about that." Tori blew out a big breath. "So how did you find out about me? Did Mr. Lancaster tell you?"

"No. When I was researching on the internet, I found our father's obituary. Your name was still Eaton then, so I did a Google search for you and found your wedding announcement."

"So why did it take you so long to tell me the truth?" She plucked an Indian paintbrush and twisted the wildflower stem around her finger until the vibrant orange-red petals graced her hand like a ring.

"To be honest, I tried to forget it—at first." He closed his eyes. "But I couldn't seem to stop thinking about you. So I took a break from my rodeo chaplain ministry and came here to Aubrey to see what would happen."

"I'm glad you did."

"Me too. I always dreamed of having a normal family—with a mom and dad and siblings. I always especially wanted a younger sister."

"From the looks of those test results, I've got a year on you, so make that a big sister." She playfully bumped him with her elbow. "What got you into being a rodeo chaplain?"

"God."

"Duh?" Tori laughed. "But why not a church? Why rodeo?"

"I was drowning in self-pity after my shoulder injury." He rubbed his shoulder. Why did talking about it always seem to make it ache? Was it in his head or did it always hurt and he never noticed except when talking about it?

"My baseball career came to a screeching halt and one of our associate pastors at my home church had begun a rodeo ministry, traveling the circuit as a chaplain. His wife had cancer and he needed a replacement. God called me."

"So you travel Texas preaching at arenas and living out of motels?"

"Actually, I only travel one leg of the circuit in that camper over there. I learned real quick motels add up fast." He plucked a bluebonnet and handed it to her. He needed to mow his yard soon, but he just couldn't bring himself to mow over the wildflowers just yet. "I've preached in indoor and outdoor arenas, sale barns and barns. I occasionally ride broncs in the rodeo so I can get acquainted with the cowboys and witness to them."

"And you stopped to find me?" She fashioned the blue flower into a ring on her other hand.

"Partially. I was suffering from burnout—because I was distracted by thinking about you. The travel was wearing on me. My mentor lost his wife a few years ago. He's remarried now and he and his new wife were thinking about going back into the chaplaincy. So it all came together for me to take a sabbatical."

"Do you miss it?"

"Not the travel part. I love the peacefulness here in Aubrey." He closed his eyes and breathed in the fresh country air. "And I'm riding in the Stockyards rodeo Saturday night."

"Really. I'll come watch you."

"That sounds great. I've never had any family to watch my competitions."

"Do you still see your grandparents?"

"I visit often. They still live in the Austin area."

Blizzard finished sniffing and bounded toward them with a faded tennis ball in his mouth and Flurry in pursuit, then dropped it at Slade's feet. Thankfully, his new adoptee had bonded with Blizzard.

"You found your ball, boy." Slade picked up the slobber-soaked ball and tossed it across the yard. Both dogs bounded after it. Raquel's tomcat shot up one of the crepe myrtle trees.

"Is that Tigger? I don't think I've ever seen him outside Raquel's barn."

"He gets semibrave occasionally. None of the dogs bother with him, but he stays on high alert—just in case one of them should suddenly decide they want yellow cat for supper. What about you—do you have any family you stay in contact with?"

"My aunt Loretta. She lives in Ponder and took me in after my mom died. Mom was a wonderful, gentle soul, and she did everything she could to shield me from my father." Her voice cracked.

"Why didn't she leave?"

"I guess he had her so cowed down she was afraid to. Afraid if she went to her family, he'd hurt them, too."

Blizzard came back and dropped the ball at their feet again. Both dogs trembled as Tori reached to get it, but Brant grabbed her arm.

"It's slobbery. And once you start, it's hard to get him to stop. Let me." He scooped the ball up.

She grabbed it from him. "I have an almost-six-month-old. I'm used to drool." Tori threw and Blizzard and Flurry bounded after the ball again.

"At least you had one good parent and I had my grandparents."

"They were good to you?"

"Wonderful."

"I had my mom until I was fifteen." She pinched the fabric of her skirt between her fingers. "She was a fabulous seamstress. All of my clothes were designer quality. In fact, everyone in school always begged me to tell them where I got my clothes. They never believed my mom sewed my clothes and thought I was holding out on some exclusive designer."

"She taught you to sew?"

"My most treasured memories are with Mom and her sewing machine." A tear slipped down her cheek and she swiped it away. "My dad came home for a few weeks before my sixteenth birthday." She breathed out a harsh sigh. "What a gift. He beat Mom up worse than ever before. When I came home the next day, I found her in the bathtub with slashed wrists."

"Oh, Tori." Slade put his arm around her shoulders and gave her a gentle squeeze.

A truck roared up out of nowhere and turned into his driveway.

"That's Brant." Tori jerked away from him and stood.

Slade jumped up and hurried to meet his sister's livid husband as the passenger door of the truck opened and Raquel unstrapped Lorraine from her car seat.

Blizzard brought his ball back, but no one threw it for him. He gave up and played keep-away with Flurry.

"Brant, calm down and put your fists away." Raquel scurried after him holding Lorraine.

"Just listen to me, Brant." Tori cut in front of Slade.

"It's not what you think. Do you really want Lorraine to see you hitting someone?"

"She's too little to understand." Brant ground out his words. "Now, y'all both stay out of the way."

"My first memory is of my father hitting my mother." Tori's tone chilled Slade's blood.

His feet stalled.

And so did Brant's.

"Now that we've all calmed down, I have news." Tori scooped Lorraine out of Raquel's arms. "Slade is my brother."

"Your brother?" Brant and Raquel echoed each other.

"Yes." Tori heaved a sigh. "Now, can we all talk about this calmly?"

"How about some coffee at my house?" Raquel squeaked, obviously shaken by the news. "I could use something to settle the nerves."

"It's about time for Lorraine's nap." Tori threaded her arm through Brant's, who was clearly shocked silent. "Where's Hunter?"

"He spent the night with Max since it's spring break." Raquel checked her watch. "Lacie's bringing him home later."

"Let's get one thing straight, Walker." Brant jabbed a finger at him. "You're gonna have to prove this news to me."

"That's not a problem." Slade handed him the paternity test results.

"What was your dad's legal name, Tori?" Brant scanned the document.

"Walter Eaton." Tori rolled her eyes. "But you already knew that."

"Just making sure. Even so, I'm sure there are other Walter Eatons besides the one who became Slim Easton.

And even if this is the same Walter Eaton, it could still be a fraud." Brant's gruff tone was intended to intimidate.

But Slade wouldn't back down. "If you don't believe me, you can check with my lawyer."

"Why would anyone go to all this trouble if it wasn't true?" Raquel sounded calm, reasonable.

"One word. Inheritance. He wants a cut of Tori's pie. He just admitted he's already got a lawyer."

"The lawyer who contacted him about the will." Tori's frustration sounded in her voice.

"Oh, really. Did he show you the money, Tori? Why should we believe anything he says?" Brant shoved the paper at Raquel. "You're a nurse. Does this look real to you?"

Raquel took the document and looked over it. "Yes. But all we have to do is check the hospital records."

"Just know, Walker, even if all of this checks out and you're on the up-and-up, you're not entitled to any of Tori's inheritance."

"Why?" Slade locked on his gaze. "Afraid your gravy train will dry up?"

"For your information—" Brant's low growl came from between clenched teeth "—I signed a prenup so Tori would know her money meant nothing to me."

Hurt reflected in Tori's eyes and Slade closed his—the fight gone out of him. His words had hurt her instead of his intended target. "I'm sorry, Tori. I didn't mean to infer that Brant would only marry you for your money. It's obvious he loves you very much or he wouldn't be so protective of you."

"Don't act all innocent with me," Brant barked. "I know this whole thing's about money."

"Brant, please." Tori's eyes grew shiny as Lorraine's fussing became a steady whimper.

"It's not about the money." Slade put a vise grip on

his temper. "I got my own cut. I didn't even want it and I haven't touched it for myself. I don't want anything from her other than for you to let her be my sister."

"I am Slade's sister," Tori snapped at Brant, "whether you *like* it or not. Whether you *accept* it or not. Whether you *allow* it or not."

"You're upsetting Lorraine." Raquel's soothing voice of reason cut through the tension.

"Raquel's right." Tori patted Lorraine's back. "Let's go home and get your nap, sweetie."

Tori headed to the truck and Brant fell in step beside her.

He opened the door for her, but she turned back to Slade before getting in. "But I will see you again. Soon."

"Sure. As long as your husband is okay with it." Even though Brant pushed all of his buttons, Slade didn't want to cause problems in their marriage.

Nervous energy zinged through Raquel as she set two coffee cups, along with creamer and sugar dishes, in the middle of the table. Tension still sizzled as she took her seat across from Slade.

He'd barely said two words since Tori and Brant had left. Poor Slade. He'd never known his father. And now his first meeting with his sister had turned into an argument. With poor Tori caught between the two men. Raquel couldn't imagine how she'd feel if she'd just met Brant and learned he was her brother.

Slade gulped his coffee black. "She'll be okay, right? Brant was so mad."

"At you. Not her. He'd never take his anger out on her." Raquel sipped her coffee. "Normally my brother is very gentle and loving, but you fray his nerves. He loves her and sees you as a threat to Tori."

In spite of her calm tone, her hand shook as she set her cup down. "He doesn't want Tori hurt again, so you're the enemy in his eyes and the hibernating bear of his temper surfaced. But he'd never intentionally hurt Tori."

"You mentioned a man hurting her once before." Concern coated Slade's voice. "Who hurt her?"

"That's Tori's story to tell. I'm terrible at keeping my mouth shut, but something I let slip to Tori last year almost kept her and Brant apart. So I'm done. You'll have to get Tori's story from her." Raquel made a zipping motion across her mouth.

"If Brant will let me. Don't you think our arguing hurts her?"

"Yes. But he'll settle down and she'll reason with him." Raquel shrugged. "It'll work out. Just give it time."

"What are the odds that I turned out to be Dylan's widow's sister-in-law's brother?"

Raquel chuckled. "How long did it take you to figure all that out?"

"A while."

"So you came here to find Tori?"

"I knew she lived here from our dad's obituary and I found her wedding announcement, so I knew her last name. At first I was hesitant to track her down. I mean, I didn't know what kind of person she was—if she'd be happy or mad to know she had a brother."

"But then you ran into her and Brant."

"And I held on to her hand too long, which got Brant and me off on the wrong foot. I fully intended to track her down after that and tell her who I was. But then you invited me to dinner."

"You didn't—" her mouth went dry "—use me to get closer to her, did you? You're not doing that now?"

"I truly had no idea you were Brant's sister until our tension-filled dinner." He covered her hand with his. "Any time I've spent with you, and Hunter, before or since, it's because I wanted to. I like your company. Both of you."

Despite the calloused strength of his hand, his gentleness showed in his touch. Her breath came in quick spurts. Could he tell she was about to hyperventilate?

"I'll help defuse Brant if you'll promise me something."

"Anything."

"Don't cause a wedge between Brant and Tori. They're still newlyweds. Don't make her choose between y'all."

"I will get to know my sister, but I'll do my best to not be a burr under Brant's saddle."

"Mom!" Hunter called from the front of the house. "I'm home."

Raquel jerked her hand away. "In the kitchen."

"Slade!" Hunter bounced into the kitchen. "Can you believe it? Our first game's in a week."

"It'll be awesome."

"Want to play catch?"

"I don't know, Hunter." Raquel interjected caution in her tone. "Slade's had a long day and you have to remember his shoulder. He's really not supposed to be pitching."

"I don't mind." Slade stood. "I'll throw you a few balls if you'll go with me to take Blizzard, Flurry and Snow for a walk. That is, if it's okay with your mom."

"Sure."

"I'll get these." Slade set both of their empty cups in the sink and ruffled Hunter's hair. "Come on, sport."

Hunter beamed under the male attention. Raquel shouldn't let him get so attached. But since Tori was Slade's sister, maybe Slade would end up sticking around.

Maybe Raquel could help ease the tensions between Brant and Slade so Slade would stick around.

But what about his calling?

Yes, she'd be supportive of Slade in his relationship with Tori, but simply for their sakes. Whether Slade stuck around or went back on the road and visited Tori occasionally—it was none of her concern. Raquel had to keep her own feelings out of the equation.

Her stomach tensed.

But how?

During Slade's chaplain years, he'd tried bareback broncs and bulls, but he had more of a knack with the broncs.

His chaps swished around his legs with each step and his spurs jangled as he headed for the chute. Manure, dirt, sweat and hay—smelled like home. Music blaring, Quinn announcing, calves bawling and horses whinnying—sounded like home.

Thoughts of Tori and Raquel wrestled for his attention. He'd had a pleasant lunch with Tori in Fort Worth one day this week. And he was pretty sure Brant didn't have a clue about it. They didn't need to do that again. He wouldn't get points with his brother-in-law by sneaking around behind his back.

And then there was Raquel. She took his breath away every time he saw her. And he'd seen her a lot this week. After the big showdown with Brant on Monday night, during practice and dinner on Tuesday and Friday, and when he'd played pitch with Hunter on Thursday.

Slade leaned against the fence railing and tried to focus on the cowboy riding a bronc. He'd planned to go to Tori's church tomorrow, but he didn't want to set Brant off. And Tori had already had Garrett Steele call him about the cowboy church.

The guy he needed to talk to was a pickup man at the rodeo and attended Wyatt and Star's church, so he could get with him after the rodeo or maybe at church tomorrow. He'd give it another week or so before he inflicted himself on Brant at his church.

"You're up next." The chute boss pointed at him.

Clear the brain and concentrate on the bronc.

Right at home, he climbed the chute, gripped the handle of the rigging and eased onto the bronc. The earthy warm scent of the horse welcomed him as the bronc tried to buck, but quarters in the chute were tight. Slade held his left arm aloft, positioned his feet high at the horse's shoulders and nodded that he was ready.

The gate opened and the horse careened to freedom, twisting and bucking. Slade stayed in rhythm with the bronc, twist for turn. The buzzer went off and he dismounted flawlessly.

"That was Slade Walker." Quinn's voice boomed over the speakers. "First-timer at Cowtown Coliseum, but obviously not a bronc first-timer with a score of eighty-one."

Applause echoed from the stands as he climbed the fence to exit the arena.

"Great ride." Wyatt Marshall clapped him on the back. "Come hang out behind the chutes. That way when the broncs and bulls are over, you can meet some of the guys. I've been witnessing to some of them for years." Wyatt made his way through the maze of contestants to a huddle of cowboys around the chutes. "Maybe they won't listen to me because they remember when I was a real rounder."

"Former rounders have the best testimonies." The change in him now blew Slade's mind. Especially when he'd learned Wyatt was married to his mild-mannered real estate lady, Star. "Sometimes I feel like mine is weak. I became a Christian at a young age. I gave up having a girlfriend, getting married and having a family for baseball. And my career ended before it even began. But God was there to catch me."

"Don't ever regret you weren't a rounder." Wyatt cringed. "And it sounds pretty powerful to me. You could have gone on a bender, turned your back on God. Instead you come out preaching for Him."

"It sounds better coming from you. Maybe you should share my testimony for me."

"But you've got something I don't. Some of these guys are baseball fans. And that one time I listened to you on the circuit, it was because I was a baseball fan."

"I was on the diamond a long time ago." Slade chuckled. "But I'll see what I can do."

They leaned against the railing watching the ride. The cowboy had good control and the bronc was giving him what for. A good ride.

"I'm up next." Wyatt strode to the chutes.

"See ya later."

"I can't seem to avoid you these days, huh, Slade," Brant shouted over the country song blaring over the speakers. "Like you're stalking me or something. Or my wife. Or my sister."

Slade's jaw tensed. "As far as I know, Raquel and Tori don't hang out at the rodeo."

"Wrong. Tori and I come quite often since I used to sing here. We like to support the cowboys."

"She's here?" Slade looked around hoping to catch a glimpse of her. She'd said she'd come watch him ride. But he hadn't planned to hold her to it, considering how Brant felt.

"She's here. But you're going to stay away from her."

Chapter 8

"Look, Brant, we got off on the wrong foot." Slade's fingers tightened on the fence until his knuckles turned white. "I should have told you who I was that first day when I ran into you and Tori. But it just didn't seem like something I needed to dump on her in the middle of the sidewalk."

"Maybe if you'd been honest from the get-go, I'd feel better about your motives. You could have contacted me—broken the news to me. And then *we* could have broken the news to Tori," Brant growled.

"Ah, I get it. So you could be in control." Sarcasm dripped from Slade's tone.

"Maybe I do like to be in control, but I'm not gonna stand around and watch you hurt Tori. Or Raquel."

"All I've done is try to get to know my sister and help Raquel and Hunter."

"Are you staying in Aubrey?"

"To tell you the truth, I'd like to." Slade lowered his

gaze to the arena floor. "But I don't know what God has in store for me."

"Tori is here to stay. And so is Rock. Neither one of them needs to get attached to you and then you end up leaving. And Hunter certainly doesn't need to get attached to you. He and Rock have been through enough."

"I'm aware of that." His gut twisted. "And that's why I've made a point to keep my relationship on a friends basis. With both of them."

"See that it stays that way."

"But there's not much you can do about blood. Tori's my sister and you can't change that."

"We'll see about that." Brant turned back toward the stands and left him standing there.

We'll see about that? There wasn't a thing Brant could do about it. Slade would get to know Tori. They would have a relationship, whether he went back on the road or not.

And with all his caution and all his just-friends talk, Slade wanted to be way more than friends with Raquel.

But Brant's remark knocked Slade back to reality. With his future up in the air, he had no right to pursue Raquel. Not unless he planned to stay in Aubrey and settle down for good. Especially since Raquel and Hunter had already been hurt by Dylan's death.

What's next, Lord? I still don't know and I'd really like it if You'd let me in on my future.

The boys lined up together, amazingly clean and spiffy in their red baseball uniforms, with their way-too-good-looking coach in the center for the team picture.

Finally April, their first game, and Raquel's insides wouldn't settle as she and Lacie leaned against the dug-out. "How do you know the photographer? She looks familiar."

"Kendra's a friend from church." Lacie was all baseball mom with her blond ponytail sticking out of the hole in the back of her cap. "You've probably seen her and her husband, Stetson, at Moms on Main. He's one of the bullfighters at the Cowtown rodeo. We're lucky to get her. She used to work for some big fancy advertising firm in Dallas."

"How did she go from there to Little League?"

"She went freelance, so she can work her schedule around her kids. Kind of like how you went from an ER nurse to a school nurse. Kids change everything."

"True." Though there was more to Raquel's decision.

"So you and Slade seem cozy."

"I told you, we're just friends." Raquel cocked her head to the side.

"Hunter told Max that Slade comes to y'all's house for supper on Tuesdays. And I know y'all eat at Moms on Fridays since you've invited us."

"I got him into this, so I figure I owe him a few cooked meals." Her stomach tumbled. Nerves over the first game or Lacie's line of questioning? A little of both. "He felt like he owed me for cooking for him. We just kind of fell into a comfortable routine. He's only here for two more months, so we don't have time for anything other than friendship."

"He's looking pretty comfy in Aubrey."

"All right, boys, take the field," Slade called, and the boys scurried to the field as he helped Kendra gather her things and then walked toward the dugout. "Thanks for doing this, Kendra."

"No problem. I enjoyed it. Hey, that was some ride the other night."

"Yeah." Slade folded her camera tripod. "Let me help you get this stuff to your car and then I'd better get to work. Let me know when the pictures are ready."

"Will do." Kendra adjusted the strap on her camera and turned toward the parking lot. "Nice to meet you, Raquel."

"You too."

Ride? Slade must have gone to the rodeo over the weekend. Brant and Tori had invited Raquel several times, but bulls made her nervous and she couldn't imagine why anyone would want to ride one. She couldn't even stand to watch. If Slade liked attending rodeos, that was just one more reason they were destined to be just friends.

Now, if she could just get her erratic heart to understand that.

Raquel and Lacie settled on the bleachers as the pregame practice started up. The other team's boys were big. Really big.

Oh, Lord, at least let our boys play well, whether they win or lose.

Praying about Little League baseball? But she knew if they lost, and especially if they lost because of bad plays, the boys would be crushed.

A familiar couple with a baby stroller crossed her line of vision. "Brant, Tori, I didn't think y'all would come."

"I wouldn't miss my favorite nephew's baseball game. Not for anything." Brant's gaze locked on Slade.

"You promised to be good." Tori threaded her fingers through Brant's and sat beside Raquel.

"Is she awake?" Raquel peered into the stroller Brant parked by the end of the stands where he sat. Bright eyed, Lorraine looked up and smiled. "Give her to me."

Brant got Lorraine out of the stroller and passed her down to Raquel.

"What do you think, Lorraine? Your first ball game. That's your cousin, Hunter, in the dugout. Just wait till you see him bat."

Another familiar couple with a stroller approached. "Mitch, Caitlyn, I didn't know y'all were coming." Raquel moved her feet so they could sit in front of her.

"We had to see Hunter's first game." Caitlyn sat down

on the bleachers. "And Mitch wanted to check out this Slade guy."

Raquel's face heated.

"Hunter talks about him all the time," Mitch whispered. "I had to come see if he passed muster. Not just anybody can get away with spending time with my favorite single mom."

"Let me hold that beautiful baby," Lacie gushed. "No worries. Slade is great. Exactly what Raquel and Hunter need."

"Excuse me?" Raquel's face steamed. "Hunter is all I need."

Brant clenched his jaw.

Thankfully, the game got into gear. The opposing team was up to bat first. After what seemed like an eternity, Hunter's team finally got the third out.

In the home team's first inning, some of the boys hit base runs, and some struck out or got tagged before they got to the base. When Hunter came up to the plate, Raquel's insides stilled.

Thwack. Hunter hit the first pitch. The home team cheered and Raquel didn't breathe until he made it safely to first base. But the next batter struck out and Hunter's team had to take the field.

Halfway through the inning, the opposing team hit a grounder and it went straight for Hunter. He bent down with his glove between his legs, but the ball rolled right between his feet.

Raquel closed her eyes. He'd be upset for days about that. The kid in the outfield missed it, too. Several minutes passed before he caught up with the ball and lobbed it back to the field. At least the bases hadn't been loaded and their opponent got only two runs out of it.

"Good try, boys," Slade called. Even tempered, calm, encouraging—not an ounce of frustration or disappointment in his tone. "Be sure and get down with your glove in the dirt, against the ground, so the ball can't get through." He squatted to demonstrate.

And her heart warmed toward him again. He really was great with the kids.

The boys ended up losing by four runs. Not bad at all, but Raquel knew exactly how upset they were. Lined up in the dugout, heads down, eyes on the dirt with the parents waiting off to the side.

"This was only our first game." Slade leaned on a bat. "And yes, we lost, but only by four runs. We learned some things about what we need to work on. All in all, I'm pretty pumped about our team. Baseball is about learning—with every game we play, we learn and develop our skills.

"And in the meantime, a very generous donor offered to buy every boy on the team a burger, fries and a Coke at Moms on Main after each game all season. I already checked with your parents on this, so let's go."

"Even though we lost?" Hunter piped up.

"Yep. And if we win, you each get an ice-cream sundae, too."

A cheer rose up from the dugout. She'd have to remember to tell Tori to thank Garrett Steele again. Food always cheered up the male species.

"And while we eat, we'll talk strategy. Everybody in."

The boys stood, piling their fists on top of Slade's.

"Go team!" they shouted in unison.

Each boy scurried to his waiting family. Hunter hurried to Raquel.

Brant and Tori and Mitch and Caitlyn had already gone. And Raquel was the only one alone. Many of the boys had stepfathers or moms' boyfriends, the result of divorces or, like Hunter and Max, death. But Max and Lacie had Quinn now. While Raquel and Hunter were still alone.

How awesome it would be to have an intact family. A husband. A father. Maybe even more children.

Who was she kidding? Her gaze settled on Slade as he approached. How awesome it would be to have Slade as a husband. As a stepfather for Hunter.

"Did Tori and Brant leave?" The object of her thoughts spoke.

"Yeah, Lorraine was tired."

"Mom, can Max ride with us?"

"Sure. Just ask his parents."

Hunter darted off.

Disappointment shone in Slade's eyes. "I was hoping Tori would go to Moms with us."

"I invited them, but Brant's still being kind of stubborn about things."

"He checked my records at the hospital. He knows my paternity test is real. I even gave Tori a copy of the will. Lancaster marked out the amount, but that's not the point anyway."

"Brant knows you're on the up and up." She closed her eyes. "But he still doesn't trust you. I'm hoping seeing you coach the kids might help."

"How?"

"You were very patient and encouraging. I have this theory that you can tell a lot about a person by watching them interact with kids."

"And I passed."

"With flying colors."

Every test. The test of her heart. The test of her son. If only he could pass the test of her brother and stay in Aubrey.

But would that test God?

The team had lost Thursday night, too. But again, it hadn't been a blowout, at least. And Slade had gotten to see Tori and Raquel several times thanks to baseball.

The bronc spun to his right and Slade cleared his mind to focus. The bronc was tough. But Slade was determined to be tougher. He kept his form in perfect rhythm with the horse until the buzzer sounded. He dismounted and landed safely, but the bronc gave a final kick. Too close. Slade dove out of the way and the horse's hoof connected with his right shin.

Pain exploded in his leg as the back of his head slammed into the metal railing surrounding the arena.

White-hot heat blasted through his crown as he collapsed in a heap against the fence. A dark tunnel widened before him, threatening to block his vision.

He blinked several times.

"Ooh," Quinn summed it up. "That was a brutal blow."

The pickup men wrangled the bronc to the exit gate. Slade's head throbbed with the pulse of the blaring rock music. Holding his breath, he managed to stand, wobble to the fence and climb out of the arena. His shin was nothing compared to his head. He didn't even hear his score as the paramedics converged on him.

The older man asked him questions about the pain and probed his head wound. Slade could barely concentrate enough to answer and pressed his face into the crook of his arm.

Deep breaths. Push the pain down. *You got this.*

No. He didn't. He really didn't.

The medic shone the flashlight in his eyes and that made everything hurt worse. "Your leg's just bruised and you have a grade one concussion."

His head pounded in agreement. Why had he thought bronc riding was a good idea?

"You're one lucky bronc rider." The medic turned off the piercing light. "I'll let your wife know you're free to go."

"I don't have a wife." He covered his face with his hands, willing the throbbing to stop. It didn't.

A hand touched his shoulder. "I can drive you home."
Tori.

"You're here." He moved his hands.

"Of course I'm here. I couldn't let my brother drive himself home after a wreck like that." Tori grinned. "I'll hog-tie you if I have to."

"Got any Demerol?"

"Sorry, I'm slap out." Humor radiated in her tone.

"You were in the stands tonight? Is Brant here?"

"No." She lowered her voice. "He thinks I'm having dinner with my aunt Loretta."

From the little he knew of her, he could picture her crossing her fingers behind her back. He grinned. But that hurt, too.

"Are you ready?" Tori helped him stand, supporting his weight with her arm around his waist.

"Past ready." He tried not to grimace. If they knew how bad he hurt, they might not let him leave.

Tiny. She was absolutely tiny. If he fell, he'd take them both out and squash her flat.

"Tori." Star caught up with them. "Let Wyatt help."

"Gladly." Tori giggled. "He weighs a ton."

"I'll drive him home in his truck and Star can follow us." Wyatt opened the lobby door.

"That would be great, but I'll take him home." Tori dug in her purse for her keys. "And probably stay the night. I'd feel better if he wasn't alone."

"I'm fine," Slade mumbled. Why were they talking around him? "I don't need a babysitter."

"Is Brant here?" Star asked.

"No. He's at home with Lorraine."

"Will Brant be okay with you taking him home?" Wyatt sounded odd as they exited the coliseum. "And spending the night?"

The rumors would start. Tori was two-timing her husband. Ugh. But they didn't know Slade was her brother.

"It's fine. Slade is my brother."

Star's mouth dropped open. "Well, why didn't either of you ever say so?"

"It never came up." Slade heard the slur in his words. Why wasn't his mouth working right? He needed to shut up before they insisted on taking him to the ER.

Tori's car waited by the sidewalk. Wyatt helped him get in.

"Drive safe." Star waved. "We'll be right behind you."

"I will. Don't worry." Tori started the engine.

The movement of the car sent a wave of nausea through him. "Tor."

"Hmm."

"I don't feel so good." His words slurred worse.

"I'm taking you to Raquel's since she's a nurse. I don't think you should be alone."

His eyes were heavy. So tired.

"Slade? What's your favorite color?"

"Why?"

"Because I want you to stay awake? Aren't you not supposed to sleep if you have a concussion?"

"I don't know. I reckon they said all that, but I can't remember." He tried to keep his eyes open, but his lids were too heavy.

"So what's your favorite color?"

"Red. You?"

"Pink."

"What's your favorite season?"

He closed his eyes. Just for a minute.

"Slade? Your favorite season?"

"Spring. The one when I met my sister."

She grew quiet a minute, then sniffled. "You better not die on me."

"It's a slight concussion."

"I don't mean tonight. I mean…the next rodeo. Or ever."

"If it was just me, I'd rather be in Heaven. But I don't want to die on you. Or Lorraine. I mean, unless I have to."

And he didn't want to die on Raquel either. Or Hunter.

Why couldn't she sleep? Raquel stared at the ceiling, slightly illuminated in the moonlight. Easter morning, well after midnight. She hadn't even slept in yesterday and should have been dreaming by now.

A loud ring ripped the silence. She sat up and stared at the phone. Who would call this time of morning?

She grabbed the handset and scanned the caller ID. Tori? "What's wrong?"

"Slade's hurt and I was driving him home. But I figure he won't keep ice on it and I don't know if he should sleep or not, so I thought he could use a nurse to keep him in line. Can I bring him to your house?"

"Of course, but what happened?"

"We're pulling in your drive. We'll try to be quiet and not wake Hunter up."

Lights flashed in her window as a car pulled into the driveway. She jumped up, slipped on her robe and smoothed her hands over her hair.

Great. Bedhead and not a speck of makeup, with sheet wrinkles pressed into her cheek. Just how she wanted Slade to see her.

But he was hurt and that was all that mattered. She hurried down the stairs. How had he gotten hurt? What had he hurt? Why was Tori bringing him home? Where was Brant?

She flung the door open to see Tori and Wyatt Marshall helping Slade walk. Raquel hurried down the walk and took Tori's spot. With his arms around both their shoulders, he still limped heavily.

Man, was he just as solid as he looked.

"What happened?"

"Horse kicked me." Slade's breath was labored, as if he had to bite back the pain. "I tried to get out of the way and met up with the fence against my noggin."

"What were you doing with a horse this time of morning?"

"Rodeo."

"How? Were you helping a cowboy unload?"

"Riding a bronc."

Her heart stilled. And her feet almost did, too. "Riding a bronc?"

Chapter 9

"Can we talk later?" Slade clenched his teeth. "It hurts too much to think, much less talk."

Fair enough. She'd direct her questions to Tori. "If he's hurting that much, should he go to the ER?"

"The paramedic at the rodeo checked him over and said he could go. He has a grade one concussion, whatever that is. He managed to jump back enough to keep from taking the full force of the bronc's kick, so his leg's just bruised."

Getting him up the porch steps would have been impossible without Wyatt, and by the time they got him inside, Raquel was praying they'd get him to her couch.

They made it and Slade collapsed with a moan.

"Lie down," Raquel ordered.

He didn't argue.

"Pain meds?"

"They gave him Aleve and said to keep ice on it." Tori gently set the ice pack on Slade's crown.

He moaned again.

"His truck's over at his place." Wyatt adjusted his hat. "Need me and Star to stay?"

"No. Thanks for helping us, but y'all go on home." Raquel slid another pillow under Slade's head.

Wyatt left.

"I didn't know what to do with him." Tori paced the hardwood floor. "The paramedic prescribed rest. I didn't think he needed to be alone and I couldn't take him to my house. I couldn't tell Brant I was going to the rodeo, so he thinks I had dinner with Aunt Loretta and decided to stay there for the night."

"It's okay. You did the right thing."

"But maybe I should have taken him to his house and you could have checked on him there."

"I wouldn't leave Hunter alone. Here is better."

"That's what I decided. But he'll have to stay here all night."

No. He. Couldn't. Especially since he'd turned out to be a bronc rider.

"I'll be fine, once that pill kicks in." Slade squinted up at them. "When the pain eases up, I'll go home."

"No." Tori tucked a throw over Slade. "I'll stay and chaperone."

"I'm hardly in any shape to need a chaperone." Slade grimaced.

His meds must be kicking in. His words were multiplying and didn't sound so bitten out.

"True. But you can't just spend the night at Raquel's. What would the neighbors think?"

"There aren't any neighbors. And it's not like his truck is in my drive." Raquel didn't want him here overnight, but Tori couldn't stay here with him.

"What will Hunter think if I spend the night here?"

"He'll think you're hurt and I'm a nurse. But I have a better solution. We're not hiding this from Brant. If he finds out, he'll be even madder about Slade. Wives shouldn't keep secrets from their husbands and Brant's gonna have to learn to deal with the situation."

"What?" Tori's voice blended with Slade's.

"Go home, Tori. Tell Brant where you've been and what happened."

"Are you crazy?" Slade groaned. "He's liable to come finish me off."

"No." Tori's tone softened. "Brant may be an overprotective bear sometimes, but he's not violent. He's all growl and no attack. And Raquel's right. I need to be honest with him."

"Go. Slade and I will be fine."

Tori nodded. "I thought you had to keep someone with a concussion awake."

"They used to torment patients by keeping them awake but finally decided sleep is better." Raquel patted her shoulder. "He'll be fine. Call me if Brant gives you any trouble and I'll help calm him down."

"I can handle him. He's really just a big softy."

Raquel sure didn't want to have to deal with Slade's pain while Brant glowered at him. Even a stupid bronc rider didn't deserve that kind of torture.

"I'll see you tomorrow." Tori touched Slade's hand. "Try to get some rest."

"Mmm-hmm." Slade was fading fast.

Tori left and tension rolled over Raquel. She wanted to chew him out for his stupidity. But he was hurt and she couldn't kick him while he was down. Instead she'd nurse him back to health and deal with her overprotective brother who couldn't seem to understand his wife and sister were both grown women.

* * *

An insistent pounding. Someone was knocking on Slade's head. He groaned.

"Slade, wake up." Raquel's soft voice.

He opened his eyes. She stood over him. Where was he? Not his camper. Not his rental house. Raquel's house?

"What am I doing here?"

"Please don't tell me you don't remember. Brant and Tori are here. It's morning. You better get it together."

He closed his eyes. The throbbing in his head was back. Oh, yeah. The horse. And the fence. And Tori.

Brant was here. This would be worse than the pain in his head. Or his leg.

"Good," Slade muttered. "I think I'm ready to be finished off."

A storm was brewing and Slade was in no shape to face Brant's fury.

"How are you feeling this morning?" Tori's gentle voice was a mere whisper.

He clenched his jaw. "You got any Demerol?"

"He's still with us." Tori chuckled. "Sense of humor and all. He was asking for Demerol last night."

"Or maybe he's addicted to pain meds." Brant's tone held no humor.

Even if the Aleve took away his pain, a bigger pain was here.

"It was a joke. I've had Demerol once," Slade barked, in no mood for Brant's brand of intimidation. "When I had my wisdom teeth cut out. I don't smoke, I don't do drugs, and I don't drink. I also don't take advantage of women. Or their money. Satisfied?"

"We'll see."

"I won't have you badgering my guest in my home." Raquel rearranged some pillows around him. "He's hurt and in no condition to deal with you."

"He's got you sucked in, too."

Lorraine whimpered.

"There's no reasoning with him, is there, sweetie?" Raquel scooped the baby out of Tori's arms. "I'll go wake Hunter. If he can go to church with y'all, I'll stay with Slade."

"You go." Tori settled beside Slade. "I'll stay."

"Over my dead body." Brant glared. "I'll cart his backside to his house and we'll all go to church."

"Can you at least tone it down for Hunter and Lorraine's sake?" Raquel shot Brant the look and headed for the back of the house.

"Brant, please." Tori sounded shaky.

If only Slade had left her alone, she wouldn't be in this difficult spot.

"Please what, Tori? Trust this guy? He showed up out of the blue claiming to be your brother."

"He is my brother. We confirmed the paternity test at the hospital."

"Okay, we learn he is your brother. And the next thing I know, you're lying to me, sneaking around going to rodeos and staying out half the night with him while I thought you were at Loretta's."

"I'm sorry." Tori's gaze sank to the floor. "I shouldn't have lied."

"And I shouldn't have let her." Slade's head throbbed with the intensity of the argument.

"He got hurt. What did you want me to do, just leave him to find his way home?"

"His family could've seen to him."

"He is my family. Like it or not, Slade is my brother. I couldn't leave the rodeo knowing he was hurt. And I deserve the right to get to know my brother." Tori stomped her foot. "And you of all people should know how much I've always wanted a family. I can't believe you're trying to sabotage this."

"I won't believe he's only here to have a relationship with you, Tori. He wants something. And I won't stand by and watch him hurt you. I have to protect you and Lorraine."

"Don't you see?" Tori's voice cracked. "By trying to protect me, you're hurting me."

Brant grew quiet for a moment, then held his hand toward Tori. "I'm sorry. I didn't realize."

She stood and the couple hugged.

"I hate fighting with you." Tori sniffled.

"This is our last." Brant kissed the top of her head.

"Just give Slade a chance. Get to know him. If you'll spend some time with him, you'll see he's a good man and he has no ulterior motives."

"I will." Brant kissed her and it turned into a lingering one.

Uncomfortable, Slade looked away. But it did his soul good to see Brant's tender side with Tori.

"Whoa." Raquel entered the room. "I'm glad to see Brant defused, but break it up."

The kiss ended, but the hug didn't.

"Sorry about that." Tori's face turned pink.

"Slade and I are calling a truce." Brant disentangled himself from Tori to offer his hand.

The two men shook on it and Tori retrieved Lorraine from Raquel.

"Wow. What did I miss?" Raquel's gaze pinged from one man to the other.

"You girls take the kids and go to church." Brant dropped a kiss on the baby's forehead and sat in the chair across from Slade. "I'll babysit Slade and when he's feeling up to it, I'll take him next door and get him settled."

"He can stay here." Raquel plumped a pillow and set it behind Slade's head. "There's no rush."

"I appreciate it, Raquel." Slade could stay camped out

on her couch forever. But staying here made him entertain thoughts he shouldn't have, even with this headache and the argument with Brant. "But my own bed sounds good."

If only God took away all those thoughts when He called a man to preach. Instead He used humans. With human desires and human thoughts. Now that his head was clearing, Slade needed to get out of here.

"At least let me feed you before you take more Aleve. Eggs, bacon and biscuits sound okay?"

Like paradise. "I'm fine. No need to go to all that trouble." His stomach growled.

"Nonsense. I always cook breakfast for Hunter."

The perfect woman. In every way. And maybe her brother was even softening toward him.

"I'll help." Tori plopped Lorraine in Brant's arms and followed Raquel to the kitchen.

"I can't remember the last time I missed church on Easter. So once they're gone, you gonna kill me in my sleep?"

"Nope." Brant propped his feet on the coffee table. "I made a promise to Tori. We're gonna get to know each other in a civilized manner."

Civilized. Slade could handle that. If he could win Brant over, all obstacles would fade between him and Tori. But what about Raquel? Slade still didn't know where his calling would lead.

Maybe his meeting next week with Garrett Steele would clear things up.

Thank goodness they hadn't set up the meeting for this week. All he had to worry about this week was baseball. Game tomorrow night. By the time he finished breakfast, the pain meds would have kicked in. He'd have to shut his spinning brain off and rest if he was gonna be up for baseball.

Hunter sprinted toward home plate, but the ball was back on the field. Raquel's heart sped faster than his feet.

"You know what to do, Hunter," Slade shouted.

The back catcher rushed the plate and Hunter slid home.

"Safe," the ump shouted, and the home crowd went wild.

"Game," the ump shouted and the home crowd went wilder.

"We won!" Raquel jumped to her feet.

"Awesome." Tori clapped. "But why did they call the game?"

"Because there are six innings."

"I'll never learn all of this." Tori rocked Lorraine from side to side.

"Yes, you will." Brant handed her a pacifier. "Did you get a chance to talk to Slade before the game?"

"Not really. Hunter was with us. Why?"

"I was just wondering how he's feeling today."

"I'm so proud of you for caring." Raquel's eyes grew misty.

Brant turned five shades of red.

"My hero." Tori leaned her head against Brant's shoulder. "I talked to Slade on the phone. He said he still had a little headache and his leg's bruised but okay if he doesn't touch it."

A cheer went up from the dugout.

"Everybody meet up at Moms on Main," Slade shouted. "And this time, we get sundaes, too."

Another cheer went up and the boys scattered, darting for their parents.

"Are y'all coming to Moms?" Raquel asked.

"Wouldn't miss it." Brant hung the diaper bag on the stroller handles.

Slade picked up his gear bag and headed in their direction. Looking way too handsome, as usual. Way too kind. Way too Christian. Way too perfect.

"Did Slade tell you about his meeting with Garrett

Steele after church this coming Sunday?" Tori strapped Lorraine into her stroller.

"No." Raquel frowned.

"They're talking about starting a cowboy church in Aubrey."

"Really?"

"It makes me wonder if Slade's thinking about staying in town."

Slade staying in Aubrey?

"Mom, can I ride with Max?"

Sure. Abandon me. Leave me alone with the cutest baseball coach ever. "Sure, sweetie. Just be good."

"I will."

Slade caught up with her. "Ready."

"Yep. How's your head?"

"A little headache never kept me out of the dugout." He fell in stride beside her.

"I guess it went okay with Brant yesterday?"

"Amazingly well. I slept and he didn't smother me. When I woke up, he helped me home without injuring me, and we had a civilized conversation." Slade shrugged. "We even watched a baseball game together."

"Leave it to sports for male bonding."

"I don't know about bonding. But the tension's gone, at least."

"I think the pod people took my brother and replaced him."

"He's not usually civilized?"

"Well, yeah, but I never really thought he would be toward you."

"We made Tori cry. That got to both of us." Slade's voice broke.

Why did he have to be so sweet?

"And he told me all about Russ Dawson and everything that lunatic did to Tori." Slade closed his eyes. "I understand why Brant is on high alert now. And I respect him for that. He'd do anything to protect my sister. And Lorraine, even though he's not her biological father. I'm glad Lorraine and Tori have Brant to watch out for them."

Even her brother was warming to Slade now and he might consider settling in Aubrey for good. Raquel was running thin on reasons to steer clear of him. And now they'd go to Moms together, since she'd driven because of his concussion. They'd probably sit together, eat together, laugh together. And then drive home. Together.

But he's a stupid bronc rider. She had to keep telling herself that. Her last defense against Slade Walker.

"I've been meaning to ask you, how is bronc riding good for your shoulder?"

"It's not." Slade chuckled. "If I land wrong, I could do a number on it. But riding uses different muscles than pitching and I always land on my feet when I dismount."

"It doesn't sound like you landed on your feet Saturday night."

"I did, but I jumped back to avoid the horse and crashed with the fence, so I fell."

They reached her car, she opened the trunk, and he stashed his gear.

"So even if you always land on your feet on the dismount, you could have hurt your shoulder if you'd twisted and crashed it into the fence instead of your head. And what happens if someday you don't land on your feet on the dismount?"

"Look, Raquel. I can't spend my life worrying about what might happen to my shoulder. I witness to cowboys. Bronc riding gets me in their circle. It's not an every-weekend thing, just when I hit a new arena."

"We better get going." She shut the trunk harder than she needed to.

Great. A stupid, honorable bronc rider.

* * *

"Watch for cars," Raquel cautioned Hunter as they trekked across the church parking lot.

But the charcoal-gray truck parked a few spaces away stopped her in her tracks.

Slade's truck. And the man himself stood just outside the door.

"You came." Hunter barreled toward Slade.

"Careful." Raquel cringed. "Remember Slade has a sore leg."

"And head." He rubbed the crown of his head. "But of course I came. You invited me and I planned to come last week, but I wasn't quite up to it."

"Come on, Mom." Hunter held the door for her.

One foot in front of the other. Calm heart. He probably wouldn't sit with them or anything. He'd sit with Tori or Garrett. But then again, he might, since she and Hunter always sat with Brant and Tori.

"You wanna sit with us?"

Raquel closed her eyes.

"Sure, sport."

Hunter led Slade into the sanctuary with Raquel trailing behind. Halfway up the aisle, Slade stopped, his gaze glued on Garrett Steele.

"He's a member here," Raquel whispered. "We usually do sit in the same pew since Tori is friends with Garrett's wife, Jenna. But we try not to make a big deal over him so he can enjoy church."

"I like his style, but trust me, I won't go all fan guy on him. I'm just interested in the cowboy church."

"I'd introduce you, but it might open the door for somebody else to go all fan girl or guy. One person approaches him and others tend to freak out."

"It's fine. I'm meeting with him today about the cowboy church."

She took her usual seat next to Brant and Tori and exchanged pleasantries. At least Hunter sat between her and Slade.

"Can you eat lunch with us after church?" Hunter asked.

Raquel closed her eyes. She had plenty of food. But she needed to distance herself from this stupid bronc rider. That was the way she had to think of him to keep her heart from revving.

"Sorry, I can't, sport. I have a meeting after church."

Thank goodness. At least she'd have to spend only an hour with Slade and her palpitating heart.

Focus on the music. "Sweet Hour of Prayer." She needed a lot of prayer to keep her safe from Slade's charms.

"Slade Walker." One of the deacons clapped Slade on the back. "Remember me? I used to ride bulls on the circuit."

"Don't tell me." Slade tapped his chin with his finger. "Buck Anderson. Right?"

"Right. You led me to the Lord. I don't know where I'd be now if not for you."

"The Lord drew you to Him. He just used me as a tool."

"It's great seeing you. Are you still on the circuit?"

"I'm taking a little break right now."

"Remember Wyatt Marshall?"

"I do. In fact, I've seen him lately at the Stockyards rodeo."

"He goes to a church down the street. Both in church thanks to you."

Color crept up Slade's neck to his face. "God orchestrated it all."

For the first time, Raquel saw the results of Slade's calling. He'd borne fruit and she had no right to hope Slade would stay in Aubrey. Obviously, the road was right where he needed to be.

It was a good service. It would have been better if Slade could've sat beside Raquel without Hunter between them.

But if she'd been beside him, her cute brown dress with turquoise stitching paired with cowgirl boots would have distracted him from the sermon.

While he lingered in the lobby unsure of where the meeting was, Raquel headed for the door.

"Raquel, can you stick around for the meeting and take care of Lorraine if she gets fussy? Poor baby girl's teething." Brant held Lorraine against his chest, patting her back.

"Sure." Raquel's eyes widened, as if it was the last thing she wanted. Not that she had a problem spending time with her niece. Just with Slade.

But at least she'd agreed.

"Where's the meeting?"

"In the fellowship hall." Brant watched the parking lot. "Garrett and Jenna are already there. Lane and Natalie are coming over from their church."

"Lane and Natalie?" The names sounded familiar, but Slade couldn't remember who they were.

"Lane's the associate pastor at the church you visited a few weeks ago and a pickup man at the Cowtown rodeo." Tori dug Lorraine's bottle out of the diaper bag. "He's the one who asked about using one of Garrett's barns for the church. Natalie is his wife and Jenna's cousin."

Slade's heart sank. Maybe this wasn't the answer. "Does Lane want to pastor the cowboy church?"

"I don't think so. Not from what Jenna said. He's happy being an associate."

Or maybe it was.

"Do you want to pastor a cowboy church?" Raquel's voice quivered.

Chapter 10

"I'd have to talk it over with God, but remember I told you I'm kind of tired of the road."

He tried to read her expression, but her gaze darted away.

Was she glad he might stay in Aubrey? Could they have a future? Was she interested at all?

She'd been a staunch supporter in his quest to spend time with Tori. But since he and Brant had settled things, Raquel seemed to be pulling away from him. Except for the Monday-night game when she was still worried about his injuries, he'd driven himself to the practices and games.

They hadn't even had supper together the rest of the week. And Hunter had said enough to let Slade know her excuses were just that. Excuses.

"Y'all can go on back." Brant rocked Lorraine in his arms. "I'll get Hunter set up with something to draw on and wait for Lane and Natalie."

"I'll show you the way." Tori linked her hand through

the crook of Slade's arm and he offered his other elbow to Raquel.

She hesitated but took his offer. Her hand trembled against him as they walked down the hallway to the fellowship hall.

Was she nervous about the meeting? Nervous about him? Or maybe she was nervous about Garrett Steele. She obviously knew him, but music stars often sent women trembling.

"Right through here." Tori pointed to the double doors.

Slade pulled free of the women to open the door for them. Garrett and the pretty woman he'd been with during church were seated at a long white table. Slade's nerves zinged. Over Raquel's tremble or the meeting? Both.

"Slade Walker, it's nice to meet you." Garrett stood and shook his hand. "I followed your baseball career."

"Really? I like your music. I've even used a few of your songs for altar calls in my chaplain work. It's nice to meet you."

"Who'd have ever thought a Garrett Steele song would factor in an altar call. God is truly amazing." Garrett gestured to the seat across from him. "This is my wife, Jenna."

"Nice meeting you, ma'am." Slade started to tip his hat but remembered it wasn't there.

"You too."

"I'd like to thank y'all for the meals for our baseball team. It's very generous. Last Monday we won our first game and got to take y'all up on those sundaes. The boys really enjoyed them."

"I'm so glad." Jenna smiled.

"I played Little League." Garrett shrugged. "I wasn't ever any good, but I remember going to eat out after the few times we won. Some of the kids didn't get to go, because their parents couldn't afford it. I always wished somebody would pay for the whole team so all my friends could go. I'm able to do that now, so I do."

"That's the sweetest thing I ever heard." A pregnant brunette stepped into the room. "Who knew Garrett Steele was such a benevolent soul."

The woman hurried over and hugged Garrett as a man settled at the table with Brant.

"Enough of that. You're just emotional because of the baby." Garrett grinned. "This is Jenna's cousin, Natalie, and her husband, Lane Grey. Meet Slade Walker. Now that everybody's here, let's talk cowboy church."

Slade turned to Lane. "I heard you asked about starting a cowboy church in Garrett's barn."

"In my work as a pickup man at the Stockyards Championship Rodeo, I've come across several Christians who work or ride there and we often witness to the nonbelievers." Lane steepled his hands. "A few months back, I invited one of the bull riders to church. He said, 'Too fancy for me.'"

Countless times Slade had heard the same from cowboys on the circuit.

"That got me thinking—there are a whole host of nonbelievers who will never step in the doors of a regular church. Because they don't feel like they belong, or a list of other excuses. But the cowboy churches are breaking down those excuses."

"People can wear what they've got, come to a barn and get baptized in a feed trough." Slade nodded. "Similar to my rodeo chaplain ministry."

"There are two cowboy churches in Fort Worth and one in Denton." Garrett ran his finger across his iPhone screen. "To tell you the truth, when Lane first came to me, I thought, Aubrey has plenty of churches and our church doesn't need any more competition. But like Lane said, some folks will never go near a typical church. I think Aubrey is ripe for a cowboy church."

"If we can find a building, would you be interested in pastoring?" Lane asked.

Slade's gut tensed. "You wouldn't be?"

"No." Lane shook his head. "I prayed about it and God convicted me, I'm an associate pastor. Period. But there is a newly called preacher at our church. Our pastor talked to him and he's willing to take my place, so I could be associate for the cowboy church."

"Would you be interested in pastoring, Slade?" Garrett sipped his coffee.

"I'd have to pray about it." Slade folded his hands on the textured surface of the table. "I've been a rodeo chaplain for several years, but I'm currently on sabbatical because I had some family concerns to take care of."

"Are your family concerns settled now?"

Slade looked at Tori, then Brant. "I think so."

"Well, I've already prayed about the matter. I'm all for a cowboy church, but not in my barn." Garrett leaned back in his chair. "Unfortunately, I have to be very careful about security and I'm very private about where I live."

"All of our property was enclosed in one fence with access from one gate. And we had a breach." Jenna patted Tori's hand.

Tori shivered and Brant put his arm around her.

The muscle in Slade's jaw flexed.

"For the last year," Garrett continued, "I've had the fences redone and added a gate so that the entrance to two of the barns are separate. They'll both open soon—one will be a bull-riding school and the other a practice arena. The only other barns on the property are too close to my residence."

"I see." Slade's heart sank.

"But Jenna and I have talked about it. We're willing to

put up the money for a building or barn that could be used. Or even buy land and build."

"Really?" Slade's mouth went dry. "I actually have some funds available. I'll donate whether I pastor the church or not."

"I could make a donation," Tori offered.

"So could I," Natalie chimed in.

"Well, then, I'll contact Star Marshall and see what she can find." Garrett leaned his elbows on the table. "Once we have a building, I'll contact Slade and we'll talk funds, then see what God says about a pastor. Since we're backing the ministry, I'm sure we'll want a pastor of like doctrine. Maybe the cowboy church could join our association of churches."

Lorraine let out a whimper. Raquel took her from Brant, stood up and bounced her niece around.

"Do you plan to attend the church?" Slade directed his question to Garrett.

"No." Garrett shook his head. "I might do a concert at the arena we'll put behind the church to jump-start the congregation, but we're happy in our church."

"This is so exciting." Natalie twiddled her thumbs. "Lane's done research and these churches don't seem to pull from other congregations—they truly draw people who don't go anywhere."

"Let's hope. Thanks for setting up the meeting, Tori." Garrett scooted his chair back and stood. "It was nice meeting you, Slade. I'll be in touch."

"I'll look forward to hearing from you."

Raquel danced Lorraine around in the corner. And her flowery scent ambushed him, drawing him like a bee to honey. Especially beautiful holding a baby.

If this worked out, if God was for him pastoring the cowboy church, he could stay in Aubrey and get to know Tori better. He could be near Raquel. If she'd let him get near.

But he had to keep her out of the equation. If the cowboy church came together, he needed to pray about it. And he couldn't let Raquel influence his decision.

She handed Lorraine back to Brant as everyone said their goodbyes and hurried out the exit.

Didn't seem as if she were interested in letting him near anyway.

Mid-April sun warmed Raquel as she stood at the plate. She hadn't swung a bat in a dozen years.

Two more games under their belt and the boys hadn't won again yet. No matter how much Raquel tried to encourage him, Hunter was starting to get down in the dumps. About half the team were decent hitters and runners. They followed the base coaches' directions well.

But playing the field killed the team every game. If one kid missed the ball, it turned into a comedy of errors while the opposing team made run after run.

So Slade had come up with a plan for practice tonight and had asked the adults who were willing to come dressed to play.

So here she stood at the plate, with a field full of seven- and eight-year-olds. And Slade pitching. "Are you sure this is okay for your shoulder?"

"I'm fine. I promise not to use my fastball on you."

"Come on, Raquel. Bring me home," Lacie called from second base.

"No pressure." Raquel deadpanned. She angled the bat back above her shoulders and leaned into her stance, remembering the tips Slade had given Hunter. Feet straight, lined up with the plate, swing level.

The pitch came low and fast.

"Strike one," Quinn announced behind her.

Raquel faced him. "It was low."

"Don't argue with my ump, ma'am." Slade grinned at her.

She gripped the bat harder and leaned into the plate, determined to knock it out of the park as Slade wound up for his next pitch.

Still a little low, but doable. She swung and connected with the ball, sending a solid vibration through her hands. She dropped the bat behind her and ran. Sam waved her on to second and Quinn stopped her there while Slade coached the boys on the field.

Okay, so it wasn't out of the park, but she'd gotten Lacie home.

"I'm gonna get you out, Mom." Hunter punched his glove with his fist on third.

"We'll see about that." She stuck her tongue out at him.

"It's not fair, coach," Fletcher whined from the outfield. "The adults can hit the ball farther and run faster."

"Yes," Slade shouted. "But it's great practice for us. That was much better. You're starting to think like a team. Each player knows where he'll throw the ball before it comes to him. If that had been a kid hitting and running, y'all would have gotten him out."

Slade turned back to the home plate. Another mom was up to bat. A solid thunk resonated on the first pitch and Raquel ran to third. Quinn waved her home. Two-thirds of the way there, Quinn dove for the ball, but it went over his head into the backstop. As Quinn scrambled after it, Slade ran in to cover home.

Mere feet away, Quinn lobbed the ball to Slade. Raquel had only one chance. She slid on her belly and touched the plate with her fingertips as Slade knelt to tag her.

"Safe," Quinn called.

Slade helped her up and the warmth of his hand numbed her brain. Lacie ran over for a high five, breaking the contact. Heat crept up her neck and she dusted off the front of her jeans and T-shirt.

"That was great, boys."

"But I didn't get her out." Hunter kicked third base.

"But Max sailed that ball straight to you. Your mom's an above-average runner. Most kids wouldn't be able to run as fast and you'd have gotten them out. You'll see. Play like we just practiced on Tuesday night and we'll get some outs. Let's wrap it up for the night."

The team scattered.

"Can Slade help us make cupcakes, Mom?"

Drat. She really needed to have a talk with Hunter about inviting Slade everywhere. "Sure."

"Cupcakes?"

"I'm making cupcakes for the game. Everybody gets one cupcake, but if they win, they get two."

"My kind of motivation."

"You can help me frost 'em." Hunter bounced up and down. "And Mom's making my favorite, chicken and dumplings."

"If you like chicken and dumplings, we've got plenty."

"If I like chicken and dumplings? You're making my mouth water."

He made her mouth water. *Stop looking. Just stop looking. Stop thinking. Stop dreaming.* "Come over when we get home from school on Thursday."

"I and my appetite will be there."

Raquel hurried to her car. At least she didn't have to be in the same vehicle with him on the way to her house. Maybe by game day, her breathing would get back to normal.

The still-warm cupcake emitted a decadent scent as Slade smeared on the chocolate icing the way Hunter had shown him. Tempting—he'd like to pop it in his mouth.

But the cupcake wasn't as tempting as the woman in the red apron beside him. Focus on the child in their midst before he did something stupid.

"Thanks for inviting me over, Hunter. I think that was the best chicken and dumplings I've ever eaten." Slade caught Raquel's gaze.

"I'm glad you liked it." Raquel turned a cupcake with one hand and slathered icing with the other.

"*Like* is a weak word when it comes to chicken and dumplings. Try *love*."

Her gaze flitted to his, then darted away.

"Wish I could have had more." Hunter's cupcake had more icing on it than it could hold.

"Not so much icing." Raquel spooned some off and started a new cupcake. "You get a cupcake after your meal at Moms. And there are plenty of leftovers for tomorrow night. If you eat too much before the game, it might get messy."

"Hey, sport, shouldn't you get your uniform on?"

"Aww, I wanna finish the cupcakes."

"Slade's right." Raquel checked the clock. "I didn't realize what time it was."

"Okay." Hunter set down the cupcake he'd just finished in the cake pan and scurried down the hall.

Finally alone. Slade stepped closer to Raquel. Side by side, they frosted their cupcakes. His arm grazed hers and heat went straight to his heart. Her perfume teased his senses.

"This is fun. I don't know how you had time to cook that meal and bake these when you just got home a few hours ago."

"The Crock-Pot is a lifesaver."

"But you had the cupcakes in the oven by the time I got here. You're amazing." He could spend the rest of his years making cupcakes with her.

"Not really. I love cooking and baking. I hope the other boys on the team get a light supper before the game."

"I'm pretty sure a few don't eat until after the game at Moms. You're a great mom, Raquel."

"Thanks." She looked up at him, her eyes misty. "I try, but I worry about Hunter not having a male influence."

"I could help you with that."

Panic filled her eyes and she took a step back. She wiped at her eyes, smearing icing on her nose.

Great, he'd scared her off, just when more than anything he wanted to kiss the icing away and then stray to her lips. "You've got icing on your nose."

She swiped at the smear and made it worse.

And for some reason, he wanted to remember this moment.

"Wait, hold it right there. I'll show you." He pretended to get her a napkin while he dug his cell from his pocket, then snapped her picture.

"What was that for?"

"To show you how funny you look." Actually tantalizing. He held his phone for her to see.

She leaned her head close to his.

"This is going on Facebook."

"No." She grabbed at his phone.

"Oh, yeah." He held it up out of her reach.

Laughing, she stepped closer and reached for the phone.

Only a breath away. Phone forgotten, his hands settled on her waist.

She stilled and her laughter died.

His gaze fell to her lips. Did he dare follow his heart and kiss her? No, she'd bolt. Better to take this slow.

"Here, I'll get it." He wiped the frosting away with his thumb.

A tiny gasp escaped her and she pushed away from him.

"And I won't put the picture on Facebook. I'm not even on Facebook. I was kidding."

"Good." She turned to the counter and began frosting the final cupcake but her hand shook.

"I've missed our dinners together. We kind of had a routine going there for a while of eating and riding together. I miss that. Maybe we could start riding to the ball field together again. And eating together."

"Well, you know where the ball field is now and your concussion is healed, so you don't need me to get you there. And we'll eat together at Moms on Main after the rest of the games, win or lose."

"I know, but I was thinking maybe we could eat together after practices too. You don't have to cook. We can go to Moms. And since we're both going to the ball field four times a week, why not ride together and save gas."

"We'll see." She set the cupcakes in the deep cake pan.

"Maybe we could have dinner on Saturday night. Alone."

Her hand stopped in mid-lid-snapping. "You mean... like a...date," she squeaked.

"Yeah, like a date. Actually, not like a date. But a date." Did that even make any sense?

"No." She shook her head and pressed the plastic lid onto the cake pan.

"No?" Slade's voice cracked.

"Do you want some chicken and dumplings to take home?" Raquel wouldn't look at him. "It's easy to warm up in the microwave."

Huh? Her chicken and dumplings were to die for. But she'd just turned him down and she was talking leftovers?

"Sure."

"I'll put it in a bowl you won't have to worry about bringing back." She dug a Cool Whip bowl out of the cabinet and ladled a generous portion of thick gravy, chunks of chicken and fluffy dumplings into it. She slid the lid into place and handed it to him.

He set it down on the counter and took both of her hands in his. She started to pull away, but he tightened his hold.

"Why are you pulling away from me? Is it Dylan?"

"Dylan made me promise to find someone new." Her gaze didn't quite meet his, stopping just at the top button of his shirt. "But that someone isn't you. You're very possibly leaving. And Hunter doesn't need to get any more attached to you than he already is."

"But I might stay. If the cowboy church comes together, I could stay and pastor here."

"I heard what Buck said at church. You clearly made a difference on the circuit. And God may still want you there. I don't want you staying in Aubrey to pastor the cowboy church to see what happens with us if God wants you back on the circuit." She pulled her hands away and turned her back on him.

"Maybe God wants me to settle down." He circled her waist with his arms.

"No." She stepped away from him. "I won't be a factor in your decision. This is between you and God. Just know if you stay in Aubrey, nothing will develop between us. You need to pray long and hard about what God wants. It's not about us."

"Mom, I'm ready," Hunter called from the next room.

"Got your glove?" She tugged her apron off.

"Yep." Hunter hurried into the room, effectively ending the conversation. "You gonna ride with us, Coach Slade?"

He couldn't do it. He couldn't ride in the same car with Raquel when she'd just stuck a pin in any hopes of a future for them.

"I need to let Blizzard and Flurry out and put these leftovers in my fridge." He picked up the Cool Whip bowl. "Y'all go ahead. I'll take my truck."

"Okay," Raquel easily agreed.

Way too anxious to get rid of him.

"See you at the game, sport." Slade's heart sank to the toes of his cowboy boots as he stepped out the back door. And out of her life.

He'd obviously misunderstood her feelings for him. *But that someone isn't you.*

Once baseball season was over in another month and a half, he wouldn't see her anymore.

Raquel washed the supper dishes while Hunter took his bath. The team had won both games this week. Hunter was happier. But Raquel wasn't.

May 1. Slade had kept his distance since cupcake night and he'd leave at the end of the month. Wasn't that what she wanted?

The phone rang, sending a jolt through her. She grabbed the handset.

"Raquel." The distress in Caitlyn's voice chilled her. "Cody was in a bad wreck at the rodeo. I thought you'd want to know."

"Oh, no." Raquel's breath whooshed from her lungs. "How bad?"

"I'm not sure, but it doesn't sound good. We're on our way to your old hospital. Want us to swing by and get you?"

"No. Y'all go on. I'll have to get Hunter situated before I can come. But I'll be praying. And text me if you learn anything before I get there."

"Will do."

Couldn't stay here. She loved Cody, and Mitch had been there for her when Dylan died. No thinking like that. Cody had better not die, but she needed to be there. She drummed the kitchen counter with her fingertips.

A few times in months past, Hunter had stayed with Slade when she had to run an errand. But sending Hunter over now wouldn't be right. Durlene Warren was usually

Raquel's babysitter, but Cody was her nephew, so more than likely, Durlene would be at the hospital.

Lacie. Yes. Fingers trembling, Raquel dialed the phone. "Hello?"

"Lace, thank goodness you're home. A friend of mine was in an accident. I need to go to the hospital. Can I bring Hunter to your house?"

"Better yet, I'll come get him and he can spend the night. You sound much too shaky to drive. By the time I get there, maybe you'll be settled down some."

"Thanks."

Fun-loving Cody. *Please, Lord, let him be okay.* She almost wished she still worked the emergency room. Almost.

Everyone loved Cody. He made everyone smile. The world needed more people like him—not fewer.

She took a deep breath and strode toward the bathroom. Hunter loved Cody. She had to hold it together. Not let Hunter know anything was wrong. She pecked on the door.

"Hunter, hurry and get out of the tub so you can pack a bag. You're going to spend the night with Max."

"Awesome!" he called.

"Hurry—they'll be here to get you soon." Raquel rushed to his room and crammed underwear and toiletries into his overnight bag.

Minutes later Hunter came back from the bathroom looking fresher.

"Pick your clothes. I got everything else. Two sets of play clothes and something for church."

Hunter pulled what he wanted to wear from the closet as Raquel folded and packed.

Lights illuminated the window. "I think they're here."

"I'm ready." Hunter zipped his bag.

"Be good." She hugged him. "I love you and I'll see you tomorrow."

"I love you, too." He called over his shoulder as he took the stairs two at a time.

Raquel hurried after him, grabbed her purse and locked the door behind them.

Next to Lacie's car, Slade's truck sat in her driveway. Her feet stalled. What was he doing here?

Chapter 11

Raquel hurried to Lacie's rolled-down window and whispered, "Hunter doesn't know anything's wrong."

"Not a word." Lacie patted her hand.

"He got his bath and he has church clothes for tomorrow. I appreciate you."

"I hope this doesn't change that. I called Slade," Lacie whispered. "You sounded too shaky to drive, so he'll take you. Keep me posted. Hunter can stay as long as you need him to."

While Raquel's mouth hung open, Lacie backed out of the drive. Leaving her alone with Slade.

"Let me get the door for you." Slade got out of his truck and went around to the passenger's side.

"I'm really fine. I can drive."

"You're worked up. Just let me drive you."

Definitely worked up and she didn't really feel like tackling Garland traffic. "Thanks." She followed him and climbed into the truck.

"Glad to help." He went back to his side, climbed in and backed out of her drive.

Besides, the last time she'd been in that hospital, Dylan had died.

Blasted hospital parking. Hospitals should be forced to build in the middle of at least a twenty-acre spread with parking decks surrounding the building. Slade eased into the only space he could find, cut the engine and bolted from the truck. A mile away from the hospital. Not really, but it felt like it as he jogged across the span of asphalt to catch up with Raquel.

Though he'd dropped her at the ER entrance, he hated to think of her entering alone and upset.

She'd been quiet in the truck and he hadn't pried. Figured she'd talk if she wanted to. He could tell she was upset and if he forced her to talk about it, the waterworks might start. And Raquel's tears were something he wouldn't be able to keep his distance from.

Almost there, he saw her. Still standing outside the entrance. When she saw him, her shoulders slumped and then began shaking. Waterworks.

He tucked her into his arms, holding her close, rubbing circles on her back. Couldn't think of a thing to say. All he could think about was how good it felt to hold her.

But she needed comfort. He had to think of something besides inane *It'll be okay.* Because it might not be okay. He did know one thing. "God's got this, Raquel. Whatever it is, however it goes, God's got this."

She nodded against his chest, pushed away from him and wiped under her eyes with her fingertips. "You're right. Cody's a Christian." She took several shaky deep breaths. "I have to pull it together. His family needs me to be strong."

Cody? Her friend was a man. Hadn't seen that coming.

Not. At. All. And for Raquel to cry over Cody, was he more than a friend? He couldn't imagine any man being anywhere near Raquel and having just-friends feelings for her.

Slade's heart splattered on the sidewalk at her feet. More than anything, he wanted to leave. Run to his truck and leave. He could not sit beside Raquel in a waiting room while she worried over another man. Maybe the man she loved.

But she needed him. And Slade loved Raquel. And even though he wasn't the man she loved, he'd be there for her. For as long as she needed him.

He offered his arm.

With another deep breath, she settled trembling fingertips in the crook of his elbow.

They entered the lobby and then the ER waiting room. Caitlyn and Mitch were there with a female version of Mitch who had to be his sister, another man and two older couples.

Mitch stood and met them.

"How is he?" Raquel's voice held that tremulous quality that tore at Slade's heart.

"Pretty bunged up." Mitch hugged her, but it was an obvious just-friends hug. "It was a bad wreck. Lots of broken bones and internal injuries. The main concern right now—one of his ribs punctured a lung."

What were the odds of Raquel losing two men she loved to car accidents? Slade found himself praying for a man he didn't even know. Praying that things would end differently for Raquel on this night.

She shook her head against Mitch's shoulder. Just as she had against Slade's shoulder. But she didn't push away. "He's tough."

"And stubborn."

Raquel's laugh came out high-pitched. "You got that right."

"Come sit down with us." He led Raquel to the rest of the gathering. "You too, Slade. Thanks for bringing her."

"I didn't think she should drive upset and all." He shoved his hands in his pockets.

"This is my sister, Tara. Her husband, Jared. Our parents, Audra and Wayne Warren, and our aunt and uncle Durlene and Ty."

He wanted to say nice to meet you, but not under these circumstances.

"Where's Michaela?" Raquel asked.

"Jenna's keeping the baby for us." Caitlyn rubbed Mitch's shoulders.

So Cody was somehow related to Mitch. Must be a brother for his entire family to be here. No wonder Caitlyn and Raquel were friends. Raquel was involved with Caitlyn's brother-in-law.

But in all the time he'd lived next door to Raquel, he'd never seen another man around. And never gotten the impression she was seeing anyone.

"I hate bulls." Mitch's mom leaned her head against her husband's shoulder.

"Me too." Tara flipped through a magazine. "He should have quit the circuit years ago. I've tried to tell him that over and over. But of course, he wouldn't listen to his little sister."

Bulls. The circuit. A bad wreck. Rodeo people called an accident a wreck. Cody Warren. Slade had probably run into him in his travels. It all made sense now. Cody's injuries and that Slade had never seen a man around Raquel's house. Cody rode bulls on the circuit. Did they have a long-distance relationship?

"He should have settled down with Raquel." Tara flung her magazine down. "So stubborn."

"Um, I love Cody, but we're just friends." Raquel's hands shook as she straightened the magazine on the table.

She loved him. But they were just friends. Had they broken up because Cody refused to quit the circuit and settle down? Or was she trying to cover her feelings for him under the guise of friendship?

But now, with him injured, he'd be home. Near Raquel. He couldn't imagine any man leaving Raquel behind. And Cody had already been stupid enough to do it once. He probably wouldn't make the same mistake again. If Cody lived, he and Raquel would patch things up.

And even if they didn't, she loved Cody. Not Slade.

Every fiber of Raquel's being longed to flee as memories washed over her. Dylan on the gurney—so still and pale. Blood everywhere. She shuddered.

But she had to stay. For Mitch's sake. He'd been with her through every excruciating moment of the night Dylan died. Even after her parents, Brant and Dylan's family had arrived. And Raquel would return the favor.

Please, Lord, I don't want to have to comfort him the way he ended up comforting me. Let Cody live.

And Slade was still here. He hadn't asked any questions and was probably terribly confused. But he stayed in the background. Her silent support. Her silent strength.

Are You sure I can't have him, Lord? Are you sure you want him back on the circuit? Hunter and I could use a good man like him.

She had to stop thinking like that. Besides, he was a stupid bronc rider. Just as Cody was a stupid bull rider. And look where that had gotten him.

A doctor stepped in the doorway. Cody's family stood and the doctor ushered them into the hall. Raquel tried to read faces, but only the doctor faced her through the glass-walled waiting room.

Slade squeezed her shoulder.

The conference ended and the doctor strode down the

hall. No one was crying as far as she could tell. That had to be a good sign. Wayne and Audra hugged as Mitch came back into the room.

"He's got a long recovery, but he'll be okay."

Raquel blew out the breath she'd been holding. "Thank goodness. When he gets well enough, I'll give him a good tongue-lashing for scaring us all half to death."

"You'll probably need to get in line." Caitlyn grinned.

"So give me specifics. How badly is he hurt?"

"They got the bleeding stopped and his lung reinflated. They removed his spleen. Grade three concussion, broken shoulder, and his knee is a mess."

Raquel winced. "Sounds like he won't be able to do anything but lie around and take our tongue-lashings for a while."

"I'm gonna get out of here." Slade touched her elbow. "Since the news is good, you don't need me hanging around."

"Thanks for driving me." Raquel swallowed hard. She did need him. "And for sticking around."

"Let me know if you need a ride home or help with Hunter or anything."

"I appreciate it."

Oh, how she needed him. She just couldn't have him.

Never in a million years would Slade have imagined he'd be anxious to get back on the circuit. But he couldn't get out of Aubrey fast enough. Raquel said she and Cody were just friends. But she'd also said she loved Cody. And Slade had seen her meltdown before they went in the ER. There had to be more to it than friendship.

During his sleepless night, he'd come to a conclusion. He couldn't stick around and watch Raquel nurse Cody back to health and end up marrying him. He just couldn't.

The suitcase sat on the bed with his clothes neatly

folded inside. He grabbed another handful of shirts from the closet. But his red team shirt slid from the hanger and stopped him cold. He ran his fingers over the heat-pressed word across the back, Coach. He couldn't let the boys down. May had just gotten here. A whole month left before the season was over. He'd have to stay that long.

Besides, he couldn't just disappear on Tori. He'd caused her upset and problems with Brant. He owed her a decent goodbye and a plan to continue their newfound relationship.

The phone rang and he glanced at the screen. Unlisted Number. He let it ring and it went to the machine.

"Hey, Slade." Garrett Steele's voice. "I've got some possible locations for the cowboy church. I'll call back—"

Slade picked up. "I'm here." He could at least help get the church set up.

"Can you look at some locations with me?"

"Sure. When?"

"Friday the fifteenth around noon. That's the first date everyone involved can make it. I thought maybe we could grab something to eat and check out three locations with Star."

"I'll be there."

"Great. See you then." The line went dead.

"A month, Lord." Slade rehung the clothing he'd folded into the suitcase. "I'll stay this month like I originally planned. Get the boys through the season. Avoid Raquel. Help Garrett set up the cowboy church. Avoid Raquel. Tell Tori I'm leaving and spend time with her. And avoid Raquel. When May is over, I'm out of here. Tori and I can connect without me living here."

Flurry cocked her head to the side.

"Just a little conversation with the Lord, girl. I'm not talking to myself. You'll get used to it, like Blizzard."

The other dog's ears perked up at the sound of his name.

"Want out before I head out for church?"

Both dogs sprang up and headed for the door.

Slade needed church today. Needed God to comfort his soul. But where? Raquel probably wouldn't be there—she'd undoubtedly stayed at the hospital all night. But just in case, he wouldn't attend her church.

He picked his clothing and headed for the bathroom. "Thanks, Lord, for this wake-up call. I thought I wanted out of being a chaplain. That I wanted to settle down. That I had a chance with Raquel. But You made it glaringly clear I'm supposed to go back to the circuit. Time for a rodeo reunion."

But his soul roiled within him.

Though everything pointed to him going back on the circuit and for the first time in months he was ready and willing, something didn't feel right.

Probably just nerves from having to stay. And avoid Raquel for a month. When all he wanted was to steal her away from Cody and make her forget any other man ever existed.

But she wasn't his. And she never could be. She didn't love him. She loved Cody. He had to get that through his thick skull.

Forget her.

Even a full week after his accident and out of ICU, Cody looked as though he'd been run over by a bull. Raquel watched the steady rise and fall of his chest as he slept. As soon as he was up to it, she still planned to give him what for.

At least it was Saturday. A nice break from Slade.

Seeing Slade at practice and the games tortured Raquel's soul. They didn't speak to each other unless they had to. Even after the boys won their game Monday night. They didn't ride together. They didn't eat together. Even at Moms, they made a point to sit as far apart as possible.

Cody's eyes fluttered and opened. He cleared his throat and coughed, then winced.

"Want some water?"

"Mmm. My hero."

She held the straw to his parched lips and he emptied the large plastic cup. "More?"

"No." He sank back into his pillows.

"How do you feel?"

"Like I had a fight with a bull. And lost. Who are you again?"

An emptiness filled her chest.

Cody grinned. "Just teasing."

"It's not funny. If you weren't in that bed—" her vision clouded "—I'd pummel you."

"Hey, take it easy." He frowned. "Every particle of me hurts, but I'll live. They're even letting me bust out of here today and transfer to rehab. What's with the tears?"

She swiped them away and shook her head.

"What's going on, Raquel?"

"Dylan died in this hospital."

"Oh, Raquel, I'm sorry." He reached toward her with his good arm. "Come on—I've got one good shoulder left."

"I don't want to hurt you." She scooted her chair closer and took his hand in hers.

"Even though you're gonna pummel me when I get better?"

Her laugh came out watery and she pressed the back of his hand against her cheek. "It just brought back memories and you were hurt so badly and Slade was here. It was all too much and I've been a basket case ever since."

"Wait a minute. Back up. Slade?"

"My neighbor."

"And?"

"Hunter's baseball coach."

"And?"

"He's a bronc rider slash rodeo chaplain. He's leaving in three weeks to go back on the circuit."

"Slade Walker? The former Texas Rangers pitcher?"

"That's him."

"I've heard him preach. Several times."

"From what I hear, he's made a lot of impact on a lot of cowboys."

"I keep hearing about everything he does, but not why you're crying over him."

"I'm not crying over him." She sniffled and dabbed her nose with a tissue. "I'm crying over Dylan. And you."

"And Slade. Why does he make you cry? Want me to hog-tie and brand him for ya?"

Another watery laugh. "I don't think you're in any shape to make that offer."

"True. But just give me a few months and I'll chap his hide. In the meantime, want to talk about it?"

She shrugged. "I made this rule to protect myself. And Hunter."

"Rules are made to be broken."

"Not this one." She dabbed her eyes. "I decided that any man I'd even consider letting into our lives had to be home every night and have a nice safe job."

"So that's why I couldn't get anywhere with you."

She laughed again and this time it was nice and dry. "You can always make me laugh. No matter what's going on in my world."

"So Slade's interested?"

"He was friends with Dylan when they were kids. He came to town to see his sister, who happens to be my sister-in-law, Tori. He moved in next door and ended up being Hunter's coach." She splayed her palms upward. "This whole time I kept telling myself he was only here for three months and not to get involved. My heart didn't wanna hear it and we started to get close."

"Until?"

"I found out he's a stupid bronc rider."

Cody laughed. "Is that kind of like a stupid bull rider?"

"Hey, I can't help it if the boot fits."

"Raquel, I know Dylan's death hurt you." He squeezed her hand. "But think about it. Dylan wasn't home every night and he was a Texas Ranger—textbook dangerous job. But he died in a single-car crash when he fell asleep at the wheel—off duty."

"I know. I've told myself that. Caitlyn's told me that and shared how many years she missed with Mitch because she didn't think she could handle his job. But I lost Dylan." She buried her face in their entwined hands. "It just makes sense not to up the odds of that happening again with a man who has a dangerous job. And on top of that, he travels the circuit. A relationship with him can't work."

"There are long-distance relationships. Maybe if he had you, he wouldn't go back on the circuit."

"He's actually looking into starting a cowboy church in Aubrey and staying here. But it's not certain yet."

"Sounds to me like he cares about you."

"But what if God wants him to stick with the circuit? I can't stand in the way of what God wants for Slade. And whether he travels the circuit or settles in Aubrey, he's still a stupid bronc rider."

"Okay, you've thought and considered and cried about all of it. But have you prayed about it? Maybe God wants Slade here."

She shrugged. "I figure my prayers are biased."

"I figure God can handle biased prayers." Cody winced. "Could you see about when I can have more pain meds?"

"Poor Cody." She pressed the call button and traced her

fingertips over the pain-induced lines of his face. "Stupid bull rider."

"Hey. Here I am putting up with hurting so I can stay clearheaded and help you out, and you keep calling me stupid."

"If the boot fits."

He chuckled and flinched.

"Stop laughing if it hurts."

"Quit making me." He squeezed her hand again. "You know, I'd gladly fall for you. I like a woman who makes me laugh. Even when it hurts. I wish we could pick who we fall for." The pain in his words came from somewhere deeper than the physical pain.

"There's someone in your life?"

"I wish. Why do women only want me as a friend? Do you have any idea how many beautiful friends I have?"

"But only one who counts. Who is she?"

"Ready for your pain meds?" A nurse entered the room.

"Yes." Cody pumped his fist. "Oblivion, here I come."

"That's not fair. Drop a bomb on me and then go off into la-la land. Nurse, can you hold off on the meds until he tells me what I want to know?"

"That's called torture. We're in America, my dear beautiful friend. Make her stop," Cody croaked.

"Mr. Warren does need to rest, ma'am." The nurse clearly had no sense of humor.

Raquel didn't remember her from her stint at the hospital. Must be new.

"I promise to be good." Raquel pushed her chair back so the nurse could tend to him.

Within minutes he was fading fast. The nurse gave Raquel a warning look and left them alone.

"Cody, who is she?"

"What? Never seen her afore?"

"Not the nurse. Who do you love?"

"Ally."

"Ally?" She knew that name. Think. Think. "Ally Curtis? The vet?"

But Cody was already asleep.

Cody was always so happy-go-lucky, cutting up and making jokes. She patted his hand and stood. But underneath, he had to be worried. About his health, his career and apparently Ally. Maybe she could move things along with Ally. Was his Ally the Ally Curtis she knew? Did his Ally even know Cody was hurt? Could seeing Cody hurt change Ally's feelings for him?

Just what Raquel needed. Something to focus on. Other than Slade.

She pressed a soft kiss on Cody's forehead and left his room.

"Hey." Caitlyn met her in the hall. "How is he?"

"Hurting. The nurse just gave him meds and he went out fast."

"I'll sit with him awhile. I know this is hard on him."

"I worry about him."

"Me too." Caitlyn sighed. "I always wonder if his jokes are a cover for what's really going on inside him."

"I was just thinking the same thing." Raquel tried to think of a casual way to bring up Ally. "Are there any friends he hasn't seen in a while? Someone who might cheer him up? An old friend from high school or the circuit?"

"I thought of that. The only person I could come up with is Ally Curtis."

"From Adopt-a-Pet?" Raquel's pulse sped.

"We all went to school together and were really great friends since we all went to the same church. But Ally's dad died our senior year and she went all hermit on us. I called and told her about Cody's accident, but I guess he doesn't have enough legs."

"What?"

"Ally rarely leaves her ranch unless there's a sick animal involved."

"Oh." Raquel pulled off a casual shrug. "Well, it was just a thought."

Maybe Raquel would pay Ally a visit and tell her how Cody felt about her. No. If she'd learned anything in the past few years, it was to keep her mouth shut. Not to let others' secrets slip—intentionally or unintentionally. To leave things in God's hands.

And that was where she needed to leave Slade. In God's hands.

Lord, I know if You want Slade back on the circuit, You'll send him there. If You want him to start the cowboy church, You'll make it happen. If You want us together, You'll make that happen, too. We're both in Your hands.

Chapter 12

The barn was pretty new. Lots of space. Slade envisioned a stage at one end with the pulpit and old wooden pews lining an aisle as Garrett and Jenna, Lane and Natalie, and Wyatt and Star walked around the space. Excited chatter echoed through the emptiness dotted with a few hay bales.

Their first stop on the potential-cowboy-church tour had been a warehouse. Plenty of space, but a lot of work. And not the best location. The second stop had a better location, but the barn had seen better days and would need a lot of work just to keep it standing.

But stop number three was perfect. Great location and solid structure. And even though Slade wouldn't be staying to pastor the church, his veins zinged at the potential this place had.

"What do you think?" Garrett scanned the ceiling. "Maybe we could buy the old barn we saw, tear it down and line the inside of this one with the wood. Maybe even have pews built from barn wood."

"That could get pricey. How much are you willing to sink into this project?"

"However much it takes."

Jenna clapped her hands. "Once people find out we're turning it into a church, we'll probably get donations, donated labor and discounts. I'd be happy to decorate for free."

"With a light touch." Garrett squeezed his wife's shoulder. "We want rodeo folk, ranch folk, cowboys and cowgirls to feel comfortable coming here. It needs to stay a barn, not a palace."

"Steak-house decor." Jenna rolled her eyes. "My favorite."

"Jenna's a froufrou designer wannabe born and raised in Texas." Natalie chuckled. "Maybe some Western stars, branding irons, horseshoes, that kind of thing."

"I like it." Slade turned in a circle, taking in the amount of space. "Lane, you're still on board?"

"I am."

"Have you considered anything other than associate, like pastoring?"

"I've prayed about it." Lane shook his head. "God's got me right where He wants me to be."

"Do we have anyone else interested in pastoring?"

"You're not backing out on us, are you?" Garrett frowned.

"I never said I'd do it. I said I'd pray about it. I'm not done praying yet."

"Well, here's the deal." Star ran her finger over her tablet. "The owner is my brother-in-law, Quinn Remington. For a church, he's willing to sell the barn for considerably less than what it's worth."

"See?" Jenna did a little bounce on the balls of her feet. "Once people hear *church*, they get very generous."

"On top of that, Quinn is willing to let you use the building for two months—rent-free. You can see how it goes, with no strings attached. If it doesn't work out, you're not obligated to buy."

"If we do that, can we make cosmetic changes?" Natalie tapped her foot on the concrete floor.

"It was used as a woodworking shop, so it already has electricity, heat and air. Quinn doesn't mind if you paint or put up interior walls. But if you don't buy, he'll decide whether he wants you to restore the barn to its original condition. So nothing permanent."

"Sounds to me like an offer we can't refuse." Garrett turned to Slade. "How about this? I'll do a hailstorm of publicity for the next week and a half. We'll have our first service May 24. You preach two Sundays, see what happens, and we'll go from there."

Slade swallowed hard. "And if we realize the church is worthwhile, but I'm needed back on the circuit, Lane can fill in until you find someone else?"

"Deal." Lane offered his hand.

The three men shook on it.

"I'll get the paperwork in order." Star tapped the screen of her tablet. "Nice doing business with y'all."

Garrett clapped him on the back.

And Slade was more uncertain of his future than ever. He wanted to go back on the circuit. Needed to get away from Raquel. But if God wanted him back on the circuit, why had the cowboy church fallen so easily into place?

The big yellow tail wagged from side to side as Raquel walked a golden retriever named Goldilocks down the rehabilitation-center corridor with Ally and Midnight—a black Lab—by her side. They had a list of three patients to visit approved by administration, staff and family members. Two down and the most important to go.

Ally had no idea Cody was on the list. All Raquel had to do was get Ally to Cody's room and maybe Ally would realize she loved Cody, too. If not, Raquel would leave it in God's hands to change Ally's heart. Or to bring Cody someone new.

This had to work. Cody obviously didn't remember uttering Ally's name in his half sleep. And Ally had no clue Cody was Raquel's depressed friend.

"I'm really glad you called me." Ally stopped and adjusted the dogs' jackets, which were emblazoned with Ally's Adopt-a-Pet. Tori had whipped them up a few days ago, and no one was onto Raquel's scheme.

"Me too. This will be good for the patients. And maybe you'll get some dogs adopted out."

"I might make this a weekly jaunt. Did you see that little girl's face light up when she saw the dogs?"

"The older woman's laughter was priceless." Which meant her devious plan was helping others as well as Cody.

They neared Cody's room and Raquel paused. What if her scheme only caused Cody pain? What if Ally felt nothing for him and seeing her again only hurt Cody?

"Is this it?"

Raquel nodded.

Ally knocked on the door and pushed it open slightly. "You have a visitor."

"Come on in," Cody called.

Ally's jaw went slack. She'd clearly recognized his voice, but she pushed the door open and Midnight led the way.

Past the point of no return. *Lord, please don't let this be a mistake.*

Memo to self—pray before you leap.

"Ally?" Cody's eyes widened.

"Cody. I, um, I thought I recognized that voice."

Oh, yeah, Ally had feelings, too. Raquel grinned. Way more than friend feelings.

"Hey, Cody, I'm helping Ally with her pet visiting project. Since y'all obviously know each other, I think I'll go check and see if it's okay to visit that lady down the hall who was begging to see Goldilocks."

"What?" Panic slammed Ally's expression.

Yep. Definitely love. "I'll be right back."

Raquel put it in high gear and left the room. *Lord, let them get past whatever fears, issues or past mistakes have kept them apart. If they're meant to be, make it happen. If not, bring them each someone new to love.*

"Hey, Raquel." Caitlyn met her in the hall. "What on earth are you doing here with a dog?"

"This is Goldilocks. One of Ally's strays."

"Is he a service dog?"

"Sort of. I was sitting on the back porch thinking about how to cheer Cody up and Snow licked my chin. And I was like, duh, dogs cheer everybody up. So I talked to my old boss about a visiting program with dogs. We met Ally when we adopted Snow, so I asked her if she'd like to help."

"That's wonderful." Caitlyn stooped to pet Goldilocks. "So Ally's here?"

"She's in with Cody."

No reaction. Caitlyn apparently didn't know about any feelings between the couple other than friendship. "Good—I'll stop in and see them both. It's been a while since I've seen Ally."

"Oh, wait. Could you help me out? I was just going to check and see if it would be okay to take Goldilocks to see a patient who wasn't on our list. She saw us go by and was begging to see the dogs. I felt terrible."

"How can I help?"

Raquel handed the leash to Caitlyn. "Stand here and hold Goldilocks. We're not supposed to take the dogs near the nursing station."

"Okay?"

"It shouldn't take long." Raquel hurried toward the nurses' station.

But everyone knew nothing moved fast in a hospital setting. If the therapists would stay away, Cody and Ally could have the uninterrupted time they needed.

And the really great thing in all of this was Raquel had barely thought of Slade today. Barely.

It took the whole morning to get caught up on paperwork and filing, but at least Raquel could see the top of her desk now. And the monotony had at least distracted her from thoughts of Slade. No, she would not think about him.

The kids had left early since it was the last day and only a handful of teachers and staff milled about, tidying their rooms. Hunter had gone home with Max so Raquel could wrap things up.

With school officially out for summer, there were no excited voices in the hall or on the playground. No buzzing to signal the next class, no announcements over the intercom.

Enough peace to let her think about…not him. Cody and Ally.

They hadn't figured out her devious plan. But she wasn't sure it had worked either. By the time Raquel had come back from the nurses' station to retrieve Goldilocks from Caitlyn, Ally and Midnight had been with her. As they took the dogs to visit the elderly lady, Ally had seemed largely unaffected by seeing Cody. Either that or she was a great actress.

By the time they'd finished visiting the elderly dog lover, Cody had been asleep. Raquel had no idea if she'd made things better or worse.

A verse popped into her head. One of her favorites— Proverbs 3:5-6. "Trust in the Lord with all thine heart, and lean not unto thine own understanding. In all thy ways acknowledge Him, and He shall direct thy paths."

Raquel released a big breath. She needed to leave Ally Cody and Slade in God's hands. God would direct their paths.

Her door flew open and the math teacher blasted in carrying an unconscious woman.

"Something's wrong with her!" Ben Smith shouted.

Annette Frasier—the science teacher. Her lips were swollen and blue. Raquel's heart lurched.

"Lay her down." Raquel sprang into action. "Did she get stung or bitten?"

"I don't know."

"Did you call nine-one-one?"

"No."

"Dial and hand me the phone." Barely breathing. An angry welt on Annette's upper arm.

Ben jabbed buttons and handed the phone to her.

"Nine-one-one, what is your emergency?"

"I have a woman I believe is in anaphylactic shock. Possible bee sting. I'm the school nurse."

"An ambulance is on the way. Have you—?"

Raquel dropped the phone, tilted Annette's head back with her chin up to keep her airway open.

"I don't know what happened." Ben trembled. "I was leaving, walking toward my car, and I saw her kneeling in the grass digging in her purse. She just fell over and I brought her here."

"You did the right thing." A siren started up in the distance. The ambulance service was only a minute away, but did Annette have a minute? She'd have given anything for an EpiPen, but the only ones she had in her cabinet belonged to students. Annette had dug in her purse? For keys? Or did she have an EpiPen?

"Her purse. Do you know where it is?"

"I guess we dropped it."

"Can you run and get it for me?"

Ben bolted from the room as Annette's breathing grew more shallow.

Minutes later Ben ran back in the room holding a black purse. "Here it is."

Raquel grabbed it and dumped the contents on her counter. An EpiPen. She jabbed it into Annette's thigh.

"What's that?" Ben was in full panic mode.

"It's for allergic reactions." But Annette wasn't coming out of it. Raquel had felt this inadequate only one other time. "The ambulance should be here any minute. Can you go show them where we are?"

Ben nodded like a bobblehead and hurried out the door.

Countless times in the ER, Raquel had seen emergency tracheotomies done. If only she had the equipment and training. Could she pull it off with a box cutter, alcohol and a ballpoint pen like in the movies?

The ambulance siren drew near.

Lord, help me.

Why wasn't Hunter in the back playing with the dogs, as he normally would be? School had let out early for the last day. Slade checked his watch and stepped inside his back door. He'd heard her car return a while ago.

The phone rang and he grabbed it. "Hello?"

"Hey, Slade. It's Lacie. I'm worried about Raquel and I can't get in touch with Brant or Tori. Do you know if she's home?"

"I heard a car earlier. Is she sick?"

"At heart, I'm afraid. She stayed to clean and organize her office after school. This afternoon one of the teachers got stung by a wasp and had an allergic reaction. Raquel did everything she could to try to save her, but the teacher died."

"Oh, no." Slade pinched the bridge of his nose. "Where is Hunter?"

"With us. She called a few minutes ago to ask if I could keep him until practice tonight so she could have time to pull herself together. She sounded really upset."

"I imagine. I'll go over and check on her." He stepped out the front door and cut across his yard to hers.

"Thanks. I just don't think she should be alone. I thought about calling Mitch or Caitlyn. But he's probably at work and she's got the new baby."

"I'm glad you called me." He hung up and cupped his hands around his eyes to peer in the window of the garage. Her car was there. He sprinted up the steps of her porch and rang her doorbell.

No sound. No approaching footfalls.

He knocked. Then pounded. "Raquel, I know you're home. Your car's in the garage and Lacie told me what happened."

A floorboard creaked. The lock clicked and the door opened.

Raquel hugged herself, her face tear streaked, her clothing blood spattered.

Blood? He scanned her for injuries but saw nothing. Not her blood.

"I'm sure you did everything you could." He stepped inside and pulled her into his arms.

Sobs shook her whole body and she soaked his shoulder. A worse meltdown than at the hospital. Small and frightened, despite her height.

He managed to shut the door behind him and when her shaking stopped and the sobs let up, he led her to the couch. "If you feel up to changing clothes, that might make you feel better."

She frowned at him as if he were crazy, then looked down. Her eyes widened as if she hadn't seen the blood until now. She covered her mouth with her hand. "You're right."

"You steady enough to handle that? Should I call a female friend?"

"I'm fine." She turned toward the back of the house.

Something to drink. Maybe food. But for now, fluids. He hurried to her kitchen and went straight to the cabinet where she kept her glasses. At least he knew where everything was. He knew she drank tea and water, so he fixed a glass of each. Or maybe she'd want coffee. He put a pot on to cover all his bases.

Just as he set the glasses on the coffee table, she came back wearing stretchy pants and an oversize T-shirt. And even in the comfortable nondescript clothing with her swollen red eyes, she was beautiful.

"I brought you something to drink. Wasn't sure which you'd want."

"Thanks." She perched on the edge of the couch and took a long drink of the water, then set the glass back down. "You can have the tea if you want."

"You hungry? I make a mean ham sandwich or hot dog. And I'm pretty good with a can of chicken noodle soup. Or I can make a Moms on Main run and bring you something back."

"Thanks, but I'm not hungry."

What could he do to comfort her further? Cody. A knife sliced through his heart.

"Do you want me to take you to Cody?"

She frowned. "Why?"

"You two are...close." He shrugged. "I thought maybe seeing him would make you feel better."

"No. I'd just distract him from his therapy."

In spite of himself, relief filled the wound in his chest. "Why don't you lie down?"

"No thanks." She scooted back and pulled her feet up on the edge of the couch. With her knees bent up under her chin, arms around her legs, she formed a tight ball of anguish.

He settled beside her and she turned slightly to lean back against him. His arm circled her shoulder, as natural as if they'd cuddled on her couch for years.

"I did everything I knew to do. I started with airway management, then realized she had a EpiPen in her purse. I used it and got nothing. The EMT did an emergency tracheotomy, but it was too late."

"I'm so sorry you had to go through that."

"She was so swollen I almost didn't recognize her. Annette Frasier." Her voice broke. "A member of my church. Only twenty-five. She has a husband, a five-year-old and a three-year-old. So today he gets to tell them Mommy's never coming home."

And she knew exactly how that felt. "You did your best."

"If only I could have gotten to her sooner. By the time the math teacher, Ben Smith, brought her to me, she was barely breathing. If I'd known about the EpiPen in her purse and used it sooner. Or if I'd tried the emergency trach. I'd seen it done, but I was afraid to try."

"Don't beat yourself up, Raquel." He rubbed his thumb up and down her forearm. "It's not your fault."

"I prayed for her to live. I felt so helpless—just like I did when Dylan died."

"It was a random accident that happened. We'll never understand why some perfectly good Christian people die young. But it's in God's hands, not ours."

"But she was so young. Her kids need her. Hunter and I needed Dylan. Why do senseless tragedies happen?" She punched the back of the couch.

"An age-old question. And the only answer I have—we live in a fallen world. But we have hope in Christ."

"I know. We'll see Dylan again someday. Annette was

a Christian. Her family will see her again someday. And there were no kids there to witness what happened." She relaxed a bit against him. "I listed all the positives I could think of to comfort poor Ben while I drove him home. He's probably a year away from retirement and was on the verge of passing out when it was all over."

Dear, sweet Raquel. Reduced to a basket case, but she'd taken care of the distraught teacher before driving herself home.

"Every time he sees me next year, he'll remember. Every time I see him next year, I'll remember."

"Time will soften the memories. You've got a whole summer to relax."

"How do I face her family at the funeral?" She dabbed her eyes. "And at church?"

"I'm certain her family will be grateful to you for trying to save her."

"They may not go this week. But I just don't think I can take the chance of facing them yet."

"Visit another church. Maybe you could visit mine?"

She stiffened. "Yours?"

Shouldn't have gone into personal areas. "I'm preaching at a barn on Quinn Remington's property on a trial basis. Sunday is our first service." He waited for her to push away from him. But she didn't. "Why don't you try to get some sleep?"

"That would be wonderful. But I don't see it happening."

"Just relax. Music always helps me sleep." He hummed the tune to "Amazing Grace."

"Are you comfortable?" She relaxed against him and stretched her legs out on the couch.

"Never better." He could stay like this for years.

Navy or black? The funeral wasn't until tomorrow, but in light of Annette's death, Raquel was in a navy or black mood. She pulled a navy dress from the hanger. If she went to her church and Annette's family was there, it might make the funeral easier tomorrow. Or worse. Maybe they wouldn't be there. But maybe they would.

She got dressed and smoothed her hair. With shoes and jewelry, she looked ready on the outside. Except for the dark circles under her eyes. She'd pulled herself together enough to wear sunglasses and go to Hunter's practice Friday night. She'd had Lacie bring Hunter home Saturday morning and Brant and Tori had spent most of the day with her—worrying about her.

But Lacie had been a treasure and invited Hunter to spend the night again and go to church with them today. Keeping Hunter none the wiser that anything was wrong. Raquel owed Max several nights at their house soon. Once she caught up on her sleep.

The best she'd slept in the past two days was when she'd fallen asleep in Slade's arms.

A knock sounded on her door. She hadn't heard a car. But then, she'd been distracted. Maybe Hunter had gotten homesick and wanted to come home. She hurried to answer.

Slade stood on her porch. Her breath caught in her lungs.

"I thought I'd check on you this morning. You okay?" He leaned on the door frame, long and lean and way too handsome for her brain to function.

She nodded, dumbstruck.

"Looks like you're getting ready for church. Wanna come with me?"

She nodded.

"Really?" His eyes lit up.

"Let me get my purse." The words sounded natural. Didn't they?

With her purse slung over her shoulder, she turned toward him. He offered his arm. Her heart rocketed.

"I can drive myself."

"Why? We're both going to the same place. Save a little gas."

A tiny smile escaped her. "It's only a quarter of a mile to Quinn and Lacie's."

He escorted her to the passenger side of his truck.

She didn't protest and got in.

"Is the funeral tomorrow?"

"At ten."

"Want me to go with you?"

"Would you?"

"Of course."

"I'll take you up on it. Brant and Tori are coming, but I'll need all the strength I can get."

"I'll lend all I can."

He really was a wonderful man. Husband material. Father material. Brant had softened toward him. He might stay for the cowboy church. And maybe that was right where God wanted him. But he still rode broncs.

Mel Gentry, Lacie's first husband, had died riding a bronc. But Cody was recovering after his tangle with a bull. And a tiny wasp had killed Annette—a middle-school science teacher, the safest job a person could have.

God, work this out however You want it.

"You okay?" Slade glanced over at her.

"I'm fine."

"You went all quiet on me. Just checking."

Because I was praying. Putting us or any possibility of us in God's hands. "Tell me about the church."

"It's amazing how easily it came together. Quinn's letting us use the barn for two months rent-free to see how it goes. If it doesn't go over, we leave and he puts it back on the market. If the church takes off, we're first in line to buy and he'll sell it to us for way less than what it's worth."

As if God was behind it all.

"I agreed to preach for two weeks and see what happens." Slade turned next to the barn just up from Lacie's driveway. "But there's nothing like an empty parking lot to wake you up."

Not one truck there. Despite the huge sign—Cowboy Church with the first service date of today. "According to the sign, it doesn't start for another forty-five minutes."

"I wanted to get here early and greet people. If they come."

"I'm sure they will." But would they? "Do many know you're here?"

"Garrett got some TV and radio spots for us. And several of the businesses in the Stockyards district agreed to put flyers up since a lot of the people who work and shop there live in Denton and Aubrey."

"I guess I live in a bubble since I didn't know."

The light dimmed in his eyes.

"But I'm not like most people. Our TV stays on cartoons and we don't listen to the radio much. I do shop at the Stockyards, but it's been a good month since I've been there. I'm sure there aren't many people like me."

"I've never met anyone like you." His gaze caught hers.

And wouldn't let go. Her breathing went all wonky. If he didn't stop looking at her like that, she'd do something stupid, like climb in his lap and kiss him.

Chapter 13

Raquel grabbed at the latch, opened the door and bailed out, gulping the fresh air. Must be lack of sleep and all the emotional turmoil of late.

"I'd have gotten your door for you." Slade met her in front of the truck.

"I want to have time to look around before everybody gets here."

He offered his arm, but she pretended not to see and strode ahead toward the barn.

Anything to resist him. And touching him sure wouldn't help.

At the door, she had to stop for him to unlock it. "If it becomes a church, we drew up plans to install some kind of glass door, windows, a lobby and classrooms. But for now, this is it."

The heavy door swung open to reveal…a barn. Square bales of hay lay stacked against the back wall with a huge pile of folded quilts on the lowest stack. A dozen long pews lined the front at an angle, facing a makeshift stage made from a single layer of pallets covered with plywood.

"It's kind of rustic, but it fits cowboys and cowgirls and that's what we're gunning for. I know the stage looks dangerous, but I can assure you the pallets are bolted together and the plywood's nailed down tight. The trough is for baptisms."

She hadn't even noticed the long galvanized man-sized watering trough. Or the barn-wood cross behind a pulpit made from a huge tree trunk with a slab of wood on top and a wagon wheel on the front. "I like rustic." She skimmed her hand over the smooth grayed-by-weather pew. "This looks like barn wood."

"It is. One of the locations we looked at was a dilapidated old barn. Garrett bought it and had it bulldozed to build the pews. Mitch's dad builds furniture and cabinets, so he did it for free. They've got enough wood to fill this whole place if we need more. And for today, if we have overflow—" Slade clasped his hands as if in prayer "—we've got hay bales and quilts for seating."

Raquel scanned the rest of the barn. Unfinished beadboard lined the ceiling and walls with branding irons, horseshoes, spurs and Texas stars strategically placed. She grinned. "Has Jenna been here?"

"We had to really hold her back, but we let her do a few things."

Silver duct work lined each side against the ceiling and fluorescent lighting hung from exposed wiring.

It was nothing like any church she'd ever seen. Yet it had a certain warmth and charm to it. A bare sparseness. Anyone who came to church here wasn't looking for comfort or opulence; they were just looking to meet Jesus.

Gravel crunched. Under a tire.

"Somebody's here!" Raquel let out a whoop and flung herself into Slade's arms.

He swung her around.

"Guess we found the party." Natalie cleared her throat. And Slade set Raquel back on her feet.

"We were excited." Raquel's cheeks warmed. "We thought somebody was actually here."

"So Lane and I aren't anybody?" Natalie propped her hand on her hip.

"You know what I mean."

"I do." Lane grinned. "And you're in luck. Another truck pulled in behind us. And then a dozen more."

"A dozen!" Now Slade let out a whoop, picked Raquel up again and spun her around.

"We'd join the party—" Natalie patted her protruding belly "—but I don't think Lane can pick me up at this point."

"Wanna bet?" Lane swooped her up and spun her in a slow circle.

"I might hurl all over you." Natalie giggled.

Slade whirled Raquel around again. Until she was dizzy from spinning. Dizzy from joy over the church. And dizzy from Slade's touch.

"Two hundred and thirteen people." Slade passed Lane a hay bale to pile back in place. "Can you believe it?"

"I only counted a dozen I knew went to church somewhere else." Natalie picked up a quilt and shook the hay out.

"That means two hundred and one people who probably don't usually go to church." Raquel grabbed the other end of Natalie's quilt and together they folded it.

"Looks like we're in business, partner." Lane offered his hand.

"I've still got some praying to do." Slade clasped Lane's hand and glanced at Raquel. "But I'll be here next Sunday, Lord willing."

"Can I do anything to help?" An unfamiliar male voice.

"Ben." Raquel's voice went all soft. "I didn't realize you were here."

Ben? Where did he know that name from? Ah, the math teacher.

Slade stopped what he was doing and strode to Raquel's side in case this reminder of Annette's death upset her. The man had a kind face, gray hair. Rugged cowboy type with a slight stoop to his shoulders.

"I, um, I don't usually go to church. But I felt like coming today. I heard about this place, so I thought I'd give it a try."

"I'm so glad you did." She turned to Slade. "This is Ben Smith. He helped me the other day."

"I'm glad you're both here." A man in his midtwenties approached. "Hello, Ben, Raquel."

"Leroy." Raquel's eyes widened. "I didn't see you either."

"I didn't feel like going to our church, where everybody knows us. Knew Annette."

The dead teacher's husband. The saddest eyes Slade had ever seen.

"I figured everybody would be sad at our church and the boys don't need any more of that."

"Where are they?"

"With my folks." Leroy motioned toward an older couple near the door with a toddler and antsy five-year-old running circles around them. "We planned to come here today anyway. Annette invited several of the teachers who don't attend church to come. I thought I'd show up in case they did."

"She invited me," Ben said, his voice cracking.

"I'm glad she did." Slade patted the older man on the shoulder and turned to the grief-stricken husband. "I'm so sorry for your loss."

"I keep asking myself why." Leroy shrugged. "I mean

she was young and healthy. We need her. And she knew she was allergic—she had her EpiPen within reach." He swiped his eyes. "I know—she was right with God and ready to go. But we weren't ready for her to go."

"I'm so sorry, Leroy." Raquel hugged him. "Everybody's praying for you and the boys. And if you ever need help with them, just give me a call."

"Thanks." Leroy sniffed. "And from the bottom of my heart, I want to thank you both for trying to help Annette."

Raquel's eyes were too shiny. She swallowed hard. "I wish we could have saved her."

"Me too." Leroy pulled away from her and shook Ben's hand. "You'll both be at the service tomorrow?"

"Of course." They echoed each other.

Leroy strode toward his family, straight and tall—a fake tower of strength for his boys.

"If only I'd brought her purse with us when I carried her to your office." Ben Smith looked as if he might fall over.

"You didn't know about the EpiPen, Ben." Raquel set her hand on his arm.

He shook his head. "I didn't even know what one was until this."

"You did the right thing based on what you knew."

"So who do we blame?"

"Blame the wasp." Slade closed his eyes. "Blame all the evil in this fallen world. But don't blame yourself. Or Raquel. Or God."

"I was there." Ben cringed. "Raquel did everything she could. And I don't know much about God. But I don't figure I'm significant enough to blame anything on Him."

"Would you like to learn more about God, Ben?" Slade seamlessly slipped into witnessing mode.

"Do you really believe Annette is in heaven, Preacher?"

"I do." Slade flipped open his Bible. "And I'd like to show you exactly how she got there. Let's start in Romans

3:10. 'As it is written, there is none righteous, no, not one.' Are you a sinner, Ben?"

"Well, I've never killed anybody. Or anything like that."

"Did you ever tell a lie, take something that wasn't yours, look at a woman in a certain way?"

Ben ducked his head with a slight nod.

"Then that makes you a sinner, just like me. And the Bible tells us in Romans 6:23 that there's a price to be paid for our sin. 'For the wages of sin is death, but the gift of God is eternal life through Jesus Christ our Lord.'

"Our penalty for sin is death, Ben. Death in an eternal hell with a real eternal flame. Hell isn't just separation from God. Mark 9:44 describes it this way. 'Where their worm dieth not, and the fire is not quenched.'"

Ben started sweating—a literal sweat.

"But God gave us a gift. A way to spend eternity with Him." Slade's pages rustled again. "Romans 5:8. 'But God commendeth his love toward us, in that, while we were yet sinners, Christ died for us.'

"And finally—" pure joy rang in Slade's voice "—God gave us instructions on how to spend eternity with him in Heaven, where Annette is now. Romans 10:13. 'For whosoever shall call upon the name of the Lord shall be saved.'"

"So what do I do?" Uncertainty coated Ben's words.

"Pray a very simple prayer. Something like this." Slade closed his eyes. "Oh, God, be merciful to me, a sinner. Save my soul from the flames of hell. I put my faith and trust in Jesus Christ, Your son, and what He did at Calvary's cross. I receive Him as my Lord and Savior. In Jesus's name, amen."

"That's it?" Ben opened his eyes.

"That's it."

"How can the difference in Heaven and hell be so simple?"

"It wasn't simple for Jesus when He had to take on our sin and die in our place. But He did make it simple for us. We choose Christ or we choose the devil."

"Now, I never said I chose the devil." Ben flushed.

"But if we don't make a choice for Christ, we choose the devil by default."

"I'm not sure I understand. But I'm getting hungry. Maybe we can talk about it some other time."

"There's no time like the present." Slade clapped him on the back. "How about we discuss it over lunch at Moms on Main? I'm buying."

Ben hesitated. "Okay."

Slade had him. How could anybody resist eternal life in Heaven? He looked around. The barn was empty. Raquel had slipped out. Along with Lane and Natalie. She'd probably caught a ride with them.

If only he could sell himself to Raquel as easily as he'd hooked Ben with Jesus.

Lunch at Moms on Main had been as awesome as usual. Slade patted his stomach as he neared his house. But not the same with Raquel at a separate table.

He drove by her place nice and slow. The garage was shut. She'd left Moms before he had. Probably went to see Cody. Once Cody got out of rehab, it would probably be a while before he went back to the rodeo. If he did. What would Slade do once Cody recovered and took her out on a date? Or worse still, when Cody married her?

You sure You want me to stay here, Lord?

Silence.

He unlocked his door, went inside and pulled off his boots. The house was as he'd found it—furnished, but he'd done nothing to personalize it. He liked his surroundings spare and neat. Probably from living on the road in a small camper. Nothing to straighten or clean. He paced the liv-

ing room, longing to go over and see if she was home
Then what? Say hi?

No. He needed to leave her alone. If he stayed in Aubrey, he needed to find another rental house. Or maybe
even buy a house. Something not right next door to Raquel

A whimper from the back of the house. He hurried to
the mudroom to let Blizzard and Flurry out. "Hey, y'all
sorry about that."

Blizzard and Flurry wagged their tails as Slade stroked
each coat and opened the back door.

A knock sounded at the front door. Strange. He hadn't
heard a vehicle. Maybe Raquel was home and Hunter
wanted to let the dogs out to play with Snow. But since he'd
put the gate between their fences, Hunter usually played
with them there.

He hurried to the front of the house and swung the door
open. Raquel was on the porch, and his pulse began to race

"Hey."

"Hey." He managed to speak around his heart lodged
in his throat.

"Can we talk?"

"Sure." He opened the door wider.

Her perfume got to him first. Then the sway of her dress
with the pink top and denim bottom paired with boots.
Flirty, feminine and fun wrapped up in cowgirl flair. A
ridiculously beautiful package. That wasn't his.

"Have a seat."

"So I'm dying to know." She perched in the middle of
his couch. "Did Ben take the bait?"

He grinned at her word choice and took a seat across
from her. Where it was safe. "He did. He accepted Christ."

"That's awesome!" Her eyes watered.

"It is. I was honored to be a part of it."

"So, if the thing hadn't happened with Annette, Ben
might never have gotten saved."

"Possibly."

"You were amazing today. Watching you fish for men was like poetry in motion. My insides were all in a tizzy while Ben's soul hung in the balance. But I knew you had him hooked and you'd reel him in."

If only he could reel her in. But she wasn't available. And he needed to focus.

"We'll be sure and tell Leroy about Ben at the funeral tomorrow. Something positive to come out of his wife's death might help him deal with losing her."

"Are you sure you don't mind going?"

"Of course not. I said I would. Until Cody's back in shape, I'm your guy." He winced. Poor word choice.

She frowned. "Why do you keep bringing Cody up?"

"Um…I figure it was his shoulder you'd have cried on after Annette died if he hadn't been all bunged up. And if he were able, he'd go to the funeral with you. I'm just a stand-in friend. When he recovers, I'll step aside."

"Why? I can have more than one friend."

What? Now it was Slade's turn to frown. "Sure. But I'm not following."

"If Cody weren't hurt, that doesn't mean he'd have been here for me after Annette died. Or that he'd go to her funeral with me. When he gets well, he'll probably go straight back to the circuit."

"He must be insane."

"The jury's still out on that. But why do you think he's insane? You ride broncs."

"No. I mean he's insane because he's leaving you behind again. And you love him."

"I do not."

"I heard you say it yourself. At the hospital. You said, 'I love Cody.'" He swallowed the hard knot in his throat. "The jig is up. So maybe y'all fought and he doesn't want to quit the circuit. But I thought maybe that bull knocked some sense into him and he'd stay here and marry you. Maybe I should sink my new spur in his backside for ya?"

Raquel laughed.

Laughed! While he was steaming mad. While he was trying to defend her honor. While he was trying to tuck his tail and hand her over to another man.

"I know one thing—if you loved me, I'd never, ever leave you."

That stopped her laughter.

Chapter 14

Slade's insides twisted. He'd laid it all out there for her. Even if Cody was too stupid to stay in Aubrey for her, she still didn't love Slade.

"Slade, have you prayed about going back on the circuit?" Her voice was almost a whisper. "About the cowboy church?"

"Three months ago, I wanted off the circuit. But I fully intended to go back because I thought that's where God wanted me. I'll admit I waffled because of you, but once I figured out you loved Cody, I actually wanted to go back on the circuit."

"Why?"

"Because I couldn't stand to stay here and watch you marry Cody." His chest hurt as if he had filleted his heart open for her. "I only agreed to help set up the cowboy church before I leave. But everything has fallen in place so seamlessly. And there were so many people. And Ben accepted Jesus. It's almost like God wants me to stay."

"What if you stay? What happens to your circuit ministry?"

"Before I came here to find Tori, my mentor showed up out of the blue without knowing anything I was going through and offered to give me a sabbatical. If I go back we'll split the territory in half or he'll travel a different circuit."

"So if you stay here and figure out later that the cowboy church isn't where God wants you, you can go back to the circuit anytime."

"Yes. But if I stay here, even though Cody's too stupid to stick around, I won't bother you. I'll probably move to a different house."

"What if I don't want you to move?" She stood and rounded the coffee table.

He held his breath as she neared, then perched on the arm of his chair at an angle facing him. "Raquel, I'm only a man." He closed his eyes. "Please don't ask me to be your friend. And please keep your distance."

"What if I don't want to?"

He opened his eyes. Man, she was close. Way too close. "I won't be your rebound guy."

"I don't want you to be my rebound guy. I want you to be my guy."

That did it. He got caught up in her eyes. Those beautiful blue eyes that made him feel as if he was her one and only. And then her lips. Her lips that kept inching close to his. Until they actually touched his.

The fire that ignited surely knocked his boots off. He hauled her against him and tasted all the sweetness she offered. While his brain screamed for him to stop. She didn't love him. And he couldn't kiss her into loving him.

He pulled away and pushed her back onto the arm of the chair.

"Wow." She sat there, seemingly dazed.

"Go home, Raquel."

"You said if I loved you, you'd never leave me."

"I heard you say you love Cody."

"Yes, I love Cody."

His thundering heart crashed against his ribs.

"But as a friend."

"You love Cody as a friend?"

"Yes. Like you loved Dylan as a friend."

"You sure?" She and Cody were just friends?

"I'm positive. And besides, even if I felt anything for Cody, which I don't, he's in love with Al— I mean someone else."

"Cody's in love with Al." Slade scrunched his face. Cody didn't seem like that type.

"No, silly. He's in love with a woman and I almost said her name. My whole life I've been terrible at letting secrets slip. I've been working on it."

"Okay, let's get back to you not loving Cody. You dated him, though."

"Yes, a few years back. Mitch tried to fix us up. We went out twice, realized there was nothing there and became really good friends."

His heart settled into a relieved, normal rhythm. "If you don't love Cody, then why were you so upset at the hospital? That was more than friend upset."

"The last time I was at that hospital—" she closed her eyes "—was the night Dylan died."

He pulled her against him again, offering his shoulder. "Then why have you kept me at bay? Until now."

"After Dylan died, I made two rules." She burrowed her face in his neck, sending shivers all through him. "Any man who would have a chance with me and Hunter had to have a nice safe job and be home every night."

"And rodeo chaplain slash cowboy-church preacher isn't safe enough for you? I promise you I'm home every night."

"But you're a stupid bronc rider." Her voice quivered.

"Oh. Why didn't you say so? I'd have quit that nonsense for you."

"I didn't want you to quit for me. And I didn't want you to stay in Aubrey for me. I want you to be you and I want you where God wants you."

"So what if God sends me back to the circuit someday?" He cupped her cheek with his hand and turned her to face him.

"We'll work it out."

"And you're okay with the bronc thing?"

"I learned a lesson lately. Cody got trampled and gored by a bull and lived. Annette Frasier got stung by a wasp and died. It doesn't matter if you're a stupid bronc rider—God's in control."

"Well, if it's all the same to you, I'd just as soon hang up my spurs. I only rode broncs to meet the cowboys where they were. But I never enjoyed it. I'm not saying I'll never ride again. But I won't if I can help it. Maybe I'll try something a little less painful like team roping."

"And you'll keep the house next door?"

"That depends." He traced the corner of her lips with his thumb.

"On?"

"You told me you don't love Cody. But you didn't tell me who you do love."

"You." Her gaze caressed his face.

And Slade wondered how he'd missed it before. She loved him.

"I love you," she repeated.

"I love you. And I'll live next door until you marry me?"

Her breath caught.

He kissed her again and it was a long, long time before he came up for air.

* * *

Raquel and Hunter cuddled on the couch—with the photo album splayed open in their laps. They'd shared the story behind most of the photos—remembering Dylan together. She'd wanted this last night before she married Slade to be special for Hunter.

"And this one." He pointed to a picture of him as a toddler leading a horse with Dylan. Both dressed in cowboy gear, Hunter adorable in his tiny jeans, boots and hat.

"That's how we discovered Aubrey. We visited a dude ranch here and Daddy took you horseback riding. You were three and I was so afraid you'd fall off—"

"You stayed huddled in our room the entire weekend." Hunter giggled. "Can we go there again?"

"Maybe." Raquel did a dramatic shudder. "But I'm kind of scared of horses."

"They're just horses, Mom, not broncs." Hunter rolled his eyes. "I bet Slade will take me to the dude ranch."

"I know you like Slade." Raquel squeezed her eyes closed. "But are you sure you're okay with me marrying him?"

"Slade's awesome."

"He is." Raquel's heart warmed. "And I wouldn't marry him if you didn't think so. But it will change things. It won't be just us. Slade will live here, too. We'll be a family."

"Like we were with Daddy."

"Yes, but Slade won't replace Daddy."

"I know." Hunter traced his fingers over the dude ranch picture. "I'm glad Slade and Daddy were friends. It's good to know Daddy liked Slade. It's kind of like he approves."

"I think Daddy definitely approves. He thought a lot of Slade."

"Will we stay here in Aubrey?"

"Do you want to?" Her heart stilled.

"Uh-huh. I like getting to have a dog and playing in the barn with the cat. And after tomorrow, we'll have three dogs."

"Oh, boy." Raquel rolled her eyes.

Hunter turned the page. "Can we look at the album with Slade sometimes?"

"I think that's a very good idea." Her vision clouded. "Slade would enjoy seeing the pictures."

"I'm gonna like having another man in the house."

"Oh, really?"

"Yep, two against one. Slade will side with me."

"You think so, huh?" She smacked him with a pillow and then tickled his neck. "We'll see about that."

Hunter dissolved into giggles. Their last night alone filled with memories of Dylan, plans for the future with Slade, and lots of love and laughter. Perfect.

The camera flashed and flashed. Kendra took pictures of Raquel with Tori, and with bridesmaids Caitlyn and Lacie. With Hunter and with her parents and Brant.

"That's most of it. I've gotten all the shots like these with Brant already. We'll only have the couple shots and the families united to finish up after the ceremony." Kendra headed into the sanctuary.

"Do I need any touch-ups?"

"Nope. You're beautifulest." Brant chuckled. "See, you've got me tongue-tied."

"See, he's just a big softy." Tori hugged her. "I was just thinking, we'll be double in-laws and our kids will be double cousins."

"I hadn't even thought about that." But she had thought of one thing that could cloud this day. "Tori, go on back to the classroom with Caitlyn and Lacie. I'll be there in a minute." Raquel waited until she and Brant were alone.

in the newly completed lobby. "Are you and Slade okay? Everything squared away?"

"What do you mean?"

"I mean, when he first came to town, you didn't like him or trust him. You toned it down for Tori and you even agreed to be one of his groomsmen, but are y'all really okay now?"

"He did something that forced me to see the error of my ways."

"What?"

"He donated most of whatever he inherited from his and Tori's dad to the cowboy church. And he didn't even have to, because Garrett was willing to back the whole thing. I realized I had him all wrong and apologized. We're buds."

She blew out a sigh. "I'm so glad."

"Trust me, I wouldn't let just anybody marry my little sis." He offered her his arm.

With no clouds on her horizon, Brant escorted her toward the classroom so she could check her appearance one more time before the ceremony.

Over the past few months, she'd met Slade's grandparents, he'd met her parents, and he had even insisted on meeting Dylan's dad and his new wife. It was heartwarming to see him happy again after losing Dylan's mom. All visits had gone well and all their loved ones had come for the wedding. Their families fit together seamlessly as if she and Slade were meant to be.

"Wait a minute." Kendra came through the double doors from the sanctuary. "I forgot one more shot. You'll love it."

Raquel was certain she'd love it, but right now she just wanted to marry Slade. "Where do you want me?"

"Brant, you go get Slade while I explain to Raquel. Do not bring him in here. Take him out through the side door and around, just outside the barn door."

"Yes, ma'am." Brant saluted and entered the sanctuary.

"We'll open the barn door." Kendra framed the air with her hands. "I'll have you stand on one side of the door with Slade standing on the other. You won't be able to see each other."

"Okay?" Raquel wasn't getting Kendra's artistic vision.

"Slade's right outside the door," Brant called.

"Wow, y'all are fast." Kendra cracked the door. "Okay, I'm gonna open the door, but, Slade, you stay behind the door."

"Huh?

"Just trust me." Kendra opened the door and peeked out. "You'll love it and you'll show your grandkids someday."

"That part sounds good," Slade said.

"Brant, hold the door open for me." Kendra disappeared around the door. "I need you right here, Slade. Like this. Perfect—now stay right there. Don't even move a muscle." Kendra popped back around the door and grabbed Raquel's arm. "And I need you right here, Raquel."

She positioned Raquel with her back to the door, looking outside. "Okay, but I still don't get it."

"You're together before the ceremony, but you still can't see each other. An iconic 'last time we were together and single' shot—without breaking tradition."

"Oh, I get it. It sounds lovely." Raquel smiled.

"You'll love it." Kendra stepped outside and fiddled with her camera.

"This is silly," Slade grumbled from the other side of the door. "I'm not superstitious. I'm coming around there."

"You better not." Raquel mustered impending doom into her tone. "I'm not superstitious either. It's just a nice tradition."

"Slade, look at the camera," Kendra coaxed. "I promise, it's a great shot. You'll love it."

"Oh, all right, but after you get the picture, I'm coming around this door."

"Slade Walker, if you come around this door, I won't marry you."

He huffed a sigh. "You win."

"You may not get to see her, but I do." Cody limped around the door with his cane, grinning like the big kid he was. "Ha ha."

"I'm gonna yank a knot in your tail, Cody. Get back over here and quit looking at my woman." Slade's laughter came through his tone.

"You sure about this guy, Raquel?" Cody grinned. "I can still light him up with a cattle prod for ya."

"Will you two stop? I don't need anyone hog-tied or chapped or spurs sunk anywhere. All I need is this picture so I can get married. Shoo, Cody. Get out of my picture."

"Oh, I see how it is." Cody moped his way back to Slade's side of the door. "Some stupid bronc rider shows up and I'm out of your picture."

"Okay, I need my bride and my groom to look at the camera. And smile." Kendra's flash blinded Raquel. "Good. One more, just to make sure. You'll treasure this picture fifty years from now." The flash went off again.

Cody limped around the door again, then jerked back. "Ouch. Stupid bronc rider."

"Don't hurt him, Slade." Raquel laughed. "They barely let him out of rehab to come today."

"I didn't touch him," Slade hollered. "He's over here jerking himself around, putting on a show."

"It's a good thing I know y'all." Kendra chuckled. "I'd be thinking the groomsman does drugs and he's hitting on the bride. That's a wrap. See y'all after the ceremony."

"Get lost, Cody. Let me talk to my woman alone."

"Are you gonna let him talk to me like that?" Cody limped around the door again.

"Get lost, Cody. Let me talk to my man alone."

"You too?" Cody did a pretend sniff and hobbled away.

"How old is he?" Slade's voice came through the door

"Twenty-nine going on eleven." She laughed. "I really appreciate you asking him to be a groomsman."

"He's growing on me, he's your friend, and he can't be in the bridal party, so I thought it was only right."

"You being so sweet is one of the many reasons I'm here. Speaking of which, I'm not sure you realize, but you're kind of holding up my wedding."

"So that's what's going on. It's like a rodeo reunion in there." He chuckled. "But this won't take long. Turn around."

"I don't want to see you before the wedding."

"Trust me. Turn around. Put your cheek against the door facing outside, like we're dancing cheek to cheek."

"Oh." She turned around and pressed her cheek against the door.

"Now give me your hand."

She reached around the edge of the door and he clasped her hand as if they were waltzing. "Do you know how to waltz?"

"I can Texas two-step. But I'd learn to waltz for you."

Her insides warmed. "My very own waltzing rodeo chaplain slash cowboy preacher."

"Just don't tell anybody. I have a reputation, you know."

"I love you."

"I love you. Ready to get this shindig started?"

"Past ready." She sighed.

"Good. I'm looking forward to dancing through life with you."

"See you in a few."

"And for the rest of our lives."

* * * * *

CONTENTS

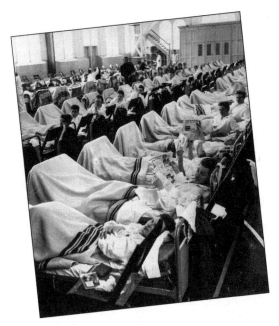

Danish personnel suffering from influenza occupy beds in temporary sick quarters in a naval shipyard. The sick beds were an emergency measure to handle the large number of patients during an epidemic in October 1957. (For more on the history of flu epidemics see page 22.)

Traders wearing masks as a precaution against SARS work at Hong Kong's Stock Exchange in April 29, 2003. The blue-chip Hang Seng Index rose 309.18 points or 3.6 percent to 8,744 during the day on news that the worst of Hong Kong's outbreak may be over. (For more on the SARS outbreak see page 48.)

On June 27, 2005, an official in protective gear pulls
live chickens out of cages to slaughter them at a
chicken farm northeast of Tokyo, Japan, where bird flu
has been detected. Officials began culling some 25,000
chickens and disinfecting the farm following an outbreak of bird flu. (For more on the story see page 40.)

A woman wears a mask to protect against SARS at a wash station at the entrance to North York General Hospital in Toronto, May 2003. (For more on the importance of handwashing as a precautionary measure see page 125.)

A man wears a mask to protect himself against the SARS virus as he walks past a billboard in Beijing, China, in May 2003. The billboard reads: "The SARS will surely be conquered by our government under the leadership of the Communist Party of China." (For more on the SARS outbreak in China see page 40.)

AUTHOR'S NOTE

This book is a gathering of information, hopefully both interesting and informative, about killer influenza and its potential to change life on our planet. There has been no effort to sensationalize, and no need to. The history of pandemic influenza is frightening enough on its own, considering that a new outbreak could kill millions.

The Severe Acute Respiratory Syndrome (SARS) outbreak of 2003 proved that the world medical community and governments were not prepared for a catastrophic outbreak of infectious viral disease. More than two years later many experts say we remain unprepared.

Some cultures favor a good measure of government control over their lives. Sometimes that includes letting government do their thinking for them. Health is too important to leave to politicians and bureaucrats. Individual citizens need to inform themselves on health matters to better judge the decisions and actions of their governments on life and death matters.

We live in times of information overload and marketing spin, and often it is hard to know who to believe on any subject. That is why it is important, certainly on matters of health, for people to gather the facts, sort them, absorb them, and form opinions based on intelligent analysis.

If a flu pandemic does strike as the experts predict, we will enter a crisis in which daily life turns upside down. Social upheaval will challenge traditions, ethics, and how we treat each other. It is important that we arm ourselves with knowledge.

I have personal knowledge of pandemic influenza. I caught the Hong Kong flu in New York City in December 1968. I returned home feeling ill but paid a Christmas Eve visit to my mother and unknowingly infected her. We were both so sick with the flu and accompanying pneumonia we didn't see each other again until March, even though we lived only city blocks apart.

The thought of infecting loved ones with deadly disease is terrifying. The heroic health workers exposed to SARS know all about that. We'll all know about it when the next pandemic hits.

Forewarned is forearmed.

Jim Poling Sr., August 2005

Preface

Ring around the rosies,
A pocket full of posies,
Atishoo! Atishoo!
We all fall down.

Children everywhere recite it, oblivious of its meaning. Rosies, the rings of rosy sores. Posies, the fragrant flowers carried to ward off the malignant odors of disease. Atishoo! the sneezing that spreads the germs that knock us falling down dead.

It's a cute nursery rhyme, but a black one, because some say, it is rooted in the pandemic deaths of times long past. Times of horrific plagues that scythed through human populations, harvesting men, women, and children by the tens of thousands. Devastating sickness we can't imagine in these days of modern medical wizardry. People dropping dead like flies in an oppressive heat. Societies so brutalized by burying countless dead—while trying desperately to save lives—that economic systems and social order break down into chaos.

It may seem unthinkable, but a modern infectious disease outbreak of Biblical proportions is a distinct possibility. A new great plague is stalking the edges of human habitation. It is overdue to break out of the shadows with a viciousness that could kill millions, tens of millions, or possibly hundreds of millions.

That's just fear mongering, some might scoff. Don't forget we live in an advanced civilization that has steadily pushed back infectious diseases and extended life expectancies. Remember how we are so well shielded with our miracles of modern medicine, and our super drugs. It can't possibly happen, at least to the extent being talked about. Perhaps, but as of today, tens of millions of chickens have died or been slaughtered in a bird influenza outbreak that is a possible prelude to a world health crisis. Respected medical experts say it is coming, and that all our brilliant technology and all our modern medicine will not stop it.

If they are right, unimaginable numbers of stricken people and an unusually high death rate could create social chaos and change our lives. It happened less than 100 years ago, when the Spanish Flu of 1918 killed more people than all the world wars put together.

Those who can't accept this macabre probability need only look back to the SARS outbreak of 2003: the masked faces on the streets, the guards at closed hospital doors, the gravediggers wearing protective suits. All this and more could be back with the next killer flu.

The smart will listen, and prepare.

SECTION ONE

A Looming Threat

CHAPTER 1

The Village Madman

Influenza is like the village madman. He prowls the shadows of our communities, emerging occasionally to disrupt our lives and hurt relatively small groups of people. Once every few decades, he runs screaming into the streets maiming and killing in much larger numbers. We fear him during these insane episodes, but we know we are incapable of killing him or even banishing him. So when he returns to the shadows, we nervously accept his presence as a distressing part of life, and then try to forget him.

Influenza has lived among us for centuries, hiding for much of the time, but reappearing annually. Most appearances are mild, but occasionally it displays its strength as a serious killer. It comes from one of 1,500 microbes that can make humans sick, but is first among these in ability to kill. Even a run-of-the-mill annual flu now kills more than one million people a year around the world.

KILLER FLU OUTBREAKS IN THE PAST 300 YEARS
• 1729–1731
• 1775–1776
• 1781–1782
• 1830-1833
• 1847–1848
• 1889
• 1898–1900
• 1918–1919 Spanish Flu
• 1957–1958 Asian Flu
• 1968 Hong Kong Flu

Hippocrates, who was the world's most famous early doctor, mentioned something like it 2,500 years ago in ancient Greece. Other medical researchers wrote of outbreaks of disease matching modern influenza during the 11th and 15th centuries. In the last three centuries there have been 10 killer flu outbreaks, three in the last 90 years.

In earlier times, the flu was a feared killer, raging out to consume undeveloped and unprotected societies. Mortality rates soared because of primitive medicine, which included questionable and sometimes outright dangerous practices, such as bloodletting. The medical community did not even know its cause until just over 70 years ago, when scientists finally traced it to a virus.

It appears every year in temperate climates when the cooler weather comes. Many people wrongly believe that cold weather causes it, but there is no proven link between cold weather and the flu. Rather, it spreads during the cold months because more people gather indoors, such as students crowded into classrooms from fall until spring.

Medical advances as well as better living

conditions have lessened the flu's impact on humans. These days it mainly leaves us aching, shivering, coughing, and running for the toilet. It is a misery that upsets our lives for a few days. All we can do is take aspirin or acetaminophen, rest in bed, and drink fluids. Yes, it still kills many people worldwide, but its victims are mainly those nearing the end of life, or those with health weakened by other conditions. Even then, the influenza does not usually do the killing itself, leaving that to pneumonia, bronchitis, or other secondary infections. Death from influenza is not an issue for the majority. The mortality rate, although it varies by year, location, and circumstances, is usually only a small fraction of one percent of those who catch the flu. Outstanding advances in human health care, including more sanitary living conditions, vaccines, and alleviation medications have reduced the flu to a mere annoyance for most people.

Influenza is a viral infection that attacks the respiratory tract. It is transmitted through

THE FLU BUG

Under a microscope the flu bug is somewhat round, but irregularly shaped. It consists of a core of genetic material called ribonucleic acid (RNA), which holds genetic instructions for making copies of the virus. The RNA is covered by a coat of protein and an outer layer of fatty substance that protects spikes of protein known as hemagglutinin (HA) and neuraminidase (NA). The proteins act as antigens that produce antibodies and immune reaction to the bodies invaded by the virus. HA allows the virus to stick to a cell and begin infection. NA allows newly formed viruses to move among cells.

the inhaling of droplets sent flying into the air by sneezing and coughing. Once the virus enters upper air passages, it lodges there, reproduces, and spreads. The result is chills, fever, digestive upset, headache, and muscle pain. Like the common cold, which is also caused by a virus, there is no cure for influenza.

The virus was isolated in 1933 by a team of scientists, including Sir Christopher Andrewes, at the National Institute for Medical Research in England. It was 10 years before scientists first saw it through a microscope. The influenza virus is 500 times smaller than the width of a human hair and millions of them fit on the head of a pin. Anyone viewing the virus microscopically surely wonders how something so small can be so complex, and so deadly.

Influenza viruses are classified as A, B, and C types according to their protein makeup. Type A tends to invade whales, chickens, and humans. It is the most deadly type, having caused some of the world's worst flu outbreaks. Type B is common in humans and although it can create epidemics, it has never reached pandemic proportions. Type C, found in pigs, dogs, and humans, causes milder respiratory infections, but has never been responsible for epidemics or pandemics.

DEFINITIONS

Epidemic: An outbreak that is widespread over one area
Pandemic: An outbreak that occurs throughout a country or the entire world

There are many different types of A viruses, and they differ because of their proteins.

These viruses have an incredible ability to change themselves. Continuous changes, called antigenic drifting, create new strains that might be unrecognizable to the human immune system. Researchers produce new vaccines every year to protect against new strains.

Type A flu sometimes makes a sudden change, called antigenic shift, reassorting HA and NA to create a new subtype. The change in genetic makeup and virulence factors make some new strains more infectious and more deadly than others. These new subtypes are the influenzas that create widespread and serious outbreaks. New viruses are dangerous because people have little or no immunity, and generally there has not been enough time to develop a vaccine against them.

The different strains of Type A influenza are classified by where they were first identified, their laboratory identification number, the year they were discovered, and the type of HA or NA they possess. For example, the bird flu virus discovered in Hong Kong in 1997 has HA5 and NA1 proteins, and is identified as: A/Hong Kong/156/97 (H5N1).

Although we can't prevent it, we can and do effectively fight the flu. Vigilance, monitoring, infection control, and medications protect us reasonably well from the scourge of our ancestors. Vaccine is by far the heaviest club we wield against it. There is a small but vigorous opposition to vaccine citing that side effects outweigh the supposed benefits. Major health organizations around the world, however, say flu vaccination lessens the annual flu toll and saves lives.

Each year the World Health Organization (WHO) predicts which flu viruses will dominate when cooler weather arrives. Then, the organization gets to work trying to prevent its spread. To create a vaccine, WHO researchers inject a target virus and a harmless virus into a fertilized hen's egg to produce an offspring virus that has the genetic material of both. They create seed-batches

of three flu strains and give them to manufac-
turers who begin the process of making vaccine,
which can take as long as six months. There's no
guarantee that an annual flu shot will prevent
the disease, but medical experts rate the flu vaccine as 70 percent effective.

One shortcoming of the flu vaccine is the
limited world capacity to produce it. The most
we can produce for any one flu season is 250 to
300 million doses. There are 6.4 billion people
in the world, so only a tiny minority can receive protection each year. That's not a big deal
because of the flu's low mortality rate. Those
most likely to be exposed and most threatened,
such as medical professionals and the elderly,
are vaccinated to check the spread and reduce
deaths. The unvaccinated majority might catch
the flu, but simply tough it out for a few days.
However, if a new and especially virulent influenza suddenly arrives, even one that responds
to a new vaccine, the world could be in serious
trouble because of a vaccine shortage.

In modern times, concern about annual flu outbreaks has been more about economic loss than large-scale deaths, at least in industrialized regions. Flu means time off from work, which affects production, and in turn affects economic output. That's why the Canadian province of Ontario in 2000 became the first jurisdiction in the world to offer free flu shots to every person over six months old, at a cost of close to $33.5 million. The provincial government is betting that free flu shots will mean fewer winter visits to doctors, hospitals and pharmacies, and therefore less strain on the government health care system.

Aside from vaccines to help reduce outbreaks, there are new antiviral medications such as oseltamivir, amantadine, and rimantadine to lessen the effects of flu. Taken within a couple of days of the onset of symptoms, these can reduce the severity of the bout and shorten its duration. All this considered, influenza has become a minor worry for most people. It's certainly far down the list of more potent threats, such as heart disease, cancer, environmental disasters, and fanatics with bombs.

Almost daily, however, there are signs that we need to adjust our attitudes about influenza. Signs that a new flu virus could explode into a major health crisis and kill millions. Signs that we should pay attention to history, and replace some of our smugness about health advances with more vigilance and hard questioning about what is really happening. Signs that every country in the world needs a higher level of preparedness, which medical experts say is the only thing that will save lives when the pandemic sweeps in.

CHAPTER 2

Signs

The voices of the world's medical experts are united and very clear: we are long overdue for a global killer flu. Dr. Lee Jong-wook, head of the WHO calls an influenza pandemic "the most serious known health threat the world is facing today. The timing cannot be predicted, but rapid international spread is certain once the pandemic virus appears. This is a grave danger for all people in all countries."

World health experts like Dr. Lee worry that a Type A virus will mutate into a rogue strain for which there is no immunity and no immediate vaccine, and will create a pandemic. It might sound like science fiction, but it isn't.

The immediate threat is the H5N1 avian or bird flu virus that WHO has monitored closely since its appearance in Hong Kong in 1997 . It has waxed and waned in the eight years since its discovery, but as 2005 dawned, WHO issued this chilling statement:

"Whereas past pandemics have consistently announced themselves with an explosion of cases, events during 2004, supported by epidemiological and virological surveillance, have given the world an unprecedented warning that a pandemic may be imminent."

The "events of 2004" refer to another disconcerting outbreak of H5N1 in Asia. Tens of millions of poultry died, or were destroyed, to stop the infection from spreading. H5N1 is a bird flu, but then it showed in a small number of humans. At the beginning of January 2005, there were 45 confirmed human cases, 32 of which were fatal. WHO describes this as "very high mortality."

Cases continue to pop up in Southeast Asia and by early August 2005, WHO reported 112 human victims, 57 of whom died. That is more than a doubling of human cases in less than six months. Ninety of the cases were in Vietnam, the rest in Thailand and Cambodia. China, Malaysia, Indonesia, and Laos all reported cases in poultry but no spread into humans, although researchers said human cases are inevitable. The human cases likely developed from extremely close contact with infected poultry. So far, there is no evidence of any human passing on the disease to another human. The great fear, and the critical factor to the potential pandemic, is that the virus will adapt itself to human-to-human transmission.

"The virus could be adapting to humans," Peter Horby, a WHO epidemiologist stationed in Hanoi has said. "There's a number of indications it could be moving toward a more dangerous virus."

As the human cases have increased, the mortality rate has fallen somewhat. Halfway through 2005 the human death rate was roughly 50 percent, down from 70 percent. That might seem like good news, but it isn't. When a disease kills most of the people it infects, it soon runs out of places to spread. So when it becomes less deadly, the better chance it has to spread and become a pandemic. Any death rate higher than a fraction of one percent could create a world catastrophe.

The Spanish Flu of 1918–19—the greatest influenza killer of modern history—had a death rate in the 2.5 to 5 percent range, killing an estimated 40 to 50 million worldwide. The world population in 1918 was around 1.8 billion; today it is more than 6.4 billion people. A death rate similar to 1918 would be catastrophic because there are more than three times the number of people to infect.

Dr. Julie Gerberding, head of the U.S. Centers for Disease Control and Prevention (CDC) in Atlanta, Georgia, told the American Association for the Advancement of Science in February 2005 that the current avian flu situation probably resembles 1918, when a flu virus was quietly mutating into the strain that became the Spanish Flu.

Dr. Michael Osterholm is one expert who says we must prepare for the worst. A world-renowned infectious disease expert based at the University of Minnesota, Osterholm is also associate director for food protection and defense in the U.S. Department of Homeland Security. He says, "If one takes a look at the 1918 pandemic that swept around the world, literally in weeks, and extrapolate those number of deaths then to what we might expect to see today, we could easily see 1.7 million deaths in the United States in one year and up to 360 million deaths worldwide."

A modern pandemic of Spanish Flu proportions could set the world back on its heels, if not knock it out. Millions of people ill with the flu would mean airplanes, trucks and trains would not deliver goods on time. The resultant shortages of food, medical supplies, gasoline, and everyday goods could set up a colossal crisis.

THE DEADLY SEVEN

The CIA and WHO's list of the most dangerous infectious diseases threatening the world today (in alphabetical order)

- E. Coli and diarrheal diseases
- Hepatitis B and C
- HIV/AIDS
- Influenza and pneumonia
- Malaria
- Measles
- Tuberculosis (TB)

The quiet anxiety about a pandemic has changed to visible concern throughout the world. Governments are bustling with action planning. WHO urges countries to draft and implement pandemic preparedness plans. Many already have, including the United States, Canada, Australia, and Britain. So have many local governments. Concern about the flu, plus the reality jolt of SARS, prompted the European Union and Canada to establish their own versions of the CDC.

Despite preparations in the developed world, there is concern about protection for the poorer, less developed nations. Many of these countries are already trying to cope with the AIDS epidemic, malaria, and exotic sicknesses, such as Ebola and Marburg hemorrhagic fever. These countries are short of the money, medical expertise, and medicines needed for a strong defense against a flu outbreak. Their exposure to killer flu is a risk to us all.

A U.S. Central Intelligence Agency report in January 2000 warned that "new and re-emerging infectious diseases will pose a rising global health threat and will complicate U.S. and global security over the next 20 years." Included in the list of CIA most dangerous diseases are "new, more lethal variants of influenza."

CHAPTER 3

The China Syndrome

The medical world has known about bird flu since 1878, when Italy named it the Fowl Plague. For thousands of years, wild birds have carried influenza viruses naturally in their intestines. Although a virus does not sicken them often, it can spread to other birds through saliva or excrement. Sometimes the viruses mutate and move to other species, infecting domesticated ducks, chickens, and frequently pigs. A pig can become a virus mixing bowl if it contracts both avian and human types of flu. The two types can then exchange genes, producing a reassorted flu virus transmittable among humans. This animal-to-human disease transmission is called zoonosis.

The new avian flu, like many other influenza viruses, got its start in China. So did SARS and the 1957 and 1968 flu pandemics. People ask why Asia, and China in particular, is so often the epicenter of new influenza. One theory is that, in Asia, large numbers of people crowd close quarters that they often share with their poultry and other farm animals. Rice farmers often keep domesticated ducks to rid the rice paddies of insects and weeds. When the farmers also keep pigs, they allow creation of the bird-to-pig-to-human transmission chain. Children pick up viruses when playing in areas shared with the animals, and additional exposure comes when the family slaughters poultry and pigs for food. Complicating the situation is the practice among farmers of quickly killing and eating birds that show signs of sickness to avoid wasting them.

Dr. Shigeru Omi, Western Pacific regional director for WHO, has expressed concern over close contact with domesticated animals and unsanitary handling of animals in live markets. Omi has called for a new set of standards to ensure human safety while living with animals. "It is vital that we achieve this objective as quickly as possible," he says. "If we do not, I fear that more threats such as SARS and avian influenza will emerge from the animal world to endanger global public health."

So far, the avian flu H5N1 has not been easy for humans to catch. It requires extremely close contact with an infected bird, and was not known to infect humans until 1997, when a three-year-old boy became infected in Hong Kong and died. Then 18 people became ill with it and required hospital treatment. Six died. Authorities ordered the slaughter of millions of birds to prevent the outbreak from growing. Six years later, a new outbreak appeared and spread in two waves into eight Asian countries. The initial wave hit Thailand and Vietnam between January and March of 2004 and saw 35 human cases, an incredible 24 of which were fatal. WHO linked almost all of the cases to people having direct contact with diseased poultry in their households. This time, 120 million birds died or were destroyed, and the outbreak subsided in late March 2004.

Another outbreak, which appeared in July 2004, affected China, Thailand, Cambodia, and Vietnam before spreading to Malaysia. One million birds died or were destroyed. There were nine human cases in Thailand and Vietnam; eight died.

Then the virus accelerated in 2005, with more than 100 human cases and a 50 percent death rate. Medical workers say the mortality rate is striking. Also noteworthy is the fact the virus picks on healthy children and young adults instead of the elderly and weakened. A hallmark of the Spanish Flu was its ability to kill healthy young adults. WHO stated in January 2005: "No explanation for this unusual disease pattern is presently available. Nor is it possible to calculate a reliable case-fatality rate, as a mildly symptomatic disease may be occurring in the community, yet escapes detection."

Scientists calculate that flu pandemics tend to arrive every 30 to 40 years, and it has been almost 40 years since the last one. In 1957, 38 years after the Spanish Flu pandemic, the Asian Flu A/H2N2 struck worldwide, killing one to two million people, including roughly 100,000 in North America.

Only 10 years after the Asian Flu outbreak, another arrived and became a new pandemic. It was the Hong Kong flu A/H3N2, a virus that is still circulating today. In 1968, it killed up to one million people around the world.

The question now is whether the avian flu can improve its ability to transmit among humans, and how quickly. If it does, the speed of modern travel will create a wildfire spread that could rapidly become a pandemic.

"We have good reason to fear the H5N1 virus that's now widely established in chicken and duck and wildfowl population in probably 10 countries. It would take only a very small genetic change or modification in that virus to make it rapidly transmissible to people," Dr. William Aldis of WHO said in April 2005.

The CDC in Atlanta says the H5N1 infection among birds has become endemic. They predict the situation will not improve in the short term, and more human cases are like-

THE NEXT PANDEMIC

WHO lists three prerequisites for the beginning of the next pandemic:
- There must be an emergence of a novel virus subtype to which humans have little or no immunity.
- The new virus must have the ability to replicate in humans and cause serious illness.
- It must be effectively transmitted by one human to another, creating sustained transmission chains that cause community outbreaks.

ly. Humans have little pre-existing immunity to H5N1, and current testing shows the antiviral medications amantadine and rimantadine are ineffective against H5N1. Two others, oseltamivir (Tamiflu) and zanamivir (Relenza), remain effective against the virus in its current form, but their effect is unknown if the virus mutates.

The world awaits H5N1's next move. Will it develop effective human transmission before medical science can get a grip on it and produce an effective vaccine? In the meantime, fears about the mutation of H5N1 to pandemic status have reached the U.S. Congress.

"We are staring at the barrel of a loaded gun

AVIAN FLU PANDEMIC

"All prerequisites for the start of a pandemic had been met save one, namely the onset of efficient human-to-human transmission. Should the virus improve its transmissibility, everyone in the world would be vulnerable to infection by a pathogen—passed along by a cough or a sneeze—entirely foreign to the human immune system."

WHO statement assessing avian flu January 2005.

ready to fire," Representative Michael Ferguson (R-NJ) said at a congressional hearing in late May of 2005. "This is nature's weapon of mass destruction."

CHAPTER 4

The Wake-up Call

It was spring of 2003 in Toronto. Not the finest of springs, but the calendar promised better weather as folks swept away the dregs of winter and nurtured blooms struggling to pull some warmth from the cool, grey skies. The city prepared for Easter, unaware that widespread fear, and anguish for some, would dampen the usual brightness and hope of the season.

Two months before Easter, in the Pearl

River Delta region of China, 7,200 miles (12,000 km) from Toronto, a 64-year-old doctor worked diligently to save the lives of patients seriously ill with an atypical pneumonia. His patients were part of an outbreak at Guangzhou Hospital in Guangdong Province. The hospital had 130 cases, 106 of which were nosocomial infections—hospital acquired infections—which made this mysterious illness even more bizarre because hospitals are supposed to cure people, not make them sick.

The third week of February, the doctor took a break from his duties, traveling to Hong Kong with his wife to attend a family wedding. They checked in to the four-star Metropole Hotel February 21, occupying Room 911 on the ninth floor. The doctor had felt a bit unwell back home but had self-prescribed antibiotics and was feeling better for the trip. The following day he went to the emergency ward at Kwong Wah Hospital with fever and shortness of breath. His condition deteriorated and he died there on March 4, another victim of this strange, unknown disease. The doctor was relatively young and healthy by today's standards, and a medical professional who knew how to look after himself. It wasn't until April that the medical community officially diagnosed a weird new lung disease they called Severe Acute Respiratory Syndrome (SARS).

Also on the ninth floor of the Metropole was Kwan Sui Chu, a 78-year-old woman who had emigrated to Toronto from China 10 years earlier. She had returned to China for a vacation with her husband, but it was a classic case of being in the wrong place at the wrong time. She returned to Toronto February 23 feeling ill, and her family doctor treated her at home. Her condition worsened daily and she died March 5. A coroner said she died of a heart attack, but other family members, including her 43-year-old son Tse Chi Kwai, soon fell ill with symptoms similar to Kwan's.

Much later, WHO investigators discovered evidence of the SARS virus in the hallway carpet outside Room 911 of the Metropole. They deduced that the ill doctor from Guangdong had coughed, sneezed, or vomited in the hallway and that others who walked in it, including Kwan, became infected. It seems incredible that anyone could pick up the disease just walking the hallway, but it is unknown if Kwan and the doctor might have passed each other in the hall or whether they rode the elevator together. Kwan was not the only one sickened by walking the hallway. At least 12 other guests and visitors to the ninth floor contracted SARS. Some, like Kwan, were international travelers and brought SARS home to Hanoi and Singapore.

Two days after his mother's death, Tse Chi Kwai went to Scarborough Grace Hospital on the east side of Toronto with a fever, shortness of breath and a dry cough. He died there less than a week later, leaving behind a wife and a five-month-old child. His SARS spread throughout the hospital, beginning the medical nightmare that all health care workers fear.

Tse's arrival at Scarborough Grace Emergency the night of March 7 was typical. Nurses put him on a bed and drew a thin curtain for privacy. That same evening, 78-year-old Joseph Pollack, a fabric dealer in Toronto's garment district, arrived with an irregular heartbeat. He got the bed beside Tse, staying only a few hours before returning home. Three days later he felt like he had the flu; he had body aches and a cough. He went to his doctor, who diagnosed pneumonia. Pollack's symptoms would not respond to the drugs his doctor prescribed, and worsened. He died March 21. His wife Rose caught it, too, and died in early April.

During one of Joseph's Pollack's hospital visits, a Filipino-Canadian family waited in emergency while the family patriarch, 82-year-old Eulialo Samson, received attention for a knee injury. The bug Pollack picked up from Tse spread to the Samsons. It quickly killed Eulialo and his wife Gregoria, 78, and sickened others. Public health officials noticed a pattern and worried that the new mystery disease had spread at the funeral visitation for the Filipino grandfather, and at a large gathering of Bukas Loob Sa Diyos Covenant Community, a Roman Catholic prayer group, with wide connections in the Filipino community.

SARS now had Toronto by the throat, and by Easter weekend, the city was in near panic. Some people refused to go to their churches, fearing SARS could be anywhere. The Roman Catholic Church even suspended the practices of taking communion from a communal cup and kissing the crucifix. It told its congregations to bow to each other during Mass instead of shaking hands as a gesture of peace.

The fear was palpable in Toronto. Chinese restaurants were empty and Chinese people shunned because SARS had come from China. Business losses were so severe that the prime minister of the day made a show of going out to eat in a Chinese restaurant, attempting to prove its safety. One major restaurant chain reported losses of more than two million dollars. The media reported the widespread alienation of Asians at work, schools, and on public transit, and of Filipino nannies dismissed or told to stay away until the outbreak ended.

Tourism collapsed. The hit musical Mamma Mia closed for the summer months because people stopped visiting Toronto.

Some funerals for SARS victims were held without family or friends present. At least one cemetery instructed staff to wear gloves and masks when handling the coffins of SARS victims. In one case, cemetery workers interred a coffin while mourners watched from another part of the cemetery.

The fear was not only in Toronto. SARS spread to five countries within 24 hours and in a few months reached 30 countries on six continents. The University of California at Berkeley announced it would not take Asian students in their 2003 summer school. Other universities asked parents from infected areas not to attend graduation ceremonies. In Taiwan, villagers blocked the entrance to a waste plant because they feared hospital waste would infect them with SARS. In Guangdong, where the outbreak began, panicked residents overwhelmed shops to buy vinegar and herbal remedies. People heated the vinegar on stoves in hopes that the acidic vapors would keep the SARS infection at bay.

Even doctors and nurses couldn't protect themselves completely from infection. Medical workers fell seriously ill; some died. This heightened the public's panic over an apparently unstoppable infectious disease. The death rate was alarming; 10 percent of those infected died. Hospitals closed to visitors, health care staff was quarantined, and rigid infection control measures were enforced, including wearing of protective gear that made medical staff look like spacemen.

No one knows how SARS got started, except that it likely had some connection to the exotic animal markets in China. No one knows why or how it stopped either, except that quarantines kept it from spreading beyond hospitals and into general populations. Fortunately, SARS was stopped before it developed into a pandemic, but by the end of 2003, it had infected more than 8,000 people in 30 countries, killing almost 800 of them, including 44 in Toronto.

The human toll of SARS was tragic, but the number of infections and deaths globally was small compared to outbreaks of cholera, diphtheria, and other infectious diseases. The economic toll however was huge, especially in the areas directly affected—those where people feared they could catch the disease. Newspapers and television showed pictures of deserted restaurants, empty airport terminals, and people on the streets in white masks. These told the story of how an infectious disease can devastate economies.

The scope of the financial losses from SARS is still not clear. One year after the outbreak,

WHO estimated losses to be between $30 billion and $100 billion, largely lost trade and foreign investment. Researchers Jong-Wha Lee of Korea University, and Warwick McKibbin of the Australian National University, calculated SARS cost the Asia-Pacific region alone $40 billion. Canada (Toronto in particular) suffered huge tourism trade losses when fear of catching the disease kept people away. At the height of the outbreak, WHO issued a warning to travelers, recommending that they not travel to Toronto. Tourists canceled plans to visit Toronto and many businesses from large hotel chains down to small business operators felt the impact. For instance, a Toronto-to-Niagara Falls transport operator's business was down a full 100 percent, forcing him to lay off workers. The city of Toronto estimated film production spending dropped 18 percent because of SARS. The Canadian Tourism Commission put the country's losses at $352 million, while the province of Ontario estimated SARS cost $641 million in additional health care spending.

SARS shocked us with its rapid appearance from nowhere, its ability to kill quickly, and its capacity for killing healthy people in the prime of life. It also revealed with brilliant clarity how unprepared the world is for outbreaks of killer disease. Ontario—the province most directly impacted by SARS—was unprepared for a major health crisis. Mr. Justice Archie Campbell, appointed by the Ontario government to investigate what happened in SARS, wrote in his first interim report in April 2004 that Ontario's public health system was "woefully inadequate" to handle such a serious threat.

"SARS showed Ontario's central public health system to be unprepared, fragmented, poorly led, uncoordinated, inadequately resourced, professionally impoverished, and generally incapable of discharging its mandate," stated his report.

What a damning indictment. One of the world's most prosperous regions initially unable to protect itself from a vicious infectious disease. In the end, the only thing that appears to have saved the province from a greater SARS disaster was the dedicated professionalism of its individual health care workers.

SECTION TWO

Killers of the Past

CHAPTER 5

The Spanish Lady

We are the dead. Short days ago
We lived, felt dawn, saw sunset glow,
Loved and were loved . . .

When enemy shelling blew apart a fellow officer, Lieutenant-Colonel John McCrae conducted the funeral service because no chaplain was available. McCrae, a faculty doctor at McGill University in Montreal, Quebec, had seen much battlefield death. He had served in the South Africa War, and in 1914 enlisted in the Canadian Expeditionary Force sent to the World War I killing grounds of Europe. That one death summed up the horrors of war for McCrae, and the day after the funeral in May 1915 he sat in the back of an ambulance near his field hospital and vented his anguish by composing the now famous poem *In Flanders Fields*.

In Flanders fields the poppies blow
Between the crosses, row on row

He saw much more death and destruction during almost four years at war but when the guns fell silent on November 11, 1918, Dr. Mc-Crae, age 45, was among the dead in Flanders fields. He was one of the estimated 12 million people—7 million soldiers and 5 million civilians—who died because of World War I. He succumbed the previous January, not of battle wounds, but of pneumonia possibly brought on by a mysterious influenza far more deadly than any war.

The influenza, called the Spanish Flu, killed

40 to 50 million people worldwide to become the most devastating infectious outbreak in human history. In fact, it killed at least four times as many people as the war in one-quarter of the time. The war and the flu together created such trauma that people tended to block those horrible times from their memory. Some historians call it the forgotten pandemic because little detailed writing for general public consumption appeared until much later in the century.

Few plagues in history caused more human misery and death than the influenza outbreak of 1918–19. It was reminiscent of medieval times when plagues consumed huge chunks of populations, overwhelmed societies, and plunged them into chaos. One of the earliest plagues was recorded by Greek historian Thucydides, who wrote of an unidentified infection that roared through Athens, creating the "awful spectacle of men dying like sheep." It was one of the first records of civilized society collapsing beneath the weight of uncontrolled disease.

He wrote: "The bodies of dying men lay one upon another and half-dead creatures reeled about the streets and gathered round all the fountains in their longing for water. The sacred places also in which they had quartered themselves were full of corpses of persons that had died there, just as they were; for as the disaster passed all bounds, men, not knowing what was to become of them, became utterly careless of everything, whether sacred or profane."

Thucydides described how funeral traditions fell apart, bodies simply tossed into fires. People ignored laws because "no one expected to live to be brought to trial for his offenses."

Similarly, when bubonic plague consumed large parts of Europe in the mid-1300s, society broke down. Giovanni Boccaccio wrote in 1348 of how Florentines fell ill with swollen lymph nodes in the groin and armpits, "some of which grew as large as a common apple," followed by the appearance of black spots on the skin, due to internal bleeding. He described people

THE BUBONIC PLAGUE

The Bubonic Plague has raged across the world, killing well over 200 million people, in three major pandemics.

Plague of Justinian:
Beginning in the Middle East and spreading north through the Mediterranean, the Plague of Justinian killed 25 million people, 40 percent of the area's population in 541–542 AD.

Black Death: History's biggest killer, the Black Death, swept Europe in the mid-1300s, killing 200 million, 40 percent of Europe's population. It returned briefly in 1665–1666.

The Third Pandemic: The Third Pandemic began in China and spread through Asia in 1855, killing 12 million people.

dying in the streets and bodies dragged out of houses so parts of the city looked like a "sepulcher."

Bodies were piled on biers, or in their absence, planks, some holding the bodies of whole families at once. Priests called upon to perform last rites on one corpse suddenly found line-ups of six or eight bodies. "Nor, for all their number, were their obsequies [funerals] honored by either tears or lights or crowds of mourners, rather, it was come to this, that a dead man was then of no more account than a dead goat would be to-day," wrote Boccaccio.

Fear was so rampant that people fled to the countryside believing they could outrun the killer infection, while others stocked supplies and locked themselves in houses, refusing all outside contact.

The plague continued to ravage Europe in the 1400s, and even the 1500s and 1600s. In 1665, the Black Plague struck particularly hard in London, where normal life ceased. Frightened citizens boarded families—sick and healthy together—into their homes, and left them to die in hopes that the plague would spread no further. Body carts carried corpses to pits for disposal. In all these great plagues, the healthy abandoned the sick out of fear, doctors and nurses dropped from exhaustion, coffin makers could not keep pace with demand, undertaking services collapsed, funeral rites disappeared, and economies flew off the rails, because so many workers were ill or dead.

It was hard for many to imagine that history would repeat itself so brutally, especially in the new and bright 20th century. Nor could anyone imagine that the agent of death, and social and economic destruction, could be something usually considered a minor illness.

The Spanish Flu changed the world in little more than a year. The death rate was an estimated 2.5 percent compared with a fraction of one percent for usual influenza, although it inexplicably varied from place to place. One medical researcher calculated that life expectancy in the U.S. dropped from 51 to 39 years in 1918 because of flu deaths.

There are several different theories about where the Spanish Flu began: China, the Middle East, Spain, and even Kansas. Some people believed that it was planted by the Germans as biological warfare, but that theory dissipated when the German army suffered from the flu as much as others. Some historians have soldiers bringing it to North America on their return from

Europe. Others have American soldiers bringing it to Europe. No one knows for sure.

The first documented reports were from west of Dodge City in Haskell County, Kansas, in January and February of 1918. There, people falling ill with aches, fever, and coughs were diagnosed with plain old influenza. This flu was different, though. It spread quickly and was two-faced, sometimes mild, other times viciously strong and followed by pneumonia.

The flu's rapid spread was due in part to the huge war mobilization of late 1917 and early 1918. The U.S. had been neutral for most of the war, but declared war on Germany in April 1917. Recruit camps popped up like mushroom patches, and soon troops were on the move through training and transport to Europe. Camps, trains, and transport ships training and carrying troops to the Sausage Factory—the western front in Europe—all featured overcrowding.

Haskell County recruits trained at Camp Funston in Kansas, where the disease arrived after smoke from horse manure fires in early March 1918 engulfed the base. The day after the fire, a Funston cook reported ill with a bad cold. Before the month was over, 1,100 soldiers crowded the camp hospital and thousands of others lined up at base clinics.

The influenza also showed at other armed forces camps throughout the States, then spread into the general population. The Ford auto factory in Detroit reported 1,000 workers ill in March of 1918. Later that spring, 500 of the 1,900 convicts at San Quentin Penitentiary contracted the influenza. However, the winter and spring outbreaks caused little alarm. People were busy with the war effort, and the flu was an annual fact. The only serious records of what was happening were kept by places where people's lives were regimented: the army, prisons, and factories, such as Ford.

Within four months of the initial recorded outbreak in the U.S., the new flu had spread around the world. In April the epidemic had a firm grip on troops in the European battlefields. Soldiers called it the three-day fever and it laid low thousands of French, British, and American troops. In May, Britain's Grand Fleet could not sail because more than 10,000 men were ill. The British First Army in France had 36,000 men too sick to fight. Battle plans on both sides fell apart because of flu-ravaged troops. German General von Ludendorff gave the flu as one reason for a failed German offensive in July.

Then the flu abated and seemed to disappear. For the most part, it had been relatively mild, with the mortality rate apparently not too much higher than usual. Once it went away, people gave it little thought. It was just another annual visit from the village madman. They were preoccupied with a war that seemed destined to destroy the world. Anyone concerned about the flu soon would forget it when the war casualty lists appeared at public places and people scanned them anxiously to learn which husband, son, or brother was dead or missing.

They did not know that worse lay ahead. This flu was about to transform itself into a killing machine that would devour more humans than all the world's rifles, artillery, bombs, and poisonous gases combined.

After a brief summer respite, the flu exploded in North America, France, and Africa. It had mutated, and the second wave was far more savage than the first. In late August, flu reports began to appear from ships on the Boston waterfront. Early victims were sailors and soldiers, but the disease moved rapidly into the city, then across the state of Massachusetts and into neighboring states. At first, dozens of cases were reported, then hundreds, thousands, and tens of thousands. During late October 1918, New York City registered 5,200 deaths in one week, Philadelphia 4,500, Chicago 2,300.

The deadly scourge had gone global. The French took to calling it *La Grippe*. Germans called it the Flanders Flu. Canadians initially called it the American Flu, probably because the earliest reports were about the outbreaks in U.S. army camps and at the Ford plant in the border city of Detroit. It later became apparent that the main source of Canadian infections was not from across the border, but from troop ships returning from Europe. Returning veterans spread the virus into the general population and within a year it killed 50,000 Canadians, and likely many more.

The Spanish Flu, or the Spanish Lady, is the name that stuck. The flu fell hard on Spain—eight million Spaniards caught it—and most of the cases were in May and June of 1918, after its appearance in the U.S. and elsewhere. The Spaniards tried to shed the name by calling it the French Flu because they said it blew over the Pyrenees in winter storms. Some historians suggest that the name Spanish Flu stuck because Spain was neutral in World War I, had no war censorship, and freely reported how the disease ravaged that country. War countries such as the U.S., Britain, France, and Germany tried to keep details of the disease secret, not wanting the enemy to take advantage of any weakness.

Regardless of its origin, the name Spanish Flu does not adequately reflect the horrors it brought. The virus left many patients bleeding from the nose, mouth, ears, and other bodily orifices. Often pneumonia followed the flu, causing victims to cough up blood. In the worst cases, their lungs filled with a frothy, bloody mixture, and the patients began to drown in their own bodily fluids. They gasped for breath, fingertips and lips turning purple for lack of oxygen, faces sometimes turning purplish brown, or black. Death was a blessing.

There is a theory that the Spanish Flu was especially deadly because of cytokine storms (overreactions of a victim's immune system). Cytokine storms happen when a person's immune system fights so hard it produces inflammatory molecules that clog lung efficiency, creating Acute Respiratory Distress Syndrome (ARDS). There is evidence that recent avian flu victims in Southeast Asia also suffered cytokine storms.

Some survivors of the Spanish Flu suffered brain damage from encephalitis lethargica, or sleeping sickness. This sickness became an epidemic of its own but it is unknown whether it was symptomatic of the Spanish Flu virus, or whether it was a separate virus that appeared coincidentally. Several million people around the world contracted it. U.S. President Woodrow Wilson caught the flu while in Paris for peace treaty talks in early 1919. Some said it affected his mental capacities. Others said a stroke came with the flu, and the arguments over whether he had encephalitis lethargica or a stroke continue to this day.

During the autumn of 1918, the Spanish Influenza became another war to fight, and the battlegrounds were everywhere. No one was safe from the scourge, although it seemed to hit harder in the larger, overcrowded cities. It usually followed transportation lines, arriving by ship or rail. The troop ships traveling both to and from Europe were flu-infested, and burials at sea became a daily routine.

Fort Devens, a military camp just west of Boston, was hit hard probably because of over-crowding. The camp, built for 35,000 troops, contained close to 50,000. A doctor stationed there wrote:

> *One can stand to see one, two, 20 men die, but to see these poor devils dropping like flies gets on your nerves. We have been averaging about 100 deaths a day, and still keeping it up. It takes special trains to carry away the dead.*

Even the most remote places were not safe. The disease wiped out entire villages in Alaska. Fourteen percent of the population of the Fiji Islands died in a period of only two weeks, and 22 percent of the population of Western Samoa died. In North America's isolated areas, where survival meant fetching wood for warmth and shooting food in forests or angling it from the waters, providers lay in their beds too ill to move. Some died of the cold, others starved. In the Labrador village of Okak, 207 of 266 people died and the religious mission there closed. There is a famous story of an eight-year-old Labrador girl who suffered the horror of watching starving dogs eat the bodies of her dead parents.

Death tolls rolled higher, but some cities were hit harder than others. The death rate in Chicago was 5.2 percent, yet in Grand Rapids, Michigan, only 200 miles (350 km) away, it was only 2.8 percent. In Montreal, deaths were so quick and numerous that officials converted trolley cars to hearses that could carry 10 coffins at a time.

Perhaps hardest hit of any North American community was Philadelphia, doubly unfortunate considering how much the city had suffered from yellow fever outbreaks in the 1790s. The Philadelphia board of health had warned of a possible outbreak several months before it arrived. Despite the warnings, the city had the highest mortality rate of any city in North America. The stricken city played out scenes from the ancient plague days: people placed corpses on their porches for death carts to pick up and carry away. The morgue, with a capacity for 36 bodies, contained several hundred at one point and health officials opened supplementary morgues. Coffin makers worked 12 hours a day, seven days a week, as did grave diggers. Why Philadelphia? One theory was that in September 1918, a war bond rally was attended by 500,000 people who crowded together in the streets. Public health officials refused to cancel the gathering and a few days later tens of thousands of people were ill.

There were no effective medicines to deal with the flu. Some doctors tried serums and so-called vaccines with boasts of success, but much of this was quackery. Others prescribed whiskey; still others said good ventilation was the key. Some people sprinkled formaldehyde on the streets in hopes of keeping the flu down. Billy Sunday, a famous professional baseball player turned evangelist, preached that the way to destroy the flu was to "pray it down."

Remedies included alcohol, opium, and cocaine. Smoking was encouraged, as people believed that it killed germs. Swallowing drops of kerosene or turpentine with sugar, supposedly killed germs also. Eucalyptus and camphor rubbed into the skin probably did nothing to stop the virus, but did push back the stench of illness and death.

Prohibition of alcohol had yet to take effect in the United States, but it was the law in Canada,where some people blamed the rising death rate on the unavailability of alcohol. A doctor in Rosedale, Nova Scotia went so far as to write the Chief Justice in Ottawa requesting his help in obtaining illegal Scotch whiskey and wine.

Later, the Canadian government allowed

doctors and clergy to prescribe alcohol for the sick, but for many people alcohol remained evil, medicinal qualities or not. In Pennsylvania, as the U.S. continued to debate whether to institute Prohibition, news that health authorities had shut down saloons and dance halls because of the flu outbreak brightened a meeting of the Christian Women's Temperance Union. The women rose as a group and sang a doxology in thanksgiving.

Home remedies alleviated some distress but were no match for the virus when it was determined to kill. All people could do was take to their beds and pray for the disease to pass, while preparing for the possibility of death. When patients died, relatives often buried them without reporting to authorities. Doctors and undertakers were too busy to keep detailed records, meaning that official death tolls were understated. For decades the Spanish Flu mortality was estimated at 20 million but research reveals the number was closer to 40 and 50 million, and some historians believe deaths might have been as high as 100 million.

The flu created massive social and economic problems as it sliced through North America, Europe, and other parts of the world. India became a living hell with an estimated 16 million deaths breaking down all usual forms of civilization. The rotting dead littered the streets and rail coaches of India because there were too many bodies to handle.

In Philadelphia, Bell Telephone had 800 operators—27 percent of its work force—down with the flu. The company appealed to people to use the telephone only for dire emergencies because they did not have enough operators to keep all lines open. The United States Supreme Court adjourned. Stock markets closed, and in many places officials banned public gatherings, including funerals. Instead, hearses and horse drawn body carts did their grim patrols through neighborhoods, where mourners draped their doors with crepe: black crepe signified an adult's death, white was for children, and grey was for the very old.

Family life changed. Spanish Flu feasted on people in the prime of life. More than half of those who died were between the ages of 20 and 40, many with children. The number of orphans around the world increased dramatically in 1918 and 1919, and many families didn't get started because so many people of reproductive age died. The disease was brutal to pregnant women; most who caught it miscarried or died. In rural areas, children struggled to feed livestock and worked in the fields while their parents lay stricken in bed. In the cities, orphaned children wandered the streets.

The tragedies brought by the Spanish Lady were appalling. One report from Boston City Hospital said everything about the epidemic:

A 14-year-old boy was ill in the hospital. When he recovered, a social worker went to his home to see if someone was there to care for him. She found the father and two children sick in bed. Two other children had died the week before. On the kitchen table was an infant who had died three days previous, the little body was not removed because everyone was too sick.

People shunned anyone, including family, who might give them the disease. One small American town that had been spared from the flu, placed a sign at the city limits that read: "This Town Is Quarantined—Do Not Stop." Some places demanded people's health certificates before permitting entry.

There were shortages of many goods and services, particularly coffins and people to dig graves. High demand and short supply drove the prices up, and there were instances of undertakers having to hire guards to prevent theft of their coffins. Burials in mass graves became common. Funerals in some places were limited to 15 minutes, with only immediate relatives allowed to attend.

There was violence. In Chicago a man screamed, "I'll cure them in my own way!"

before slitting the throats of his wife and four children.

In Philadelphia, people stripped pharmacies, and colleges suspended pharmacy classes so students could help fill prescriptions and prevent riot. A group of weeping women surrounded a doctor making a house call. They wouldn't let him leave until he had treated 57 neighborhood children.

In San Francisco, where wearing a mask was the law, a health inspector shot a man who refused.

Social problems grew from the economic troubles spawned by the pandemic. Businesses failed because so many workers were sickened or killed, and because consumer confidence fell. The insurance industry took a hammering as it paid out thousands of death claims. Per capita income plummeted, especially in areas hardest hit by deaths.

A glance at one newspaper page tells much about daily life, and death, during the worst days of the flu. The *Halifax Herald* reported the following on October 14, 1918:

New York City—New York State makes sneezing and coughing without covering nose and mouth a criminal offense. The fine is $500 or one year in jail, or both.

Montreal—20,000 cases reported in the city. All shops, stores and bars ordered to close by 4 p.m. Churches, theaters, bowling alleys and public baths must remain shut. No gatherings of more than 25 people allowed. Fifteen men brought before the courts charged with spitting.

Ottawa—Six hundred cases reported in one day.

Toronto—Hospitals almost full. Conventions, including the Baptist Convention of Ontario and Quebec, and the Ontario Sunday Schools convention, canceled. Only immediate relatives allowed at funerals. Urgent call issued for nurses and orderlies to handle the sick and dead.

Winnipeg—Sunday services and Thanksgiving Day services suspended.

As in every crisis, people stepped forward to perform acts of mercy. Volunteers changed bedding, did laundry, and cooked meals in temporary hospitals. People took in orphaned children. Doctors and nurses worked until they were exhausted, many contracting the disease themselves. Teachers frequently became volunteer nursing assistants when school closures left them without work. Often their efforts put them in grave danger, and sometimes killed them.

The worst of the flu in North America was the fall and early winter of 1918. It continued into 1919, finally fading as spring approached. There was still enough of it around in April 1919 to create a remarkable note in sporting history. Montreal and Seattle fought a titanic struggle for the Stanley Cup, the Holy Grail of professional hockey. The championship series was tied and the deciding game was set for April 1. Organizers abandoned the series and the Cup was not presented when the entire Montreal team, except one player, was too ill with the flu to play. Until the 2004–2005 hockey season, when a National Hockey League labor dispute canceled all play, 1919 was the only year the league did not present the Stanley Cup.

The tragedy of the Spanish Flu was that it caused so much grief at a time when the world was taking its first steps to recovery from the horrors of the great world war. No story illustrates this point better than that of Alan Arnett (Bus) McLeod, a teenage flying ace who won the Victoria Cross medal for his aerial battle heroics. McLeod, who was from Stonewall, Manitoba, survived dog fights with German fighters, a crash and explosion when he was shot down, and wounds from machine gunners in the German trenches. He received the revered Victoria Cross on September 4, 1918. Two months later, he caught the Spanish Flu and died at age 19.

If there was any good brought by the Spanish Influenza, it was the recognition of the need for central public health agencies. The killer flu showed the world that it was unprepared for a large magnitude health crisis. The U.S. Congress quickly approved $1 million for flu vaccine research and followed that with improvements to public health. In 1919, Canada established the first federal health department, and more funds were freed for hospital expansion and public nursing courses.

When the flu and the war passed, people moved on with their lives. They carried the pain of the Spanish Flu in their personal memories, but the world's collective memory buried it. Was there ever such a world catastrophe about which so little was written and remembered?

Medical researchers have revived interest in the Spanish Flu because they believe it might hold information vital to the battle against the next pandemic. Expeditions into far northern areas where the ground is perpetually frozen have exhumed bodies of people who died in 1918 or 1919, presumably of the Spanish Flu. Tissues from bodies taken from the permafrost in Brevig Mission, Alaska, along with tissues kept from World War I soldiers, are being used to reconstruct parts of the virus. The goal is to gain information to develop new vaccines, medications, and tests that might prove to be important defenses against future outbreaks.

CHAPTER 6

Visitors from Asia

The Spanish Flu burned itself out by the summer of 1919, but some isolated cases lingered. Although people tried to forget the combined horrors of the influenza and the war, the pain of remembrance never left individuals who lost loved ones, or those who were sick themselves. Not only did millions die, the high death rate among prime adults changed the structures of families around the world.

Influenza remained an annual fact of life, but killer strains with pandemic capabilities stayed hidden in the shadows. Medical advances, including the identification of viruses, indicated that the war against infectious diseases was being won, and public health efforts focused on preventative health and safety. Four decades passed without a killer outbreak, creating a feeling that, perhaps, killer influenza had been defeated.

Not quite. In March 1957 there was news of a serious flu sweeping out of China. It began in Yunan Province and world health authorities predicted it might spread to other parts of the world. One of the places it showed up was the quiet prairie town of Grinnell, Iowa.

Well past the usual winter flu season, it arrived in Grinnell by rail on June 26, 1957. The chartered rail coach carried 100 young people out of California, who would join 1,600 others gathering at Grinnell College for a religious conference. The youths were from 43 states and a number of foreign countries.

Someone on the California coach carried the Yunan flu. Others were infected on the train, and when the coach spilled its passengers into the Grinnell meeting, many of the delegates fell ill. By July 1, health personnel documented more than 200 cases. The conference closed early because of the outbreak, and delegates returned home, many bringing the virus with them.

Although the first outbreaks were scattered in June of 1957, health authorities took them seriously and a limited supply of vaccine was available later that summer. When children returned to school in the fall, the Asian Flu broke out in earnest. hitting hard at children, young adults, and pregnant women. It brought with it bacterial pneumonia and a high death rate among the elderly.

By December the worst seemed to be over. Then a second wave hit in January and February of 1958, picking mainly on older people. Records kept in the U.S. indicated that

80,000 Americans succumbed to the 1957–58 Asian Flu and its complications. Worldwide deaths were estimated at 1 to 2 million people, and possibly more.

Only 10 years later, the next pandemic arrived. In early 1968, authorities detected a new flu and named it Hong Kong A/H3N2. It made its way to North America in September, and peaked in December and January 1969. The death toll was mercifully low compared to the Spanish and Asian influenzas, but still devastating. Roughly 36,000 died in the U.S., 4,000 in Canada, and at least a million globally.

The Hong Kong Flu qualified as a pandemic, but it was the mildest of the three seen in the 20th century. The Hong Kong virus was similar to the 1957 Asian strain, and the earlier exposure may have provided some immunity that reduced the severity. Also, there was better treatment for those who did become ill, including antibiotics to knock out secondary infections, such as bacterial pneumonia. A third factor was that the flu was at its peak when schools closed for the Christmas holidays.

During the last 300 years, the intervals between pandemics have ranged from 10 to 50 years. When the Spanish Flu struck in 1918, it was almost 20 years after the previous pandemic. The Asian Flu arrived about 40 years after that, and there were only 10 years between it and the Hong Kong pandemic of 1968. It has been almost 40 years since then, and that's one of the reasons medical researchers are so concerned: we are due for an outbreak at any time.

However, much of the developed world has yet to share that concern, living in the comfort and relative safety that modern medicine provides. We have been lulled into believing that the only big medical battles left are against cancer and heart disease. Better surveillance, better living conditions, better medicines and medical care will take care of any infectious outbreaks, or so we think. Evidence of our complacency towards an infectious disease pandemic is found in some authoritative sources. For example, an entry from a relatively current encyclopedia reads that although influenza is a yearly affliction, it is unlikely that another epidemic of such magnitude could occur today.

It couldn't be more wrong.

SECTION THREE

Who Will Protect Us?

CHAPTER 7

Accepting Reality

The bad news is, the next killer flu pandemic is on the way, and there is nothing we can do to stop it. The good news is, we have time to prepare, and possibly reduce the severity. The warning signs of the last few years have "opened an unprecedented opportunity to enhance preparedness," says the World Health Organization. And accepting the coming pandemic is an important defense against it.

The question now is how seriously we take the warning and to what extent we commit to preparing for the next outbreak.

Past pandemics have given little or no warning. In 1918, there was no surveillance system to warn about the coming Spanish Flu. It was not identified until too late; the new virus was already tearing around the world before anyone realized the possibility of a catastrophe.

Infectious disease terrifies people, and many deny its presence, until it is too late. Spanish Flu provided many examples of this. So did SARS. Some newspapers and some health and military authorities in the U.S. and Canada tried to downplay the 1918 outbreak, either because they wanted to stop panic, or because they were in denial. The Ontario Board of Health, even when warning about the 1918 influenza, issued a notice that said closing schools would be "economically wasteful" and that there was no need to close public places if they were well ventilated. In an astonishing example of trying to maintain status quo in the face of disaster, the Board added: "Health officers should do nothing consistent with the welfare of the public likely to dislocate business or the ordinary affairs of life."

A Philadelphia editorial complained about closures of churches and theaters, and asked if the authorities were trying to scare people to death. In San Francisco, a newspaper said there was less danger from the Spanish Flu than from German propaganda.

That attitude reappeared in Toronto in the 2003 SARS crisis when some public officials became indignant over WHO advisories against travel to Toronto. There were suspicions, although no direct evidence, of political interference in some public health decisions made during SARS, and the public had an impression that much of the political concern over SARS related to economic, not human, suffering.

In fact, SARS got its toehold on the world

because China initially tried to cover up its existence. During the crisis, WHO researchers said Beijing probably had twice the number of SARS cases than were reported. Chinese government officials blacked out news of SARS, eventually admitting under pressure that the disease had created a serious situation. Almost a year later, in January 2004, police in Beijing raided the Southern Metropolis Daily newspaper and detained seven employees, likely in retaliation against the newspaper's reporting on a possible new SARS outbreak.

Today, the World Health Organization is concerned about Vietnam's reluctance to provide complete information on human cases of the H5N1 bird flu.

This is highly illustrative of why we need an international effort against the next pandemic. It is dangerous for citizens to trust that their individual national governments will protect them from pandemic infectious disease. National governments tend to be parochial, doing what they might think is best for their own, and not always best for the rest of world. In today's world of rapid transportation, a bug that gets loose in a country where controls have been sloppy, is around the world in hours. World defense against pandemic is only as strong as the weakest link.

As the Commission investigating the SARS outbreak in Ontario noted in its Second Interim Report in April 2005: "It takes only one dysfunctional health unit to incubate an epidemic that brings the province to its knees."

The weakest link won't necessarily be an impoverished and undeveloped country. Canada's handling of SARS showed how an advanced industrialized nation can threaten others. Canada exported SARS to the Philippines when a nursing assistant from Toronto arrived there April 4, 2003 for a vacation. She had contracted the virus from a woman she had been nursing. She infected at least eight others in the Philippines and set off a public health emergency there. An

American visitor to Toronto brought SARS back to Pennsylvania. Fortunately, he was isolated and caused no new infections.

SARS shook the public's confidence around the world. It showed that affluence, layers of developed government, and advanced medical systems do not guarantee defense against a new infectious disease.

Some experts continue to worry about whether we have learned lessons from SARS.

"SARS wasn't even a dress rehearsal," Dr. Louis Francescutti, director of the Alberta Centre for Injury Control and Research, told a meeting of the Canadian Association of Emergency Physicians in late May 2005. "You're going to have just about everybody trying to get into the health-care system, which will slowly collapse."

The same meeting heard from an American doctor who said that even after witnessing Canada's SARS crisis, the U.S. "still didn't get it."

"When I look at our level of preparedness in the United States ... we'd better pray it doesn't happen," said Dr. Art Kellerman, chair of emergency medicine at Emory School of Medicine in Atlanta. "Plans are half-baked. We've known about this threat for years. We really now have very little time to be able to cope with this in an appropriate manner."

There has been almost daily news on the developing avian influenza in Asia and warnings about the need to prepare. There is some question, however, about whether our politicians, so easily distracted by the issues and polls of the day, will remain focused on this threat.

The performance of politicians and bureaucrats during health crises has not been inspiring. In 1918, New York City's health commissioner announced "no need for our people to worry" about the Spanish Flu because there was no danger of an epidemic. At the same time, Canada's Parliament did not even meet during the worst of the most devastating health crisis in the country's history. It stood adjourned from May 1918 until February 1919. Eighty-five years later, at the height of the SARS crisis, Canadian Prime Minister Jean Chrétien took a 12-day vacation to the Dominican Republic, returning to a swirl of criticism about absentee leadership during a national crisis.

CHAPTER 8

Loss of Trust

Two post-SARS incidents further eroded confidence in governments and health care systems, leaving people wondering about the ability of leaders to protect them in the next pandemic.

As the 2004–2005 flu season approached, the United States government announced a serious shortage of vaccine. The shortage developed when a Liverpool, England vaccine plant owned by Chiron Corp. was shut down by the British government because of evidence of contamination. The U.S. had ordered between 46 and 48 million doses of 2004–2005 vaccine from the Liverpool plant. It had planned to distribute 100 million doses, but the Chiron problem left it nearly 50 percent short. Word of the shortage led to panic with people fearing an outbreak and not nearly enough vaccine to go around.

Americans formed overnight lineups to get a shot, or traveled to Canada to pay $50 or more per injection. Some areas of the U.S. imposed fines for giving flu shots to healthy people, and a debate broke out in Canada over whether Canadians should share their generous supplies of vaccine with the Americans. In Aurora, Colorado, police reported that thieves broke into a pediatrician's office and stole 620 doses of vaccine. In Wichita, Kansas, distributors sold the $80, 10-shot vials for $600.

Then, in March 2005, incisive detective work by Winnipeg's National Microbiology

Laboratory revealed that the College of American Pathologists had mistakenly sent a pandemic flu strain to laboratories in 18 countries. The vials shipped to more than 3,700 labs were supposed to contain an innocuous strain for quality control testing but instead contained the deadly H2N2 Asian flu virus that killed between 1 and 2 million people in the 1957 pandemic. Most, but not all, of the virus samples were tracked down and destroyed. Tracing efforts continued throughout the spring without 100 percent success. Even one lost vial has the potential to create a new pandemic. Anyone born after 1957 would have little or no immunity against the strain.

Incidents like these, plus an ever-growing distrust of leaders of any kind, increase anxiety about our capability to handle a global health crisis. The World Economic Forum reported in late 2002 that a global survey showed a major decline in trust of leadership in democratic institutions and large national companies. A

Canadian Broadcasting Corporation poll in May 2005 found that a stunning 65 percent of Canadians have little or no confidence in their political leaders. Forty percent had little or no confidence in their religious leaders, 36 percent little or none in their business leaders.

The pharmaceutical industry, and the North American government agencies that watch over them, give people cause to worry about who is minding the medical store. There has been a litany of harmful drugs pulled from the market during the last decade. Health authorities banned the miracle stomach drug Propulsid, called the champagne of anti-heart-burn drugs, after it caused heart problems that killed at least 300 people. They also pulled Seldane, the popular antihistamine, because it caused fatal heart arrhythmias when combined with some other drugs. Then there were antibiotics that caused liver failure and pain-killers believed capable of causing heart or circulatory problems.

This is good reason for people to look to independent medical leadership, free of big business and big bureaucracy.

Many believe the World Health Organization is our best first-line defense against the next killer influenza. WHO is a United Nations agency, acting as a coordinating authority on international public health, with headquarters in Geneva, Switzerland. Since 1948, it has operated a global influenza surveillance system. This system comprises 112 national influenza centers in 83 countries and four WHO collaborating centers in London, Tokyo, Melbourne, and Atlanta. They receive reports from a global flu network made up of hospital emergency departments, clinics, private physicians, and public health departments. The idea is that if a new virus appears, or an old one appears to be mutating, the world medical community will know quickly and be able to jump into action. Rapid detection allows a better chance of isolating a potential new pandemic virus.

WHO has developed an Influenza Pandemic Preparedness Plan designed to guide world medical communities, to harmonize global, regional, and national preparedness plans, and to offer tools to assist in plan development. The hope is to reduce medical and economic impacts by implementing plans and measures before the pandemic occurs. SARS took public health officials by surprise and they made up their responses as the emergency developed. Fortunately, their responses stopped the infection in hospital settings before it could run wild in general communities.

Says Dr. Klaus Stöhr, director of the WHO global influenza program: "The objective of pandemic preparedness can only be damage control. There will be death and destruction. National pandemic response plans are the key."

Preparedness plans try to address all the situations that might arise in a pandemic and make a start at planning how to handle them. For instance, some plans note that special arrangements might be necessary to handle unusual numbers of bodies. They suggest that temporary morgues might be established in arenas or curling rinks. They also note that funeral homes might not be able to cope with increased demand and this requires planning.

Preparedness plans also address dozens of other issues, from transportation of bodies to effects on religious and ethnic death traditions, to laboratory testing, vaccine distribution, the use of antivirals, and infection control in medical settings. What happens if an outbreak closes public transportation? How do we handle millions of kids if schools are closed?

Ethical issues will abound during a pandemic. Do we quarantine and if so how will we address infringements of individual rights? Will we force workers in essential services to work, exposing them to infection? Who will receive the already-restricted supplies of antivirals and vaccine? Will ability to pay be one criterion for who gets vaccine or antivirals? How do we monitor and control the use of emergency power by pressured authorities who might use a sledgehammer to drive a tack?

The answers to many of these questions will not be known until the real thing arrives, but the Secretary of U.S. Health and Human Services, Mike Leavitt, says that preparation will save lives.

"The more we prepare now, the more lives we will save in the event of a pandemic," he says. "There is a time in the life of every problem when it is big enough to see and small enough to solve. For flu preparedness, that time is now."

On his recommendation, U.S. President George W. Bush has already added pandemic influenza to the list of "quarantinable events," giving the government power to force people into quarantine, if necessary.

Plans are not worth much without commitment and resources. The world's future health depends to some extent on what resources governments commit to preparedness. Every country has a list of urgent priorities and never enough money to meet them, so planning for something that has not yet happened can be difficult to justify. The costs of trying to eradicate bird flu in Southeast Asia, developing a human vaccine, and stockpiling antivirals and medical supplies run into billions of dollars.

It will be even harder to keep politicians and governments focused on the threat if its imminence begins to fade. Mr. Justice Archie Campbell, the Ontario judge investigating the SARS outbreak, addressed this issue in his Second Interim Report: "More financial and professional resources are needed; otherwise all the legislative changes and program reforms will prove to be nothing but empty promises. The test of the government's commitment will come when the time arrives for the heavy expenditures required to bring our public health protection up to a reasonable standard."

WHO argues that pandemic preparation

spending is not wasted even if the pandemic does not arrive. It says spending will provide benefits now, such as improved medical infrastructure, and will help against other epidemics or infectious disease threats. Part of the plan is to strengthen the ability to respond to annual influenza outbreaks through surveillance of animal and human viruses and vaccination programs.

Some plans include stockpiling antivirals, other medications, and medical supplies. WHO has recommended that countries stock enough oseltamivir (Tamiflu) for at least 25 percent of their populations. Not all governments accept that. The U.S. and Canada are more focused on getting the right vaccine, while using antivirals as a stopgap measure. Right now, Canada has enough Tamiflu to treat 2.2 million citizens infected by influenza, about 6.7 percent of the Canadian population. The U.S. has set aside enough for 2.3 million treatments and is negotiating for another 2 million. That's enough

Tamiflu to treat less than 1.5 percent of the population, and critics say it's not enough. The Infectious Disease Society of America has called on the U.S. government to stockpile enough Tamiflu to treat at least one-third of the U.S. population—100 million people. Tamiflu tablets cost $40 in the U.S. for one treatment of 10 pills, and buying enough for 100 million people would cost $1 billion.

The U.S. and Canada's stockpiling philosophies differ vastly from other countries. For example, Britain plans to buy 14.6 million treatments of Tamiflu, enough for about 24 percent of its population.

Stockpiling raises an important question: will countries that have medicines be willing to share with countries that don't? The poorest countries with the least resources stand to suffer the most, and open risk for the rest of the world.

The *Washington Post* reported in July 2005 that the main hospital for treating bird flu in

Jakarta, Indonesia, had enough antivirals on hand to treat only eight patients. Thirty-three other hospitals across Indonesia had enough to treat two patients each. At the same time WHO confirmed the first H5N1 human death in Indonesia, and suspected two others, setting off alarms that Indonesia could become a starting point for an outbreak.

The great risk in this have-and-have-not situation is allowing an emerging outbreak to get a grip on the world through a poorly protected country. WHO scientists estimate they can extinguish an outbreak if 80 percent of an infected community receives antivirals quickly. Chances are the outbreak will start in an underdeveloped country with limited influenza fighting resources.

Because vaccine production is so limited, some countries are planning to increase their own domestic production so they don't have to rely solely on imports. The U.S. is trying to attract more vaccine manufacturing plants and to create a system that allows more surge capacity. Canada's federal government gave $24 million in the spring of 2005 to help the University of Saskatchewan in Saskatoon develop an international vaccine center that could become a world leader in development and testing of new vaccines.

There is no vaccine yet for the current strain of avian flu that might become the next pandemic. Even if one is developed soon, there will not be nearly enough of it to protect everyone. No one should be led to believe that any vaccine can prevent a pandemic. All a vaccine can do is limit the sickness and death.

Vaccination is the only truly powerful weapon that we have against influenza, even though vaccine success varies by individual. The CDC says flu vaccines are 70 to 90 percent effective in young adults. They are less effective for the elderly and people with existing medical conditions, but still help reduce the severity of the flu and the risks of major complications.

Studies show that flu vaccines reduce hospitalization by about 70 percent, and death among elderly people by about 85 percent.

Opponents of vaccination say influenza shots are more about making money than protecting people. They point to the 1976 Swine Flu scare when medical authorities warned that Swine Flu would produce the greatest epidemic in history and convinced the U.S. Congress to fund development of a vaccine. The vaccination program started October 1, 1976 and President Ford himself went on television to receive his shot. Swine Flu did not develop, and instead, hundreds of people who took the vaccine fell ill with Guillain-Barre paralysis. Others suffered impotency and vision problems; a few dozen died. The U.S. government suspended the vaccination program on December 16.

Skeptics say that any flu vaccine has the potential to cause these problems. However, for most people, evidence of flu shot benefits is too overwhelming to ignore.

The benefits of vaccine are one issue, but producing a timely, safe, and adequate supply is another. The egg vaccine technology we still use is 50 years old, and it takes many months to produce a new vaccine. If a novel strain appears in September, there's no chance of developing and producing a vaccine to cover it before the winter flu season erupts in temperate climates. Also, because universal vaccination is non-existent in most of the world, manufacturing capabilities are small, and difficult to ramp up in a hurry.

Dr. Osterholm of the University of Minnesota, one of the strongest voices calling for urgent action against the coming pandemic, says vaccine availability must become the top priority in pandemic planning. He calls for a cell-culture technology that would produce more vaccine, faster and cheaper than the egg system. The egg-based system requires 350 million chicken eggs and at least six months following isolation of the new strain to produce 300 million doses of vaccine. That's not enough to vaccinate even five percent of the world population. But, right now, the technology and manufacturing capability are not there to do any better.

In the egg vaccine process, flu strains are injected into fertilized eggs that incubate and essentially brew the viruses. The viruses are then killed and bottled in vials. Facilities that produce vaccines are old, and piled with tens of thousands of eggs requiring many workers to keep things organized.

In a cell culture process, cells from insects and certain animals are infected with the flu virus strain. The cells with the virus are brewed in fermenting vats. Walking into a cell culture factory would be like entering a new brewery filled with shining stainless steel vats and computers. There is disagreement about how much production time cell culture saves, but certainly one advantage is that the process allows for faster production without waiting for chickens to lay millions of eggs.

The cell culture process needs huge

amounts of new investment and most investors would rather deal in pharmaceuticals that millions of people take every day, not a low-return flu shot received once a year. So, if cell culture is needed, taxpayers will likely have to subsidize it. The U.S. has signed a $97 million contract with European vaccine manufacturer Sanofi Pasteur MSD to accelerate cell culture development.

CHAPTER 9

Paying Attention to Hygiene

When confronted with the thought of a flu pandemic and vaccine shortages, the first reaction of most people is: What can I do to stop it? The short answer is: Nothing. The experts say it is coming and we'll all have to deal with it. However, there are ways that people can protect themselves from getting the flu.

An immediate concern is for travelers

visiting areas where the bird flu is active. The
CDC warned travelers throughout the spring
and summer of 2005 to avoid all contact with
poultry in Asia. It advised against visiting live
poultry markets, and
eating undercooked
poultry or poultry
products, including
dishes made with un-
cooked poultry blood.
Cooking poultry prod-
ucts thoroughly at heats of 150 degrees Fahren-
heit (78° Celsius) kills the virus.

IT IS THERE. KILL IT!

The influenza virus can live
up to two days on a hard
surface but dies instantly
with a wipe of a cloth
soaked in a solution of nine
parts water, one part bleach.

Other than that, common sense hygiene
taken seriously, is an effective defense against
influenza.We've all been in this scene: In a public washroom a person steps quickly up to the
sink beside you, turns on a tap and dribbles
water over a few fingers. After a quick wipe with
paper towel, or a partial drying under a blower,
the person is off and running.

We live in a world swarming with microbes.

Door handles, toilet seats, towel dispensers, and tap handles are crawling with germs that we can't see. Most of them don't hurt us because our bodies are used to them, but when microbes do lead to illness, they have often come from our hands.

Good hygiene is not just for times of flu danger. Infectious diseases are always around. The 2000 CIA report on the infectious disease threat said that infectious disease deaths in the U.S. have nearly doubled to 170,000 per year after reaching a historic low in 1980.

Public health authorities keep telling us that thorough hand washing is an important defense against infectious disease. We have known this for more than 100 years, and the message gained a renewed prominence during SARS. Yet despite being told time and time again that hand washing helps prevent illness, many of us don't make it a habit.

In fact, a survey sponsored by the American Society of Microbiology found that roughly one-quarter to one-third of people using U.S. airport washrooms don't wash their hands. The survey, done just as the SARS scare was ebbing in 2003, found that 30 percent of people using New York airport washrooms did not wash their hands. In Miami, 19 percent didn't wash, and neither did 27 percent in Chicago. The survey also asked Americans if they wash their hands after coughing, sneezing, or changing a diaper. Seventy-seven percent wash after changing a diaper, but only 58 percent wash after sneezing or coughing.

Probably one of the best pieces of advice for avoiding colds and flu doesn't come from any medical authority. It is based on pure survival instinct and can be summed up in two words: Be Rude.

Many of us tend to place social graces ahead of infection control. We feel obligated to shake hands, hug, kiss, and mingle close even when we know others might have a cold or flu. Crowding creates perfect environments for

SAFETY PRECAUTIONS

Dodging the flu involves a few things as simple and obvious as hand washing. Here are some other ideas collected from a variety of health sources:

- Avoid touching your nose, mouth, and eyes. That's where viruses hang out and touching spreads them.
- Cover your nose and mouth when you cough or sneeze. Use a tissue and don't carry it around after you've used it. Get rid of it because it contains germs. Handkerchiefs are germ containers.
- Don't let air in your living and working spaces dry out. Drink lots of fluids. Mucous linings of the respiratory tract are the body's first line of defense against cold and flu viruses. Keeping them moist protects them. Dry air compromises the body's defense systems.
- Disinfect bathroom and kitchen countertops. The more germs you kill around your home, the fewer there are to bother you.
- Children's toys are also the playthings of many germs. Kids share them and spread the germs around. Disinfect toys as often as reasonable.
- At daycare, ensure personnel use a new shoulder cloth for every baby they pick up.

spreading infections. If you have a cold or suspect someone else has, refuse to hug or shake hands, and stay back a distance. Simply explain this behavior with: "I'm sorry, I have a cold and don't want to spread it around." Someone might think you are rude, but it's better than getting sick.

The more time you spend in crowded places, and the closer you are to people, the more likely you are to get the flu. Even people who look healthy can transmit the flu because the virus is infectious for 24 hours before symptoms develop. During flu season, minimize home visitors, cancel family outings, shop in off-peak hours, use online banking and bill paying, visit smaller shops, or even order groceries by telephone. If a family member becomes ill, keep his or her personal items separate and do not share towels, utensils, or drinks.

In a pandemic, we will all rely upon our public health systems to protect us. However, public health will sacrifice the individual to

WASHING YOUR HANDS SAVES LIVES

The Clean Hands Coalition in the U.S., which promotes hand washing and even sponsors a Clean Hands Day in September, says 22 million school and work days are lost every year to illness. A good portion of those 22 million could be prevented by washing hands thoroughly after using the toilet, before preparing food, after blowing your nose, or after touching animals, garbage, or things that many other people have touched.

Likewise, the Centers for Disease and Control and Prevention in Atlanta says, "The most important thing that you can do to keep from getting sick is to wash your hands."

Hand washing is effective only when you do it the way mom showed you. Using *hot* water and soap, thoroughly scrub your hands for 15 or 20 seconds, between the fingers, into the palms, and up past the wrists. Rinse for a full 20 seconds to wash away the soap and the germs.

Alcohol-based hand cleaners have become popular because they are portable and quick, however they must be applied thoroughly—squeeze a generous amount on the palms and rub all over the hands and between the fingers until the hands become dry.

save the herd, if necessary. Individuals need to protect themselves, and that means being well informed and armed with enough facts to make intelligent decisions.

Politicians, bureaucrats, and journalists will have much to say in the event of a public health crisis, but it's not all going to be the gospel truth. Facts will get spun, twisted or confused. Statements get misconstrued or misinterpreted in the heat of stressful situations, and there will be plenty of controversy over what people should or should not do. The best any individual can do is listen closely, gather information from a variety of sources, and make informed decisions. That includes asking questions and challenging what the media say. Each individual's health is too precious to leave solely in someone else's hands.

Thailand provides an example of the importance of how individuals working with each other can strengthen health care protection. The backbone of Thai health care is the Village

Health Volunteer system in which 800,000 volunteers regularly check on community health conditions and the health of their neighbors. In early summer of 2005, the Thai government held meetings of volunteers to tell them how to educate their communities about an influenza pandemic.

Education helps people better understand the disease and how to make informed choices about how to protect themselves. The Spanish Flu pandemic provided many examples of how vulnerable people become when panicked. They were desperate for protection and looked to serums, air purifiers, lotions, and syrups to ward off the flu germs. The snake oil salesmen prospered, but many of the therapies were useless.

During the next pandemic, there will be a marketing flood promoting goods and services that will claim to protect you, cure you, or at least make you feel better. Companies are already advertising classes on building a better immune system to help protect people against the pandemic. For roughly $100, you can learn how to strengthen your immunity through a healthier body and mind. There was also a recent study that revealed the chemical resveratrol, found in grapes and some other fruits, inhibits the reproduction of influenza viruses.

Like everything else, some of these goods and services will be valuable, others might be useless. The key is to be a smart consumer of health information.

SECTION FOUR

The Future

CHAPTER 10

Sooner, or Later?

There have been tens of millions of words written about the coming killer influenza, in books, government papers, medical research notes, newspapers, and web sites. They pile up hourly, like wind-whipped snow building impossibly high banks of information so overwhelming that no one person could go through it all. None of this vast knowledge has yet to answer definitively the two key questions about the future pandemic: When will it come? How bad will it be?

The answer to the first question is easy, but not comforting. No one knows. Perhaps it has already begun. Despite worldwide surveillance efforts, someone might be sneezing and coughing a killer flu virus right now in a remote Asian farm village, a chicken rookery in North Carolina, or somewhere else. It could sweep the globe in a matter of months. Or, it could be 10 years away.

"It is impossible to anticipate when the next pandemic might occur," states WHO's updated global influenza preparedness plan released in May 2005. The organization notes that on average there have been three documented pandemics per 100 years since the 16th century and they have occurred at intervals of 10 to 50 years.

The avian flu is now a serious epidemic among birds in Southeast Asia, and the number of human cases, although still very small, has passed the 100 mark. The virus is evolving into the final stages of what could produce a pandemic. Several clusters of human cases are being studied in Vietnam to determine if person-to-person transmission is occurring, or about to occur. The CDC says that spread of H5N1 from one person to another is rare, so far, and transmission has not continued beyond one person. But there is much anxiety that we will awaken one morning to hear the news that one person has infected another with the new flu. Then the panic to control the spread will begin.

"You can sort of see it happening," Dr. Earl Brown, a virologist at the University of Ottawa said in the spring of 2005. "But our predictive power is so crappy that even when you see it happening you don't know what the next step is, unfortunately."

"H5N1 has been knocking at the door pretty hard for 10 years," he added in a later interview. "I think there is some barrier keeping it from getting into people. It seems to be trapped deep down in the body."

By that he means the virus lives deep in the lungs, an area from which transmission is more difficult. To improve its transmission ability, he feels it needs to reside higher in the respiratory system where it is more easily coughed or sneezed out. If that happens, will it be a repeat of the Spanish Flu of 1918 or the SARS scare?

Despite the worry of the experts, it is appropriate to ask: Can there really be a monster pandemic at this advanced stage of human development?

Cynics say pandemic fears are good for the medical research business. Pandemic planning is becoming an industry. Governments are pouring financial and human resources into pandemic research and preparations. As concern builds, spending increases. The best time to squeeze money from people is when something, particularly disease, frightens them.

A former chief medical officer of health for Ontario says the pandemic alarms aren't justified. Dr. Richard Schabas was Chief of Staff at York Central Hospital in greater Toronto when a SARS outbreak forced it to close in 2003.

"Our science just isn't strong enough for us … to be making these kinds of alarmist predictions that we're hearing from the WHO and others," says Dr. Schabas. "This is the third time the WHO has told us we're on the brink of an avian influenza pandemic. They said it in 1997 and they were wrong. They said it a year ago and they were wrong."

He believes there will be a pandemic in the future but it will be milder, more like 1957 and 1968. The medical community's ability to deal with pandemic flu is much stronger than it was in the 50s and 60s, and "a bad scenario" will not be nearly as bad as 1918. Spending on stockpiling drugs and equipment "is more or less foolish," Schabas says. Developing infrastructure for annual flu vaccines and for more vaccine production facilities is more worthwhile.

Others say we should not be complacent because the evidence of a coming pandemic is very real, but that panic about a huge toll on humans is not justified.

Christopher Wills, doctor, professor, and author, is one of the experts who does not believe a pandemic as horrid as the Spanish Flu will return. In his 1996 book *Plagues. Their Origin, History and Future*, he argues that emergence of a new killer virus would quickly be thwarted by the "frenzied marshalling" of modern epidemiology and medicine.

"I am confident that no terrible disease will appear that slaughters us by the billion," he writes. "The reason is that we can now respond very quickly to such a visible enemy. Any disease that spreads like wildfire will have to do so through the air or the water, and there are many immediate steps we can take to prevent such a spread. If the people of fourteenth century Europe had known what we know now, they could have halted the Black Death in short order."

Dr. Wills, professor of biology at the University of California (San Diego), wrote those words in 1996, the year before avian H5N1 appeared in Hong Kong. The events since, and growing anxiety about the virus's spread, have not changed his opinion: "I am still convinced that a terrifying plague like the Black Death or the great flu pandemic of 1919 is unlikely, unless, of course, society breaks down and our technology founders as a result of war or famine. In the case of the bird flu, quarantine will be difficult, especially in places like Vietnam, but it should be controllable with Tamiflu and with quick diagnostic tests for the H5N1 virus to follow how it is spreading. There is no cause for complacency, because in the worst case there may be thousands of deaths, but also no cause for gibbering panic."

Still others caution about throwing massive resources at one virus strain. They recall the panic over the Swine Flu and how it turned into an incredible fiasco.

"[The avian flu is] the most likely bet right now, but we just don't know what could happen," said Dr. Frank Plummer, scientific director of the National Microbiology Laboratory in Winnipeg, the lab that uncovered the H2N2 Asian flu shipping error. He made the comment at a global health conference in late 2004.

There are few experts who doubt whether there will be a pandemic in the future. The real question is about its severity, and how well the world will be able to stand up against it.

Dr. Stöhr from WHO has said repeatedly that a pandemic is on the way.

"During the last 36 years, there has been no pandemic and there is a conclusion now that we are closer to the next pandemic than we have ever been before," he told reporters in Thailand in the spring of 2005. "There is no doubt there will be another pandemic."

He presented estimates of sickness and

death to WHO meetings early in 2005. They are
frightening:

- The sick will number in the billions because
  the flu will hit 25 to 30 percent of the world's
  population. Thirty percent of the world's
  6.4 billion people is roughly 2 billion.
- Between 2 and 7.4 million of the sick will die
  (WHO's best-case scenario).

Frightening as they appear, the numbers
might be low. WHO's estimate of 2 to 7.4 million deaths assumes a mortality rate of roughly
0.1 to 0.37 percent. The mortality rate for the
Spanish Flu was 2.5 percent, and SARS was a
stunning 10 percent.

Death estimates are all over the chart. The
European community is preparing for a pandemic that would kill up to 30 million worldwide.
The Centers for Disease Control and Prevention
in Atlanta has estimated that a medium-level
pandemic, in which control measures such as
vaccination were not available, would infect

tens of millions and kill 89,000 to 207,000 in the United States. A Russian scientist has predicted 1 billion deaths. The Canadian government has estimated that as many as 8 to 10 million Canadians could become sick in a pandemic and deaths could number 11,000 to 58,000. Some experts and observers say many of these estimates are low.

WHO agrees that potential illness and death figures do vary wildly, but says there are valid reasons for the variances:

"Central to preparedness planning is an estimate of how deadly the next pandemic is likely to be. Experts' answers to this fundamental question have ranged from 2 million to over 50 million. All these answers are scientifically grounded. The reasons for the wide range of estimates are manyfold."

Some of the estimates are based on past pandemics but illness and death tolls in those, even the most recent, are not exactly known.

For instance, WHO says deaths in the 1968 Hong Kong flu were anywhere from 1 to 4 million. No one knows for sure. Also, estimates involve extrapolations and the world has changed dramatically since the last three pandemics. Air travel has changed the world significantly since 1918, and even since 1968.

Other factors affecting estimates are unknowns like the specific characteristics of the virus that will cause the pandemic, or what age groups it will attack most viciously. How well the world has prepared itself for the pandemic will be a major factor in the toll.

Timing is critical in predicting the severity of the next pandemic. The experts say that if it has started, or starts soon, the world is in serious trouble. The longer it stays away, the better our chances of lessening its toll because we will have had time to develop vaccines, stockpile antiviral drugs, and make other preparations.

WHO says that if the virus strain is especially virulent, its optimistic estimate of 2 to 7.4 million deaths "could be dramatically higher." In fact, WHO's Dr. Shigeru Omi has broken from the organization's line on mortality and said deaths could go as high as 100 million.

Trust for America's Health, a non-profit organization that aims to protect community health, projects a moderate pandemic would infect 67 million Americans, force 2.5 million into hospitals and kill more than 500,000. Their estimated death toll matches 1918 deaths in America.

Dr. Osterholm says the evidence today suggests that if H5N1 becomes a pandemic, it will be similar to the Spanish Flu. If the 1918–19 mortality data are applied to the 2005 U.S. population, then 1.7 million would die of the new flu, half of them between the ages of 18 and 40. Extrapolated globally, the world deaths would be between 180 and 360 million.

"Victims of H5N1 have also suffered from

cytokine storms, and the world is not much better prepared to treat millions of cases of ARDS today than it was 85 years ago," he says.

A pandemic as severe as 1918 would be the most devastating event in modern human history, because there are unprecedented numbers of people to infect and kill, and because economic and social structures rely on relative world stability.

North American planning estimates say that up to 30 percent of transportation workers, such as truck drivers, would become ill. Others might balk at working in any areas or conditions that they fear might put them in contact with the disease. Global transportation would slow or even halt. International borders might close out of fear. The result would be shortages of food and medical supplies. The majority of medical supplies used in North America are produced in other countries, and transport slowdown or closed borders could stop the flow of these important items.

Wholesale illness and death would overburden health care systems, weaken essential services, and cripple industries and services with staff shortages—all of which could lead to government instability and social chaos. The investment firm BMO Nesbitt Burns issued in August 2005 a special report on the potential economic effects of a pandemic. It warned that an outbreak less virulent than the Spanish Flu could have an economic impact comparable to the Great Depression of the 1930s. The air, land, and water transport industries would collapse and the effects on the tourism, hospitality, and import–export trade would be devastating. Large swaths of the population would be unable to work, resulting in economic disruption that would trigger financial panic, bankruptcies, and foreclosures.

Dr. Osterholm asks: "How are we going to handle our everyday lives here in this country to make sure that we can deal with sick people? What do we do to assure that people continue to have a food supply if transportation stops? How will we manage the basic business of life when up to half the population may become ill and five percent of those will die?"

The Centers for Disease Control says economic losses in the United States could range between $71.3 and $166.5 billion in a "medium–level" pandemic. A medium pandemic would affect between 15 and 35 percent of the U.S. population. It could cause 314,000 to 734,000 hospitalizations, 18 to 42 million outpatient visits, and another 20 to 47 million people to become sick.

If the avian flu improves human transmission and breaks out into the world as Dr. Osterholm and others expect, it will be on us suddenly. It won't poke its way around the world on slow boats from China. It will arrive within hours on passenger jets that cover more than 500 miles (900 km) every hour. When it comes, preparation time will be over, and whatever contingencies exist then will be what we have to deal with.

It will come quickly, but will not be over quickly. People of the developed world have become accustomed to quick catastrophes. An earthquake kills thousands, but then it's over. A hurricane rips through Florida, then is gone, leaving death and devastation behind. The TV images appear, and then disappear, and we move on to the next thing. It is unlikely that the next killer flu will be like that. It will not be here then gone quickly, and its damage will be sustained. The experts predict the pandemic could last 12 to 36 months. Other pandemics have come in waves, with strong second and third outbreaks following a lull after the initial infection.

Staff shortages will demand a high level of volunteerism. Some people will be too frightened to risk their health helping others, but as seen in Spanish Flu, SARS, and other health crises, volunteers will step forward. One impediment to volunteering, liability for someone else's health or even death, will have to be overcome.

Risking your health, and even your life, to help others is one thing, but the possibility of being sued later for your help is another. Someone must find a way of removing this impediment.

Home nursing, reduced to an anachronism in the age of high-tech medicine, will be important during the next pandemic, especially if it is severe. There will not be enough doctors and nurses for all the ill, so good home care will be vital. The Canadian province of Alberta put into place a self-care strategy for the start of the 2005–2006 flu season. It is an important part of its pandemic response, and involves looking after yourself and others at home and not burdening health care facilities until necessary.

Material shortages, a critical feature of any catastrophic event, would be felt particularly in the medical field. The shortage of proper masks was a critical issue during SARS, and there are still not enough. The same might apply to syringes and other supplies used in treating the sick. Dr. Osterholm says there are 105,000 mechanical ventilators in the U.S., 100,000 of which are needed during an average flu season. He estimates that the U.S. alone might need several hundred thousand during a pandemic.

If vaccine is limited, those who have it will likely nationalize their supplies. Only nine countries—Canada, United States, Britain, Japan, Australia, France, Germany, The Netherlands, and Italy—have the ability to commercially produce vaccine, and they represent just over 10 percent of the world's population. Will they give some of their limited supplies to the other 90 percent, leaving some of their own citizens unprotected?

There is optimism that antivirals will help in a pandemic of the avian flu strain. Oseltamivir phosphate, marketed as Tamiflu by Roche in Switzerland, is expected to be effective against H5N1, but there is only enough to cover a tiny part of the world population, even though the company is opening a new plant in the U.S. Tamiflu attacks an influenza virus and tries to stop it from spreading through the body. One drawback is that it must be taken within the first 48 hours of acquiring flu symptoms, making timing a crucial part of its success.

The distribution issue also exists for antivirals. Who gets them first when supplies are limited? This issue will be a hot one during a pandemic and will have repercussions long after it is over. It has the potential to intensify differences between the world's wealthy and poor nations. The latter will be short of not just vaccine and antivirals, but all kinds of other medical resources. It could even cause serious differences between developed nations bent on solely looking after their own interests.

CHAPTER 11

Dealing with the Fear

There will be no shortage of fear. SARS, which killed relatively few people, showed us the type of psychological impact we can expect. Health care workers were traumatized by the fear of infecting their families, while members of the public went to extremes, avoiding Asian people and refusing to attend church services. A survey by the Harvard School of Public Health found that the fear was widespread with 42 percent of Torontonians worried that they or someone in their family would get SARS. That is significant, considering the virus was mostly contained to hospitals, and chances of transmission outside them were low.

SARS was new, had a relatively high fatality rate, spread rapidly over great distances, and seemed to be beyond the control of the medical establishment. All these factors, plus the use of quarantine, contributed to what some saw as unreasonable fear. Similar conditions might exist during an influenza pandemic, and experts want more research to find ways of dealing with psychological distress during an outbreak.

A valuable lesson of SARS was the need for better public communications during a health crisis. Few will argue now that poor communication helped to create unreasonable fears about SARS. There was little to balance the reports of doctors and nurses in protective "space suits," undertakers in gowns, masks, and gloves, and hurried burials without memorial services.

All investigations into what went wrong in Ontario during SARS said poor communication compounded the problems. The Walker Report, written by a panel of experts who investigated SARS, stated: "Moreover, we heard that poor communications contributed significantly to heightened confusion and anxiety for providers and the public; limited the ability of health care providers and the Ministry to deal with media sensationalism; and compounded sometimes unclear direction. The province cannot allow again a situation whereby the Ministry lacks the basic communications capacity to deal with a health emergency."

A study by the University of Toronto found that hospitals did a poor job of explaining visitor bans and canceled surgeries during SARS. Hospitals did not tell people clearly what was happening and this caused frustration among the public.

"In the midst of a crisis such as SARS where guidance is incomplete, consequences uncertain and information constantly changing, where hour-by-hour decisions involve life and death, fairness is more important rather than less," the report stated.

Study after study has shown the need for effective communication to control panic during public emergencies, but communication usually slips to a lower priority during the heat of crisis. Rudy Giuliani, New York's mayor at the time of the September 11 terrorist attacks, provided the classic example of how to do it right. He put himself out front, gathering the facts and honestly reporting the situation to his citizens, and indeed the world. His style of communication leadership is what will be needed during a serious pandemic, but will be difficult to find.

Many world governments still practice censorship, or at least tightly controlled and managed information. Even in western democracies, some politicians and bureaucracies still believe that information can be dangerous and distributing it requires extreme caution. For example, Canada's Information Commissioner often has referred to the "culture of secrecy" that exists in its federal government.

Various governments said they have learned from Canadian SARS communications failures. The U.S. pandemic preparedness plan notes "effective communication with community leaders and the media also is important to maintain public awareness, avoid social disruption, and provide information on evolving pandemic response activities."

The U.S. preparedness plan says the goals of their communication strategy are to be accurate and comprehensive; to instill public confidence; to address rumors, inaccuracies, and misperceptions; while maintaining order and avoiding panic.

However, there is a huge question of just how open the communication will be. The challenge of all governments will be to get a balanced message out: reassuring people who are more concerned than they should be, while informing other people who are not taking enough notice.

Dr. Donald Low, Microbiologist-in-Chief at Toronto's Mount Sinai Hospital and a member of the Walker expert panel on SARS, is skeptical about whether it will be possible to keep the public well informed or well assured during a pandemic.

"The next pandemic will be really difficult to give people reassurance when we really won't know what's happening. It will be painful," he said during a panel discussion on scaremongering and SARS. "There will be no shortcuts. I don't see how other than providing accurate information and balance we can do much. There's no soft way to sell it."

Excellent communication during a pandemic will entail providing accurate and honest information that the public can use for effective decision making. Competent communicators trusted by the public must deliver it. The public must be involved in the bigger concerns and issues, such as ethical decisions involving vaccine or antiviral distribution. Too often governments plunge ahead doing what they think is best for the people without trying to engage the public in the debate and decision-making process. Too often politicians and bureaucrats decide to put the best face on a crisis. Communication during a pandemic will demand unadulterated facts, not spin doctoring. Governments that understate or overstate the threat will have much to answer for later.

As the news stories and speculation about the next pandemic continue to grow, it is interesting to reflect on what has changed in the four decades since the last flu pandemic. Doctors and other health care workers are much more knowledgeable about the spread and management of infectious disease. Treatments of all kinds have improved immensely. Diagnostic equipment employs the world's latest high technology, allowing for more comprehensive surveillance and detection. Living conditions are better in many parts of the world, and so is the general health of most people.

What has not changed, though, is the danger presented by the influenza virus. The virus remains present, appearing every year in one form or another. It retains the ability to transform itself into a killer pandemic strain. Our technology and our medicines have not been able to eradicate it.

Even if the avian flu does not develop into a human pandemic in the next few years, the world will live with the threat for a long time. The United Nations Food and Agricultural Organization predicted during the summer of 2005 that it will take up to 10 years to eradicate bird flu in Southeast Asia. The threat to humans will continue as long as this flu is active in birds.

Researcher C. W. Potter summed up the human relationship with the influenza virus in a paper that appeared in the Journal of Applied Microbiology in 2001: "Nothing has been introduced during the past 100 years to affect the recurrent pattern of epidemics and pandemics. And our future in the new century is clearly indicated by our past."

Sir Christopher Andrewes, one of the scientists who isolated the influenza virus in the 1930s, expressed a similar view: "I can believe that virus goes underground and perhaps does so all over the world, causing odd subclinical infections and not much more, but able to become active and epidemic when the time is ripe."

So our global village madman is not going to go away. He will continue to lurk in the shadows, making his annual appearances, and occasionally going on an especially vicious killing streak. The only remaining question concerns our ability to predict and better control his rampages.

More than 20 years ago, Eileen Pettigrew wrote *The Silent Enemy*, a book about the Spanish Flu. At the end of that book she refers to Sir Christopher Andrewes' remark and ponders how the human race will fare the next time the virus is "ripe."

Medically, then, we should have every confidence of a less terrifying and lethal situation," she writes. "We can only hope that we would be as wealthy again in terms of human kindness."

Time will tell.

A Pandemic Timeline

The Last 100 Years

Winter 1917–18
> Reports of pneumonia-like illness in Europe.

Spring 1918
> First documented cases of what becomes known as Spanish Flu appear in Kansas.

Early Summer 1918
> More cases appear in U.S. army camps, prisons, and factories.

Summer 1918
> Flu seems to disappear.

Late August 1918
> Spanish Flu returns with explosive force in U.S., Europe, and Africa.

October 1918
> Close to 200,000 Americans die of flu in one month.

Spring 1919
> Flu abates and disappears.

1933   British researchers identify
> influenza as a virus.

1943   Influenza virus first seen under
> a microscope.

Spring 1957
> Serious flu sweeps out of
> Yunan, China, as precursor to
> the second influenza pandemic
> of the century.

Winter 1957–58
> Second wave of Yunan Flu
> becomes a pandemic in which
> 1 to 2 million people die.

Fall 1968
> Hong Kong Flu becomes third
> pandemic of the century,
> killing more than 1 million
> before peaking in January
> 1969, then abating.

1997 Bird flu typed H5N1 appears for the first time in a human, a child who dies in Hong Kong. Eighteen people are infected, six of whom die. Hong Kong's chicken population slaughtered to prevent more spread.

2003 H5N1 re-appears in humans in Hong Kong, creating alarm in health communities.

2004 H5N1 explodes across South-east Asia affecting millions of birds, infecting some humans.

August 2005
Total of 112 human cases reported, almost half of whom die.

Late summer 2005
World health community holds its breath while governments race to prepare for a widely predicted pandemic.

Amazing Facts and Figures

- Every year in the United States, on average, between 5 and 20 percent of the population gets the flu; more than 200,000 people are hospitalized from flu complications; and about 36,000 people die from flu.

- During the 2004–2005 U.S. season, influenza activity occurred at low levels from October to mid-December, steadily increased during January, and peaked in mid-February.

- Symptoms of flu include: fever, headache, extreme tiredness, dry cough, sore throat, runny or stuffy nose, and muscle aches. (Stomach symptoms can occur but are more common in children than adults.)

- U.S. federal spending on influenza research increased in 2005 more than fivefold to $400 million annually.

- The flu virus took three to four months to spread from Southeast Asia to Europe and North America during the pandemics of 1957 and 1968. The SARS virus reached North America in a few days.

- The U.S. Centers for Disease Control and Prevention in 2005 increased the number of quarantine stations used to block infectious diseases and bioterrorism from 12 to 18. More are due to open in 2006.

- Dr. Julie Gerberding, head of the CDC, says that H5N1 is more infectious than SARS, which caused considerable panic before being stopped in 2003.

- The 1983 Pennsylvania outbreak of bird flu took two years to control. Some 17 million birds were destroyed at a direct cost of $62 million. Indirect costs have been estimated at more than $250 million.

- Projections Chart (following pages) provided by Trust for America's Health, Washington, D.C.

Potential pandemic influenza deaths and hospitalizations from a mid-level pandemic flu*

State	Projected dead	Projected hospitalized	Number of cases	Number of cases without Tamiflu
Alabama	8,886	38,591	1,079,789	994,263
Alaska	886	4,558	152,328	140,263
Arizona	9,223	39,675	1,138,742	1,048,547
Arkansas	5,350	22,660	630,705	580,749
California	60,875	273,090	8,067,075	7,428,119
Colorado	7,192	32,978	973,161	896,081
Connecticut	7,054	29,932	817,465	752,717
Delaware	1,507	6,560	182,895	168,409
Dist. of Columbia	1,155	4,974	132,241	121,767
Florida	35,737	142,386	3,663,486	3,373,318
Georgia	13,655	62,912	1,871,561	1,723,323
Hawaii	2,446	10,571	296,651	273,154
Idaho	2,279	10,157	302,558	278,594
Illinois	23,720	103,738	2,973,962	2,738,408
Indiana	11,817	51,711	1,466,027	1,349,910
Iowa	6,233	26,090	713,106	656,624
Kansas	5,373	22,946	654,335	602,508
Kentucky	7,930	34,748	977,031	899,645
Louisiana	8,334	37,148	1,087,942	1,001,771
Maine	2,651	11,333	310,513	285,918
Maryland	9,958	44,500	1,273,572	1,172,698
Massachusetts	13,136	56,038	1,529,313	1,408,183
Michigan	19,622	86,005	2,443,473	2,249,937
Minnesota	9,304	40,786	1,171,387	1,078,607
Mississippi	5,362	23,531	682,625	628,558

*Projections are based on CDC's FluAid 2.0 program. The estimated deaths are for a pandemic strain three times more lethal than the 1968 pandemic, on which the default FluAid numbers are based. The hospitalization rate is three times the default 1968 rate. The "Dead" and "Hospitalized" numbers represent the *most likely* FluAid projection at a 25 percent rate of contraction. The "Number of cases" is the projected number of residents contracting the flu, based on a 25 percent rate of contraction. State population numbers are from FluAid, using 1999 U.S. Census data. Updated

State				
Missouri	11,274	48,240	1,350,515	1,243,546
Montana	1,804	7,787	219,703	202,301
Nebraska	3,441	14,697	414,218	381,409
Nevada	3,243	14,455	419,202	385,999
New Hampshire	2,333	10,301	293,177	269,956
New Jersey	16,980	72,791	2,013,212	1,853,755
New Mexico	3,244	14,504	432,438	398,186
New York	37,701	162,490	4,534,307	4,175,165
North Carolina	14,987	65,637	1,856,296	1,709,267
North Dakota	1,371	5,795	160,221	147,530
Ohio	23,197	99,979	2,796,583	2,575,078
Oklahoma	6,833	29,376	829,273	763,590
Oregon	6,724	29,047	810,872	746,646
Pennsylvania	27,185	112,658	3,004,915	2,766,910
Rhode Island	2,234	9,263	246,857	227,305
South Carolina	7,474	32,983	940,045	865,589
South Dakota	1,559	6,599	184,493	169,880
Tennessee	10,875	47,678	1,342,050	1,235,752
Texas	35,124	160,648	4,859,834	4,474,909
Utah	3,393	15,906	514,787	474,013
Vermont	1,185	5,213	147,245	135,582
Virginia	13,104	58,872	1,683,499	1,550,157
Washington	10,910	48,610	1,402,591	1,291,498
West Virginia	4,049	17,014	453,947	417,992
Wisconsin	10,620	45,842	1,292,419	1,190,053
Wyoming	915	4,086	119,936	110,436
U.S. Totals	**541,433**	**2,358,089**	**66,914,573**	**61,614,573**

population data were not used to ensure consistency with estimated "Dead" and "Hospitalized" numbers. "Number of cases without Tamiflu" is based on state-by-state proportional distribution of the 5.3 million courses of Tamiflu ordered or currently in U.S. federal government possession. For example, California, with approximately 12 percent of the U.S. population, receives 12 percent of the Tamiflu in the above projection.

What Others Say

"This is a critical point in history. Some day, after the next pandemic has come and gone, a commission much like the 9/11 Commission will be charged with determining how well government, business, and public health leaders prepared the world for the catastrophe when they had clear warning. What will be the verdict?"

Dr. Michael Osterholm,
University of Minnesota

"This is arguably the most serious threat to human health in the world. Are we ready? Unfortunately, we are not."

Rep. Henry Waxman D-California

"We now know that domestic ducks are playing a silent role in the transmission of the virus. The ducks are spreading the virus without showing any signs of illness. The public health implications of this are very serious. How can people avoid exposure to the virus when they don't know which ducks are infected and which ones are not?"

Dr. Shigeru Omi, WHO regional director for the Western Pacific

"This is not a drill. This is not a planning exercise. This is for real. Americans are being placed needlessly at risk. The U.S. must take fast and furious action to prepare for a possible pandemic outbreak here at home."

Shelley A. Hearne, executive director Trust for America's Health

"Evolution of a pandemic strain of virus may be preceded by numerous small steps, none of which is sufficient to signal clearly that a pandemic is about to start. This poses a difficult public health dilemma. If public health authorities move too soon, then unnecessary and costly actions may be taken. However, if action is delayed until there is unmistakable evidence that the virus has become sufficiently transmissible among people to allow a pandemic to develop, then it most likely will be too late to implement effective local, national or regional responses, and opportunities will be missed to 'Get Ahead of the Curve' and prevent large numbers of infections and deaths."

World Health Organization statement explaining decision-making dilemmas regarding pandemics, May 2005

"Many of the public health interventions that successfully contained SARS will not be effective against a disease that is far more contagious, has a short incubation period, and can be transmitted before the onset of symptoms."

World Health Organization statement, 2005

"The disease [H5N1] has become endemic in many parts of the Asian region and its eradication cannot be considered a short-term objective. Even more worryingly, the disease has given rise to concerns that an influenza pandemic is imminent. All it would take is that the deadly virus currently circulating in Asia acquires the capacity of being transmitted from human to human."

Markos Kyprianou, the European Union (EU) health commissioner

"The countries that have the weakest health systems are in need of most support, and [are usually] the poorest countries who have the least resources to invest in health."

Bjorn Melgaard, WHO,
Southeast Asia office

"Another example is wet markets, where animals that would not normally encounter each other in the wild are kept in close proximity to each other and are often slaughtered on the spot, normally with very little regard for hygiene. We know that practices such as these can set the scene for the emergence of new zoonoses [animal to human disease transmission]."

Dr. Shigeru Omi, WHO regional
director for the Western Pacific

"If these H5N1 viruses gain the ability for efficient and sustained transmission between humans, there is little pre-existing natural immunity to H5N1 infection in the human population, and an influenza pandemic could result, with high rates of illness and death."

Centers for Disease Control, Atlanta

"Although many levels of government are paying increased attention to the problem, the United States remains woefully unprepared for an influenza pandemic that could kill millions of Americans."

Dr. Andrew Pavia, chairman of the Infectious Disease Society of America's Pandemic Influenza Task Force

Bibliography

Barry, John M. *The Great Influenza: The Epic Story of the Deadliest Plague in History.* New York: The Penguin Group, 2004.

Crosby, Alfred W. *America's Forgotten Pandemic: The Influenza of 1918.* Cambridge: Cambridge University Press, 2003.

Duncan, Kirsty. *Hunting the 1918 Flu: One Scientist's Search for a Killer Virus.* Toronto: University of Toronto Press, 2003.

Garrett, Laurie. *The Coming Plague: Newly Emerging Diseases in a World Out of Balance.* New York: Farrar, Straus and Giroux, 1994.

Kolata, Gina. *Flu: The Story of the Great Influenza Pandemic of 1918 and the Search for the Virus that Caused It.* New York: Farrar, Straus and Giroux, 1999.

Pettigrew, Eileen. *The Silent Enemy*. Saskatoon: Western Producer Prairie Books, 1983.

Powell, J. H. *Bring Out Your Dead: The Great Plague of Yellow Fever*. Philadelphia, 1793.

Web sites
World Health Organization:
www.who.int/csr/disease/influenza/pandemic/en/

Centers for Disease Control and Prevention: www.cdc.gov/flu

General Flu Resources:
http://books.mongabay.com/health/conditions/Influenza.html

Canadian Broadcasting Corp.:
www.cbc.ca/news/background/flu

Ontario Commission Investigating SARS:
www.sarscommission.ca

Canada Public Health Agency:
www.phac-aspc.gc.ca

U.S. Health and Human Services:
www.os.dhhs.gov

Acknowledgements

The author would like to acknowledge the help of the Saskatchewan Western Development Museum in researching the Spanish Flu; the New England Journal of Medicine; the Canadian Association of Emergency Physicians for allowing me access to its 2005 conference notes; and the Trust for America's Health in Washington, D.C. for granting permission to use its chart estimating the effects of a mid-level pandemic.

Special thanks to Doctors Michael Osterholm, Earl Brown, Christopher Willis, and Richard Schabas for taking time to help me understand the workings of influenza viruses.

Thanks also for reprint permission for *The Silent Enemy*, 1983 by Eileen Pettigrew, publisher, Greystone Books, a Division of Douglas & McIntyre Ltd. (Originally published by Western Producer Books.)

Photo Credits

Cover: AP Photo/Richard Vogel; AP Photo: pages 8, 9 (Vincent Yu), 10 (Koji Sasahara), 12 (Greg Baker); CP Photo: page 11 (Kevin Frayer).

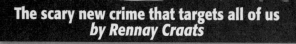

LATE-BREAKING
AMAZING STORIES™

IDENTITY THEFT

The scary new crime that targets all of us
by Rennay Craats

www.amazingstoriesbooks.com

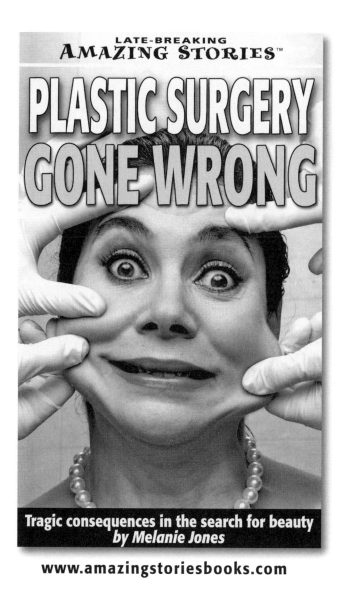

www.amazingstoriesbooks.com

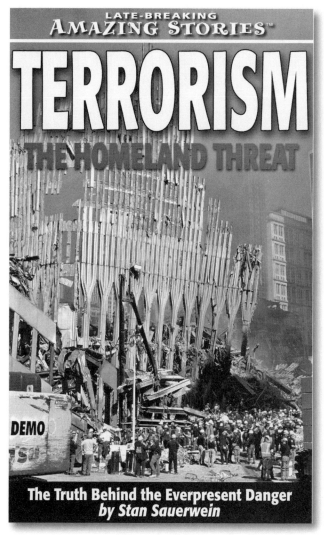